CORRUPTED

Matt Rogers

"Do not be dismayed to learn there is a bit of the devil in you. There is a bit of the devil in us all."

- Arthur Byron Cover

CHAPTER 1

The Kamchatka Peninsula

Russian Far-East

Sarah Grasso could hardly feel her face.

The rural village at the edge of the Kamchatka Peninsula — her temporary home for the past five days — seemed like it belonged on another planet. Before touching down on Russian soil, her superiors had warned her of the extreme climate.

Nothing could have prepared her for it.

She crouched against one wall of an *izba*, a traditional Russian dwelling made of logs and complete with a thatched roof. The small building shielded her from the biting wind howling across the plains. With each breath forming a cloud in front of her, she tucked the cold-weather mask up over the lower half of her face, then shoved her gloved hands under her armpits and rode out the shivers.

It was mid-winter in the Russian Far East.

On the horizon, a storm brewed.

She had been holed up in the *izba* for the last two hours, helping an elderly woman through a particularly nasty case of tuberculosis. The old girl's symptoms had been severe; fatigue, coughing blood, sweating, chest pain. The outbreak had spread like a medieval plague through this village, no thanks to its primitive technology and outdated medical supplies.

That was the reason she had been tasked to visit this desolate corner of the globe.

She clenched her teeth and made for the gravel track in front of the *izba*. An unassuming grey four-wheel-drive thrummed idly by the side of the road, headlights cutting through the swirling darkness. She rounded the vehicle and threw open the passenger door, ducking into the seat as soon as there was enough space. The heat of the cabin struck her. She slammed the door closed and turned to the driver — a European man in his late twenties.

'She'll live,' she muttered, removing the cold-weather mask. Her breath fogged the windshield almost immediately. 'But this isn't good.'

The man sported a resigned expression. 'I know.'

'We're fighting a losing battle.'

'The weather isn't helping us.'

'Neither is the location,' Sarah said, gesturing out the windshield. 'The disease is endemic out here. I didn't believe WHO when they told us how isolated the region was.'

The man shrugged. 'At least we were put in the same detail.'

She smiled. 'I'm glad, Léo. Someone's here to keep me composed.'

They leant over the centre console and pressed their lips together. Sarah closed her eyes in an attempt to wash out the stress and the unease and the exhaustion churning through her system. She felt his warmth and tried her best to tune out everything else.

Léo was the only person keeping her from going insane.

The Kamchatka Peninsula had single-handedly pushed her to breaking point. She knew she was a naturally introverted person, and — despite her occupation — she had managed to keep control of the nausea that often came with being thrust into inhospitable regions to combat disease and poverty.

This, however, was a little too overwhelming.

Nevertheless, she didn't take her job lightly. The demonic winds and mind-numbing cold didn't matter. The residents of this village needed her help, and she would do everything in her power to ensure they came out of their battle with tuberculosis unscathed.

The newfound romance with Léo had instilled a sense of calm within her. They had never met before being assigned to the same detail and sent to Russia. There were eight others back at the makeshift HQ that had been assembled in the rundown town hall. Their ten-person detail had formed a bond over the last few days that could only rise out of the situation they had been tasked to deal with.

Her and Léo, especially.

Léo shifted gears and the four-wheel-drive rolled off the mark. The chains laced around its tyres bit into the icy road and they set off back to the town hall. It was approaching ten in the evening. Sarah was utterly exhausted.

'How's the morale?' she asked.

Léo raised a palm and tilted it back and forth. 'So-so. I don't think many of us were expecting these kind of conditions.'

Sarah stared out the grimy passenger-side window, peering into the darkness. The winds tearing across the road rattled the thin pane in its sill, bombarding their vehicle as it trawled along the empty gravel track. Frail trees with twisted branches dotted the sides of the road at random. Beyond that, visibility ceased abruptly, cut off by the night.

Out here, street lights were a foreign concept.

Out of the corner of her eye, she saw Léo bite his lip in what appeared to be frustration. He blinked hard and flashed a glance out his own window. She could tell he was on edge.

'You okay?'

He blinked again. 'Just a bit nervous.'

'Why?'

Silence.

'Léo...'

'This place is getting the best of me,' he said, motioning out the windshield. 'It's probably nothing. We're all just exaggerating.'

'What is it?'

He shrugged. 'We haven't heard from Marcus yet. He was supposed to check in an hour ago. It doesn't take much for us to get worried — sitting around in that building.'

'Where'd he go?'

'Outskirts of the village. Delivering Isoniazid to the families out that way — apparently that area took the brunt of the symptoms. Nothing notable. He's probably just caught up with administering the supply.'

'Probably,' Sarah said, refusing to outwardly display her concern. 'You're right. This place is causing too much stress. I'm sure he's fine.'

But inwardly, her stomach constricted and a chill ran down her spine.

They continued to the end of the road and turned onto an even narrower track that sliced between a cluster of *izba*s. Ahead lay the town hall, a decrepit wooden building that had seemingly gone unused for decades before they had been allowed to take up temporary residence within its walls. Missing tiles and rotting portions of the exterior enabled the wind to seep into the building, creating an almost constant wailing that unnerved even the most resilient members of their party.

Sarah couldn't wait to experience the comfort of her own bed back in Michigan.

Dusting snow off her boots into the footwell, she heard Léo let out a grunt of concern. She raised her head and peered out into the night.

Instantly, she realised something was awry.

She noticed the bulk of the strange vehicle an instant before its enormous headlights flickered off. It was some kind of all-terrain truck — so large that for a second she mistook it for a tank. It was parked facing the hall, four gigantic tyres resting in the rudimentary parking lot out front. The headlights — two powerful white beams that obliterated the darkness around the hall — vanished, switched off by the driver.

The surroundings returned to night.

'What the hell is that?' Léo whispered, his voice barely audible.

Sarah said nothing.

She had no answers.

He touched his foot to the brake out of instinct, and their four-wheel-drive slowed. He approached the town hall cautiously, engine idling as it coasted closer to the lot.

The massive vehicle looming out front remained stationary.

'What do we do?' Sarah said, her voice cracking.

'Nothing,' Léo said. 'It's probably Russian military. We have all the documentation we need. We're supposed to be here. We've done nothing wrong.'

She let his words hang in the air, aware that he was speaking more to reassure himself than anything else.

As they left the gravel track and crawled into the lot, the gargantuan truck began to move.

Already jumpy from the tense situation, Léo panicked and stamped on the brakes. They jolted to a halt. Sarah felt the leather of her seatbelt bite into her shoulder. She let out a deep breath and waited for what would come next.

Headlights still shut off, the vehicle rolled gently past them. Sarah stared with wide eyes as its massive wheels — almost as large as their own car — rumbled in the opposite direction.

It turned onto the same gravel track they had come from.

A moment later, it disappeared from sight.

Silence descended over the lot. Their own headlights were significantly less powerful. The twin beams washed over the front of the town hall, casting vast shadows across their surroundings.

It did nothing to help the ominous feeling in the pit of Sarah's stomach.

It was then that she began to notice the problems with the view ahead. Before, the vehicle's presence had consumed her attention entirely. Now she saw the entrance doors to the hall hanging wide open, exposing the interior to the elements.

Carmen wouldn't dare leave the doors open, she thought.

A few seconds later, something wafted out of the entranceway and spun away into the night, separating as the wind carried it out of the hall.

Sarah gulped back apprehension as their headlights illuminated a cluster of documents, fanned out by the wind, disappearing into the darkness…

Something was seriously wrong.

She flashed a glance at Léo, and noticed his face had paled. The usual colour in his cheeks from the Hungarian sun had all but disappeared, replaced by a white sheet of fear. A drop of sweat ran from the corner of his forehead down the side of his face.

'Léo…' she said.

He turned to her. 'Let's find the others.'

They parked diagonally across the lot and stepped out into the night. Léo left the engine running and the headlights on, aiming them towards the hall.

Then, Sarah realised there were no lights on inside the building…

It was late. Marcus should have been the only one still out on assignment. The other seven WHO workers were supposed to be in the hall, preparing for a quick night's sleep before an early start the following morning.

The building seemed deserted.

Léo led the way, one hand cradling a bulky LED torch that he had fished out of the rear footwell. As they moved away from their four-wheel-drive, he flicked the torch onto full capacity, activating 240 lumens of artificial light. A white LED beam cut through the open entrance, revealing the hallway within.

Nothing seemed out of the ordinary so far — except the darkness.

She followed him inside, cutting off the wind lashing her clothing. This hallway led into the vast main hall that took up the majority of space within the building. Five days ago, they had established their base of operations in the middle of the hall, unloading their medical supplies and communication equipment across a sea of trestle tables they'd found in a back room.

As she and Léo stepped into the open space, she couldn't suppress a gasp of shock.

She barely recognised their workstation anymore.

Léo cast his torch beam over the destroyed surroundings. Sarah hurried past him to get a better look at the carnage. All the tables had been overturned violently, and all breakable equipment had been smashed. In the corner, a cluster of plastic chairs rested in pieces against one of the walls.

There had been serious commotion here…

More importantly, there was no sign of any of their co-workers.

Carmen. Jessica. Marcus. Ethan. Aaron. Diego. Seth. Eli.

All gone.

The beam floated over to the pile of broken chairs — likely used by the crew as rudimentary weapons to defend themselves from…

…*from what?* Sarah thought.

She spotted a dark brown patch smeared into the floor beyond one of the tables. As the torchlight hit it, she noticed the distinct flash of crimson.

Dried blood.

With a pang of terror arcing through her chest, Sarah spun on her heel. She hadn't heard a word from Léo this entire time. She needed to voice the emotions tumbling through her head…

'Léo,' she said in a voice barely above a whisper. 'Where are—'

Then she saw it.

Standing behind Léo.

A bulky figure, hunched over, illuminated ever so slightly by the faint light spilling off the edges of the torch beam. With limited visibility, she couldn't quite make out the features. She thought it was a man — his face covered by some kind of gas mask...

Then the figure lurched forwards and wrapped an arm around Léo's exposed neck.

She watched Léo's eyes boggle as he was wrenched backwards by the motion. He lost his footing and let go of the torch. It clattered to the ground loud enough to echo off the surrounding walls...

...and the beam flickered out.

Her heart racing so fast she thought she might pass out, Sarah screamed as her vision went black. The darkness washed over her. She heard Léo struggling against the attacker's grip.

A powerful hand seized the back of her jacket.

Charged with indescribable terror, she felt her limbs take on a life of their own. The fight-or-flight mechanism kicked in and she tore away from the grip, racing across the room in the direction of the entrance hallway.

She couldn't see anything.

She couldn't hear anything above the noise of her heart pounding in her ears.

Thump.

She ran directly into something.

Someone...

The impact took her off her feet. She sprawled to the cold wooden floor, scrambling for purchase. Two strong hands clamped down on her shoulders and pressed her to the ground. She screamed again and thrashed wildly, bucking and jerking as fear tore through her veins.

It was no use.

This time, her attackers were prepared.

A thick cloth slammed against her mouth and was held there, cutting off her outcry. Panicking, blind to what was unfolding, she sucked in a deep breath of air.

She noticed the chemicals far too late.

It tasted like a mixture of red wine and rot, both fruity and sterile like an artificially-flavoured hospital disinfectant. The acrid flavour stung her throat as it flooded her airways.

The terror gave way to drowsiness and Sarah Grasso slipped into a different kind of darkness.

CHAPTER 2

Stockholm

    Sweden

It had been three weeks since Jason King's services were last employed by Black Force, and the injuries sustained over the course of a gruelling one-man war in Egypt had only just begun to fade into relative obscurity.

He let his breathing settle as he jogged back into the confines of the Mariatorget. He had spent the last week growing accustomed to the pleasant city square in Södermalm, one of the more desirable boroughs in Stockholm. It was calm, residential, tranquil — the polar opposite of what he was used to.

No automatic weapons.

No bloodthirsty extremists.

No fighting and killing.

Just peace.

He took caution not to grow used to the serenity. He knew it would only be a matter of time before he was sent back into hell.

He had come to learn that Södermalm was largely populated by locals, distinctly separate from the busier tourist districts in Stockholm. He had only been in Sweden for seven days, but it felt like it had been an eternity.

Day-to-day civilian life moved slow.

He had moved fast for as long as he could remember.

The orange glow of dusk filtered over the treetops as he came to rest in front of the square's centrepiece — a large statue of the Viking god Thor. He lifted his wrist and concluded the evening run at twelve miles.

He felt his lungs burning in his chest and the veins in his neck throbbing as they sent blood where it was necessary. It was uncomfortable, but discomfort had become so common in his life that he felt strange if he wasn't experiencing it.

Besides, he had learnt to balance that discipline with enjoyment of life.

A short-lived retirement had assisted with that endeavour.

It had been tough to take a sabbatical. Every fibre of his being had begged to head straight back into action. He had entrenched the habit of constant motion so firmly in his psyche that it took great effort to refuse the lure of operations.

But his handler — Isla — had offered him a short vacation to recuperate from the damage he'd sustained in Cairo, and there had been someone he needed to see...

He found the building he was looking for — a residential apartment complex facing out over the Mariatorget — and strode into its lobby. He exchanged a nod with a tired-looking receptionist at the end of his shift who had seen King leave over an hour earlier. The daily run had become something of a staple in the brief period of time that King had spent at the complex.

Even though it went against the urges ingrained into him, he almost dreaded returning to active duty.

He took the stairs two at a time. The hooded sweatshirt draped over his muscular frame was plastered to his skin, damp with sweat. As he reached the fifth floor and made for the quaint wooden door at the end of the hallway, he peeled the shirt off and scrunched it into a ball.

On an average day, he churned through enough laundry to keep a full-time maid busy.

Maintaining this level of physical fitness had its requirements.

The door was locked. He slipped a silver key out of his back pocket and let himself in quietly.

The apartment was *art nouveau*, sporting a vast, sweeping main room complete with a high ceiling and a predominantly white colour palette. A marble kitchen bench swept along one wall, behind a dining area and adjacent to spacious living quarters. A four-poster bed lay against the opposite wall.

He shuffled silently across the oak parquet flooring and ducked into a connecting bathroom. He took an ice-cold shower to wash away the sweat exerted on the run and crept back into the main room, calmed by the serotonin flooding his brain after the exercise.

'I'm awake,' a soft voice said, chuckling. 'You don't need to sneak around like a mouse.'

Klara was stretched out across the four-poster bed by the window, half her lithe frame covered by the stark white duvet. Her skin was paler than usual, weeks removed from the Corsican sun that King had first met her under. There was little opportunity to tan in the freezing Swedish winter.

King preferred the lighter skin tone. Every day, he still found himself taken aback by her beauty.

He smiled. 'This is new. Usually I don't hear from you for hours.'

'What can I say?' she said, rolling on her side to face him. 'Afternoon naps are getting shorter. You're curing my habits.'

'I wish I wasn't,' King said, tapping the side of his head. 'Can't help myself.'

'You're missing out,' she said as King dropped onto his side of the four-poster bed. 'Naps are one of life's greatest experiences.'

'I could list a couple of better experiences,' King said as she threw the duvet off her lingerie-clad body and rolled on top of him.

* * *

An hour later, the final rays of daylight filtered in through the traditional bay windows beside the bed.

Lying naked side-by-side, they both dozed.

King stirred as the room darkened and cast his gaze across the apartment's contents. Klara had done incredibly well for herself. Over the time he'd spent in Sweden, he had come to learn so much more about her than their brief whirlwind romance in Corsica had revealed.

He had started to fall for her even harder.

She certainly hadn't been born with a silver spoon in her mouth. No-one purchased an apartment in one of the most sought after addresses in Sweden without a certain level of wealth. Klara's had been made through a determination and work ethic that King deeply admired. It turned out her modelling in Corsica had been the last leg of a worldwide campaign covering glamour magazines and international brands.

That last leg had almost proved disastrous. How close she had come to an unspeakably horrendous fate at the hands of a corrupt politician still sent shivers down King's spine…

She came to not long after he did. He watched her piercing blue eyes as she stirred.

She smiled. 'This is nice.'

He couldn't argue.

He knew that the closer he got to her, the more devastated she would be if he were to die in the service of Black Force. Even still, he couldn't help himself. After over ten years of embracing pain and fear as a part of his life, he wasn't about to refuse a burst of happiness amidst the carnage.

She noticed his hesitation. 'You need to go back soon, don't you?'

He nodded. 'I wish I didn't.'

She raised an eyebrow. 'Do you?'

He paused.

It was the most complicated puzzle he had ever attempted to disassemble. He knew where she was coming from. When they had first met, he had been retired. Now he was back working for the very same organisation he had fled from — and he couldn't deny that it felt right. The time he'd spent away from Black Force had been just as chaotic as his previous career, and it had taken a dire situation within their ranks for him to return.

It felt like he had never left.

'It's hard to explain,' he said.

'I think I get it.'

'I'm not really sure if I understand it myself.'

'You've done this your whole adult life,' Klara said. 'It's what you're best at. You don't feel like you're doing the right thing when you sit around and don't put that talent to use.'

'Yeah,' King said. 'But there's more…'

'The addiction?'

'I guess you could call it that.'

Klara smirked. 'Regular life is too boring?'

He leant over and kissed her slowly, savouring her taste. He didn't think it was something he would ever grow tired of. 'It's not boring. Truth is, there's nothing I'd rather do than spend the rest of my life here. It's just…'

'The itch?'

'The itch.'

She said nothing. He wasn't sure how she would respond. The silence grew unnerving.

'Do you think I'm insane?' he said.

She smiled. 'That itch — for adrenalin or fighting or whatever the hell it is you do — is probably the most useful one to have.'

'You think?'

'You help people.'

'I struggle with that too. It's hard to do the right thing all the time. My field is so far from black and white…'

'If it wasn't for you, I don't even want to think about where I would be right now. That boat in Corsica was hours away from leaving forever.'

'I know.'

'Think about how many people you've assisted that probably feel the same.'

'I try not to think about anything that's happened in the past,' he said. 'Keeps me sane.'

'Yet you keep going back.'

'You're not angry that I feel I need to?'

She kissed him again. 'Just the opposite.'

'If I leave—' he said. 'Are we committing to each other?'

'I am,' she said. 'I was willing to do that ever since Corsica.'

'Same here,' King said. He paused, then shook his head and chuckled. 'I have no idea how you deal with me.'

'You're the one throwing yourself into danger,' she said. 'I'll be worried, but you've got it so much worse.'

'Voluntarily,' King reminded her.

'Voluntarily.'

He rolled off the bed and slipped on a pair of designer jeans and a thick woollen jumper. 'I'll go pick up some stuff for dinner. The pantry's empty.'

'Don't kill anyone on the way,' Klara ribbed.

He snatched his wallet off the kitchen bench and scoffed. 'I'll try my best.'

* * *

Mariatorget had come alive by the time he made it out into the open air. The square — previously devoid of life — was filled with locals hurrying home to their luxury apartments, dressed to the nines in perfectly-tailored corporate attire.

King knew he stood out amongst the general population. Two-hundred-and-twenty pounds of muscle on a six-foot-three frame stood out almost anywhere. He kept his head bowed as he strode through the square and onto Hornsgatan Street. The sidewalks were lined with maidenhair trees and the roads were congested with hundreds of civilian vehicles resting almost bumper-to-bumper, in the midst of the evening rush.

He decided to spend a little more time than usual out of the apartment. The cold air felt good against his skin, and he was acutely aware of the time he could spend away from Black Force steadily ticking away.

Isla had been lenient in letting him take a short vacation. She had no requirement to do so. The contract he had signed back in New York made it clear that his services were available twenty-four-seven, three-hundred-and-sixty-five days a year.

Every minute he did not spend reporting for duty felt like borrowed time.

Which it was.

So he decided to stroll onto Centralbron, a major traffic route that connected Södermalm to the tourist-filled borough of Gamla Stan. He had made the journey across the waters a couple of times now, and he found the architecture of the old town took his mind off whatever troubles were plaguing him.

He certainly had no shortage of those.

He entered the town's jurisdiction and walked along cobblestone streets, passing buildings that had been constructed as far back as the thirteenth century. He turned onto a narrow thoroughfare — mostly empty in comparison to the rest of the town — and began a slow trek through the heart of the town.

Halfway along the path, he shivered.

Somehow, it felt like he was being watched…

He passed a bank of pay phones that seemed like they hadn't been used in years. Graffiti was scrawled across their dial pads and they were overshadowed by the lip of a neighbouring building, tucked away and abandoned in this quiet corner of Stockholm.

Then, the phone at the very end of the bank began to ring.

King froze in his tracks, more than aware that it couldn't be a coincidence. He stood and watched the phone without moving, weighing up his options, knowing the call was for him but unwilling to answer it.

Finally, unsure as to why Black Force couldn't have got in touch with him in an easier fashion, he lifted the cheap plastic receiver off its cradle and pressed it to his ear.

'Enjoying the stroll?' a deep male voice said.

King recognised it.

Because it's not Black Force, he thought. *It's a friend.*

'Hey, Slater,' he said. 'It's been a while.'

CHAPTER 3

Will Slater was perhaps the only man on the planet as dangerous as King — if not more. Black Force had tasked him to eliminate King back in Corsica, a request that had proved futile after the two had teamed up to take down a corrupt politician in brutal fashion.

King never would have imagined that Slater had shared his sentiments about the organisation that they had both devoted their lives to.

He hadn't spoken to Slater since the man had commandeered a chopper atop a billionaire's superyacht and gone AWOL. It was one of the reasons King had resolved to come out of retirement.

Because Black Force needed him.

Slater had left a gaping hole in their ranks.

'I hear you're back at work,' Slater said. 'I hope that wasn't all for me.'

'If it was simply to replace you, I wouldn't have done it,' King said. 'You know that. I had personal reasons.'

'So I don't need to thank you?'

'I think you do,' King said, smirking. 'I'm probably going to be the one to talk Black Force out of killing you when they find you.'

'They won't find me.'

'You sure?'

'I'm taking it a little more seriously than you were.'

'Hiding was never my goal. I told them I was leaving, remember?'

'Touché,' Slater said. 'How are you holding up?'

King thought about the last week and how truly happy he was with Klara. 'Could be worse, brother.'

'Recovered from Egypt?'

King paused. 'How do you know that was me?'

'Over thirty dead. Half the Giza Pyramid Complex blown to shreds. Who else would it have been?'

'I've been keeping busy.'

'I can see that.'

'How are you finding retirement?' King said. 'Hopefully yours isn't as eventful as mine was.'

'I'm enjoying life,' Slater said. 'Had to spend a couple of weeks making sure my tracks were covered. After all, I didn't want Black Force sending you after me…'

King scoffed. From Slater's end, he thought he heard the sounds of splashing water and the faint laughter of children.

'You in the sun?' King said, leaning one shoulder against the pay phone stand.

'Antigua,' Slater said. 'Thought I'd spend a few days in St. John's.' He hesitated, contemplating something. 'I have your word not to share that with Isla?'

'Share what?' King said.

Slater laughed. 'Thank you.'

King picked at a nail, wondering whether to prod. 'Have you got the itch yet?'

Slater paused. 'Not yet. I'm hoping I don't.'

'Combat was your life,' King said. 'Like it was mine. Don't be surprised if you feel the urge to come back.'

'I'm never coming back.'

King heard the weight in Slater's tone and knew the man was telling the truth. He was done. 'I'm glad to hear that. Really, I am.'

'You were out,' Slater said. 'Why'd you go back?'

'Three times. Three times I tried to start fresh and ran into more trouble than I could imagine. I guess I decided that it was inevitable.'

'I hope you get out before it's too late.'

'So do I.'

'Good to talk to you, King.'

'How the hell did you know where to call?'

'CCTV's a wonderful thing,' Slater said. 'Keep in touch.'

The line went dead.

King lost track of the time he kept hold of the phone, long after the call had ended. He stayed immobile by the bank of pay phones. There wasn't a soul around to watch. He sunk deep into thought, wondering if he really had done the right thing to fill the gap left by Slater's abrupt departure.

It hadn't been his responsibility.

It hadn't been expected of him.

Maybe he should have kept as far away from Black Force as possible. Every day he seemed to grow more conflicted about whether he truly wanted to be there. In the end, it all came back to the simple fact that he had never known anything else, and an attempt to distance himself from that life had failed spectacularly.

Now, he was in too deep.

He set off back the way he had come, suddenly yearning to see Klara. The jarring nature of Slater's observation had rattled him. He flicked his eyes over every nook and cranny of the archaic laneway as he made for the T-junction at the end.

He felt like everyone was watching him all at once.

If tracking him via CCTV had been so effortless, he didn't want to consider who else might be watching.

As he strode back out onto the main road and spotted the bridge leading back to the borough of Södermalm, he made up his mind to get back to the apartment as quickly as possible.

Although the medieval town had previously felt like a breath of fresh air, now it was plagued by a certain sinister feeling.

He didn't like being observed.

He shoved his hands into the pockets of his jeans and pressed forward.

He didn't make it to the bridge.

For a split second, King took his eyes off the sidewalk and glanced down at his feet — more an instinctual reaction than anything else. He imagined all manner of security cameras trained on his face and intuitively cast his eyes to the cobblestone underneath his shoes.

When he looked back up, a man had materialised out of nowhere.

The guy was taking measured strides in the opposite direction to King, only a few feet from passing him by. He had short brown hair — much like King's — close-cropped and cut in the atypical military style. He couldn't have been much taller than six feet, and his thick winter clothing covered gangly limbs. Hard lines were creased into his forehead, signifying years of stress.

He seemed unassuming.

King knew better.

The guy met his gaze and King instantly noticed the recognition. This man was not here for a stroll. He had come for a single purpose and that purpose had something to do with King.

The man glanced away in an attempt to disguise his intent. He carried on strolling toward King, pretending to scrutinise the architecture of the 17th and 18th century buildings running the length of the lane.

King zoned in.

He had no idea what would happen next. He felt a shot of cortisol flood his system like a jolt of fire. He made sure not to reveal the fact that he was on edge.

The fact that he was onto the man heading straight for him.

Then the guy stopped a foot away, as if he knew that it would be dangerous to try and close the distance.

'Jason King,' he said softly. 'My name is Carter.'

King ground to a halt. 'Have we met?'

'No, sir.'

'Okay.'

Carter raised a hand slowly, fingers splayed, indicating that he was unarmed and meant no harm by the action. King watched carefully, anticipating a sudden lunge at any moment.

Then Carter gestured down the entrance to the narrow cobblestone trail they had come to rest beside. It curved between a cluster of Renaissance-era buildings, running through to destinations unknown.

'If you would, please,' Carter said.

King raised an eyebrow. He kept his mouth shut, electing to prolong the uncomfortable silence until the man in front of him was forced to provide an explanation.

Which proved unnecessary.

A woman stepped out of the shadows a dozen feet inside the lip of the alley. She wore an expensive puffer jacket and khaki trousers tucked into high-topped combat boots. Her hair had been pulled back into a rudimentary ponytail.

She looked different to when King had last seen her — two weeks previously in New York.

'Should have known,' he muttered.

Isla seemed more on edge than usual. She wore a terse expression and stared at King like he was her last lifeline, a final hope amidst a sea of confusion. It didn't take much deductive reasoning to understand that something was awry.

She took a step in King's direction and beckoned him into the alley. 'Your vacation's over.'

CHAPTER 4

'Nice to see you again too,' King said. 'Who's this guy?'

'That's Carter,' Isla said, her tone monotonous.

'I'm aware of that. Anything else you might care to share about him?'

'No. Follow me.'

With that, she wheeled on the spot and set off down the deserted laneway. King flashed a glance at Carter, who shrugged apologetically and indicated for him to follow.

He had little other choice.

'Is this another one of those situations where you give me the barest amount of detail and then throw me into the thick of it?' King said, stepping into the alley with measured strides. 'I really didn't appreciate that last time.'

Isla scoffed and turned to face him as she walked. 'King…'

'What?'

'Egypt was on you. I don't recall telling you to butcher a small army along the way. All we needed was a single dead extremist.'

'I think you know stealth isn't my forté.'

'I've come to learn that.'

King grabbed her by the arm and stopped her in her tracks, pausing in the centre of the cobblestone path. Carter almost ran into him from behind.

'What the hell is this?' he said, gesturing in a wide semi-circle.

Isla glared at him. 'We need you. Right now.'

'I'm visiting someone,' he said. 'You can't just whisk me away to do your bidding without giving me a single hour's notice.'

'Of course I can,' she said. 'That's what you signed up for. And we don't have an hour's notice, King. We needed to be in the air an hour ago.'

'To where?'

She flashed a glance at her digital wristwatch. 'Russia.'

They pressed on into the old town of Gamla Stan.

* * *

One hundred feet later, the cobblestone lane opened out into a spacious two-way street lined with residential buildings. Two orderly rows of civilian vehicles ran along each side of the asphalt, all sporting permits on the dashboards to signify that they belonged to residents.

Except for one.

Isla and Carter led him to a brand-new Saab 9-3 Turbo X, so pristine that King thought it might have come straight from the dealership. Isla unlocked the 4WD and ushered him into the back seat.

'Rented?' he said as he slipped into the interior.

'Yeah,' she said. 'On loan from the airport. We came straight to you as soon as we landed.'

'Am I going to get even the slightest hint of an explanation?'

'Sorry,' Isla said, pressing two fingers to her eyes in a rare display of something resembling emotion. 'There's a million things running through my head right now.'

'Feel free to share them with me at any time.'

She spun in the passenger seat to meet his gaze as Carter reversed the Saab out of the parking space and stamped on the accelerator. King felt the power of the engine kick in as he was thrust back against his seat.

'Why are we in a hurry?'

Isla breathed out hard and closed her eyes for a moment, clearly attempting to gather her wits. 'Okay, where do I start...?'

'Why I'm headed to Russia. That might be good.'

She pursed her lips. 'Cut the sarcasm.'

'Give me answers.'

'The Kamchatka Peninsula,' she said. 'What do you know about it?'

'Never heard of it.'

'Great.'

'It sounds remote.'

'It is. It's a stretch of mountains and volcanoes in the Russian Far East. The whole region's barely populated, and those who do live there are predominantly ethnic Russians. Many of them live in rural villages with little modern technology. Makes it a clusterfuck of a situation when any kind of disease starts to spread.'

'I bet.'

'There were ten World Health Organisation workers stationed at one of the villages. It's so isolated that it doesn't even have a name. They were fighting an outbreak of tuberculosis amongst the locals.'

'What happened?'

'No-one knows. They had strict check-in policies that they haven't adhered to for over thirty-six hours. Given the somewhat dangerous location, it's sent alarm bells ringing.'

King let the words sit for a moment before proceeding with a response. 'Stop the car.'

'What?'

'Pull over right now unless you want me to do it for you.'

Isla exchanged a tense glance with Carter. Then she relented, giving a slight nod to indicate that he should follow King's orders.

Carter screeched to a halt between two parked sedans.

Isla spun in her seat the second the Saab had stopped. Her glare had fury behind it, clearly outraged that King would be so brash in the face of such concerning news. 'What the hell are you doing?'

'I should ask you the same,' King said. 'A party of health workers don't get in touch with the people they need to for a day and a half? They're in the middle of nowhere. They've probably lost their signal. Maybe they're in a bad storm.'

'We don't think so,' Isla said.

'Don't the WHO have protocols in place for this sort of thing? What is this, Isla? This isn't what Black Force is for.'

She locked eyes with him, and he sensed anger there. 'I don't think I need to lecture you on the tensions between Russia and the U.S. right now. You're a precautionary measure. We drop you in there and you make sure everything is okay. If the worst has happened, the consequences will be disastrous. You're the closest thing our country has to a one-man wrecking machine. I've been given express orders for you to sort this mess out before *anything* makes it to the media. Understood?'

'Not really.'

'You don't have a choice, King,' Isla said. 'This is what you signed up for.'

'Not exactly.'

'Pout all you want,' she said. 'But you do what we tell you to. Consider yourself lucky. In all likelihood they're fine, and you can get back to your girlfriend as quickly as possible. Okay?'

'Why do I get the feeling that's not going to happen?'

'Because you're a Black Force operative,' Isla said. 'Something will always come up. You know that. This recuperation period was a one-off.'

Carter exchanged a look with Isla, who gestured for him to continue. He reversed out of the lot and veered back into the Stockholm traffic.

King felt an icy resignation washing over him. He knew there was nothing left to argue. The switch in mentality from vacationing romantic to cold-hearted killer took some time to settle in.

But now it had.

His instinctual response to the situation had been resistance. Now he shook away the odd sensation and embraced what was to come. His services were needed — it was not his business to question his orders. He assumed the finer details of the situation involving the WHO workers had been stressed over and considered by officials ranked far higher than him. He settled back into his seat and studied the passing scenery as they skirted around traffic.

He was unsure what lay ahead.

The detail had been scarce, but he assumed there was still plenty of time to be properly informed.

'Where are we headed?' he said.

'Stockholm Bromma Airport,' Isla said.

King cocked his head. 'Haven't heard of that one.'

'It's a smaller number. Not as busy. We have a plane waiting. You'll be fully briefed once we're in the air.'

King grimaced. 'Wonderful.'

Carter switched lanes and picked up speed, roaring closer to an operation that King subconsciously knew would not be as easily resolved as Isla anticipated.

CHAPTER 5

Near Shiveluch Volcano

Russian Far East

The gold mine had been abandoned by its crew over eight years ago, skewered into the craggy plains of the Kamchatka Peninsula. A cocktail of frequent volcanic eruptions, devastating floods and the sheer difficulty required in transporting ore back to civilisation had resulted in its owners closing the doors after a single shaky year of mining operations.

Vadim Mikhailov knew precisely when it had been abandoned.

He was a man of opportunity.

A man of preparation.

A man of painstaking and meticulous scrutiny.

He did not commit to anything without being confident of its success in advance.

He cast a glance at the thick storm clouds that hung ominously over the towering Shiveluch Volcano in the distance. It caused him to grip the handlebars of his ride a little tighter. Even a man with his horrific past couldn't help but shiver at such a sight. He slowed the Taiga-551 snowmobile to a crawl as he approached the familiar building resting in the shadows of a sheer cliff-face.

This far off the beaten track, no-one would have a hope of discovering it at random.

Which was precisely why he had selected it for his most recent business endeavour.

Mikhailov felt the sheer silence of the region as he killed the engine and the snowmobile's whine faded into nothingness. He clambered off the seat and dropped into the snow. The three layers of high-end winter clothing did nothing to stop the cold leeching into his bones. Out here, the temperature hit such extreme lows that any effort to avoid it proved futile.

He had grown used to the sensation long ago.

The cold-weather gear covered a hardened frame covered almost entirely in savage tattoos. Six years in the KGB a couple of decades ago had transformed Mikhailov. He had come out of the agency a cold shell of his former self. He happily admitted that. It had proved lucrative in the new Russian landscape following the dissolution of the Soviet Union.

The forty-five-year-old had high aspirations.

This operation would help him achieve them.

He touched a gloved hand to the jagged scar running underneath his eyelid, surrounded by burned skin and mangled flesh. An error of judgment, three long years ago. The old wounds still troubled him when the freezing cold seeped into them.

He'd refused skin grafts.

He'd wanted to remember his moment of weakness for the rest of his life.

He trudged through the snow as the wind howled all around him, slicing across the sloping plains. The region was uninhabited for dozens of miles in any direction. Even reaching the mine via land was a dangerous task, achievable only by those who knew the area like the back of their hand.

Another reason why it was unoccupied.

Mikhailov unlocked an enormous steel padlock clamped over the sliding warehouse door and wrenched it open. The door ground against its tracks, iced over from the elements pounding the building. He felt the veins in his forearms pumping from the exertion. When he finally forced the gap wide enough to fit a vehicle through, he stepped into the space within.

The warehouse had a single feature — a giant steel cage set against the far wall that contained a rickety elevator suspended from a hoist. Beside the cage rested the hoist motor, connected to the elevator by thick steel wire rope.

It descended six thousand feet into the bowels of the earth.

Aside from that, the warehouse was empty. It was a vast space with a concrete floor, surrounded by four towering walls — nothing but a housing facility to protect the mine cage from the elements. Mikhailov cast his eyes around the room and imagined the warehouse filled with gold mining equipment many years ago, bustling with activity as miners toiled to earn an honest paycheque.

His paycheques were anything but honest.

Not that he cared.

In his experience, honest paycheques had a distinct lack of zeroes.

Deep in one of the pockets of his jacket, a satellite phone began to vibrate. Mikhailov peeled off one glove and fished it out. He pressed the device to his ear.

'*Da?*'

'Everything went smoothly,' a gruff voice said in Russian. 'We have them. We'll be there in five minutes.'

'Perfect. No trouble?'

'None.'

'The door's open.'

He ended the call and tucked the phone back into his jacket. He kept his hands inside the insulated material, shivering in the sudden quiet. To anyone unaccustomed to the mine's remote location, the noises emanating through the warehouse would be nightmarish. The storms raging across the peninsula were faintly audible, howling and wailing like ghosts disturbed from an eternal slumber. The rocky outcrop behind the warehouse protected its surroundings from the wind, so that the storms in the distance sounded like an approaching apocalypse.

Mikhailov wasn't bothered by such things anymore.

This place was his second home.

He stayed completely still in the centre of the abandoned building, watching the entrance intently, waiting…

Not long after, the throaty chugging of a powerful engine drowned out the distant wailing. Mikhailov knew everything about the approaching vehicle — because he had purchased it.

He did not part from his hard-earned money without careful consideration.

He did not throw millions of rubles at an armoured blast-resistant tank-on-wheels without knowing exactly what he was getting.

The Otokar Kaya-II — painted midnight black upon its arrival in Mikhailov's arsenal — could officially carry up to ten people and traverse almost any kind of terrain you could throw at it. That had been the main selling point when he had secured the carrier vehicle four months ago — whatever he decided on had to be able to make it to the mine with ease.

The maximum road speed of sixty miles per hour was not an issue.

The bulletproof windows, welded steel armour and NSV 12.7mm heavy machine gun mounted on the roof hatch had seized his attention instead.

Mikhailov had effectively acquired a tank.

Once he had his targets inside the vehicle, nothing would be able to break them out.

The Kaya-II rumbled into the warehouse and stopped beside Mikhailov, chunks of snow falling from its massive wheels. The driver's door opened and a man in combat khakis stepped down from the front compartment. A thick woollen balaclava covered his face, exposing only his eyes. Normally cold and hard, Mikhailov could now see the stress leeching from the man.

He didn't blame him.

The drive would have been nerve-wracking, guiding a thirty-thousand pound tanker through the Kamchatka Peninsula, home to all manner of frozen lakes and unstable ground. They had charted a route through the terrain many times before, but that wouldn't have shaken the nerves.

The driver would spend the trip imagining the ice beneath the Kaya's wheels giving way, a moment before the armoured behemoth sunk to a watery grave.

Nevertheless, the man was being paid handsomely for his endeavours.

'They're in the back?' Mikhailov said.

The man nodded. 'All ten.'

Mikhailov crossed to the rear of the Kaya-II and wrenched open the steel hatch leading into the body of the vehicle. He heard a chorus of whimpering from inside, accompanied by sharp inhales.

They're scared, he thought. *Good.*

He cast his eyes over the shivering bodies, sprawled across the metal floor of the compartment, their hands and feet bound and their mouths gagged. He made eye contact with the woman closest to him. She stared up at him with terrified eyes, groggy from the drugs that had knocked her unconscious.

'Did we do well?' the driver said. A second man in an identical balaclava emerged from the passenger door. Mikhailov exchanged a nod of approval with the pair.

'Where are the others?' he said.

'On the outskirts of the village,' the driver said. 'There wasn't enough room for all of us to fit. We thought we'd drop this lot off and then pick them up on the way back.'

'Why do you need to go back?'

'To clean up the scene.'

Mikhailov paused. 'What's to clean up?'

'We had … some difficulty. Ten people are hard to subdue all at once. We had some resistance.'

'I assume you handled it.'

'We did.'

Mikhailov slammed the hatch closed, locking the ten WHO workers inside the Kaya. 'You did well. Get back to the village and sterilise the hall. If you caused commotion there might be some undesirables poking their noses around.'

The driver hesitated. 'I thought you paid the authorities off...'

'I have. But you can never be too careful. We're dealing with foreigners here.'

'What do you want us to do with them?'

'Leave them here,' Mikhailov said. 'I'll take them underground. The viewers are ready.'

CHAPTER 6

Twenty minutes out of Gamla Stan, Carter turned onto a winding potholed road that led away from the more populated regions of Stockholm and twisted through an industrial zone on the way to the airport.

King spent the journey in absolute silence. He shunned Isla's infrequent attempts at small talk. It was none of her business how his holiday had gone. He had a task ahead and that task would involve a return to the savagery and brutality of his past.

He was sure of it.

He concentrated on preparing for that and watched Stockholm flash by on either side of the Saab. Then he had a thought.

'You got a phone?' he said.

Isla twisted in her seat. 'You don't?'

'Left it back at the apartment. Wasn't expecting such an … abrupt departure.'

'Why do you need one?'

'You just dragged me away from someone who I've grown quite fond of. Let me tell her why I'm gone, at least.'

Isla nodded and tossed him a military-style satellite phone that she fished out of the footwell. He dialled Klara's number and waited for her to pick up.

'Hello?' she said, her voice quiet.

'Hey. It's me.'

She said nothing for a while, likely putting two and two together. Connecting the unknown number to the sound of King's voice. 'You're not coming back for a while, are you?'

'I'm afraid not. Business … came up.'

'Did you know before you left?'

'No. Otherwise I would have said goodbye properly.'

'They were following you?'

'Maybe it's best we don't talk about that,' King said.

'Of course. Well, you know where to find me. Thank you for the week, Jason.'

'I'll be back,' he said. 'I promise.'

'I know you will. Go do what you do best.'

'I love you,' King said on a whim.

It took her by surprise — he could tell. They hadn't said it to each other yet, and King hadn't intended to say it for a long time. He wanted to be sure before committing so hard to a relationship, but he didn't want to suppress how he felt before potentially dying in the service of his country.

He wanted her to know…

'I love you too,' she said, and ended the call before either of them could say anything more.

He knew she would be fighting with emotions. He scolded himself for letting it out, aware that if he happened to meet his demise in the coming operation it would prove harder for Klara than he could imagine.

He listened to the silence from the speaker for a couple of beats before passing the phone back to Isla's outstretched hand.

She grimaced as she took the device.

'I'm sorry to have to pull you away on such short notice,' she said. 'I hope you know that.'

'I know,' King said. 'You don't have a choice.'

The conversation died. King wasn't in the mood to talk. He considered the gravity of what he had just said, surprised that it had come out like that. He considered himself a man of few words, and even fewer emotions.

He was surprised that she had understood his departure so quickly. Perhaps it had been caused by witnessing the violence that he and Slater had dished out in Corsica.

She knew what he was.

She had chosen to be with him regardless.

He knew he might not find anyone else like that in his lifetime.

Finally — after ten minutes of silence — Isla turned back around and made sure to make direct eye contact with him. 'You haven't heard from Slater, have you?'

King didn't miss a beat. 'Not a word. I take it you haven't?'

She didn't respond for a lengthy duration, scrutinising the expression on his face, trying to ascertain whether he was really telling the truth.

He knew she wouldn't find anything there. He could put on a mask of stone when he wanted to.

Satisfied by the answer, she turned back around. 'Not yet. We're hoping he makes contact.'

'You're not looking for him?'

'Of course we are.'

'To kill him?'

A pause. Isla let the statement hang in the air, weighing up its implications.

'King,' she finally said. 'I want you to know that it wasn't me who made the decision to send Slater after you in Corsica. We never really addressed that.'

'Because it doesn't need addressing,' King said. 'You had the wrong idea — I get it. You thought I'd turned psychotic in retirement. If I was in your position, I probably would have done the same.'

'If you do want to talk about it…'

'Maybe,' he said. 'Not right now. Sounds like there's more pressing matters at hand in Russia.'

'Like you said, it could be nothing.' Her tone had softened since they'd first run into each other in the laneway. King wondered if she felt guilty about Corsica. 'But we need you to check it out.'

'I'll be compensated?'

'Of course.'

'Then that's all that needs to be said. I'll do my job.'

The airport loomed ahead — a vast expanse of land with a maze of lined runways and a couple of weather-beaten terminals in the distance.

'I take it we're not heading to the Russian Far East via the civilian route?' King said.

'Not this time,' Isla said. 'It's quite difficult to reach. We need the assistance.'

Carter pulled up to a cramped security guard's booth built into the wire fence skirting around the perimeter of the property. He flashed a knowing look at the waiting guard, who promptly stabbed a button on the console in the booth. The gate grated open, inch by inch. As soon as there was space, Carter shot through and sped toward a secluded corner of the airport's grounds.

King spotted the aircraft well before they reached the otherwise-deserted stretch of runway. He studied its exterior from afar, struggling to comprehend the size of the plane. From this distance it looked like an alien spacecraft — jet black in colour, with two sweeping wings and a smooth body that seemed to be designed for high altitudes.

'What the hell is that?' he said. 'Is that ours?'

'It's a B-1 Lancer,' Isla said. 'And yes — it's ours.'

The knot in King's stomach that had formed after Isla's appearance twisted a little tighter. He grimaced as they pulled up to the enormous aircraft and Carter killed the engine. Silence filled the car. No-one moved.

'Correct me if I'm wrong,' King said, 'but isn't that a supersonic bomber?'

'It is.'

'Why the hell do we need a supersonic bomber?'

Isla shook her head. 'Don't worry. We're not starting a war. In fact, quite the contrary. That's why we need something like this.'

'An explanation would be good.'

She pointed at the vast underside of the Lancer, where two steel doors rested firmly shut. 'That's the forward bomb bay. It's currently empty. That's how we're getting you into Russia undetected.'

King grimaced. 'I'm jumping?'

Isla nodded.

'From what altitude?'

'Thirty thousand feet.'

'A HALO jump?' King said.

It stood for "High Altitude, Low Opening." He had only made a handful in his lifetime. They required the use of a plethora of apparatus, including oxygen masks and gear capable of withstanding temperatures well below zero.

In almost all cases, he preferred to avoid them. A traditional skydive provided more than enough of a rush.

'Yes,' Isla confirmed. 'It's important that no-one knows you're there. We want you in and out before any alarm bells start ringing. The less their government know about American black-ops soldiers on their soil, the better.'

'Hence the bomber.'

'Exactly.'

'They need quite the crew, if I'm not mistaken,' King said.

Isla gestured across the centre console. 'Carter here is an Air Force enlisted bomber pilot. That's why he's here.'

'And the others?'

'On board. A co-pilot and a defensive systems officer.'

'I take it I keep my mouth shut around them?'

'You're damn right,' Isla said. 'You don't exist, remember?'

'Let's get in the air,' Carter muttered.

King followed them out of the Saab. He stepped down onto the tarmac and felt the wind in his hair, thick and unruly after the lack of maintenance. He made a mental note to return to the familiar buzzcut as soon as he could.

It seemed that would have to be after Russia.

Still largely uninformed on the details, he trailed along behind Isla and Carter, heading for the bomber. Despite the pit in his stomach, the nerves felt normal. His track record was long and storied and rarely ever non-violent. At this point, he anticipated carnage in the Russian Far East. He expected nothing less.

Any alternative would be greatly welcomed.

But it never seemed to turn out that way…

They were met by an unassuming middle-aged man underneath the Lancer. He was well below average height and dressed in a stained olive jumpsuit.

'I'm the co-pilot,' he said softly, exchanging a nod of greeting with Carter. He didn't elaborate. King shrugged it off, agreeing that knowing as little about the man as possible was probably best. Carter seemed to be the only crewman aware of Black Force's existence.

The co-pilot shook their hands in turn before leading them up a shaky entrance ladder. King went last, following Carter and then Isla into the bowels of the bomber.

They climbed up into a cramped, low-ceilinged room behind the main cockpit. It was windowless and humid, with the only light coming from a dim bulb fixed into the metal roof.

There were three hard seats taking up the majority of the floorspace — one occupied by another middle-aged expressionless man in a jumpsuit.

The defensive systems officer, King thought, recalling the crew members Isla had rattled off before.

'There's no offensive systems officer?' he muttered to Isla.

She grit her teeth. 'We weren't able to find one in time. Besides, we're not attacking anything.'

'Wha—' he began, but the co-pilot cut him off with a glare, as if to say *"I already tried."*

King shrugged off the haphazard approach and dropped into one of the available seats, positioned in the centre of the space. It provided a clear view through to the cockpit, where Carter was busying himself firing up the bomber. Hundreds of indecipherable buttons and switches and flashing lights splayed across the console in front of him.

Isla dumped herself into the seat next to him — usually occupied by the offensive system officer.

'Something about this whole thing gives me the feeling that it was thrown together at the last minute,' King said.

'It was,' Isla said. 'We're improvising here. But that's what you're best at, isn't it?'

King sighed. 'I guess.'

Twenty minutes later, strapped into the seat so tight that he thought the circulation might be cut off in his limbs, he felt the

B-1 Lancer rocket down the empty runway and lift off with a swooping stomach lurch.

King closed his eyes and composed himself.

Earlier that day, he had been anticipating a relaxing evening spent indoors with Klara, cooking and eating and talking about life.

Now, he was shooting toward the darkest corner of Russia at seven hundred miles per hour.

Just another day at the office, he thought.

CHAPTER 7

The silence that gripped the cockpit as the Lancer left the runway and began its ascent into the night sky gave King time to think.

Ultimately, he concluded that nothing about this situation made any sense.

Black Force was made up of the very best operatives on the planet, used to achieve the impossible and act decisively when unnaturally high stakes presented themselves. King recalled his whirlwind career before his short-lived retirement.

He remembered battering his way through a Mexican drug cartel — one of his first operations under the command of Black Force. He remembered waging a one-man war against a vicious Ugandan warlord and his army of hired thugs. He remembered coming within a hair's breadth of death in the jungles of the Amazon Rainforest.

He certainly didn't remember babysitting a party of international relief workers who had gone missing for a grand total of thirty-six hours.

Despite the situation that *might* have unfolded, it felt unnatural to King. He had never undertaken a task like this before. The stakes felt incredibly low.

Which is good for your health, he reminded himself. *About time you got an easy gig.*

Still, it unnerved him.

Black Force didn't exist to dispense easy gigs.

It wasn't in his job description.

As they reached altitude and levelled out near the top of the lower atmosphere, King flashed a glance at Isla. She sat rigid in her seat, palms flat against her knees, hands white and clammy.

'Afraid of flying?' King said, pointing at her hands.

She shrugged. 'A little.'

'So talk to me about what the hell's going on here.'

She leaned over and checked on the defensive systems officer to King's left, making sure he was out of earshot. The cockpit was loud as hell, and the man had his gaze transfixed on the screen in front of him. His ears were covered by a bulky headset. Satisfied, she sat back.

'It's rare that Black Force is required in a situation like this,' Isla said.

'I'm aware.'

'This came from the very top,' she said. 'Usually there are endless protocols in place for this sort of thing. None of them involve us.'

'So what's different about this?'

Isla shrugged. 'I know as much as you do. Tensions are high, apparently. The upper echelon of government wants to be assured that everything is okay, and they don't want the Russians to know that our operatives are snooping around in places they're not meant to be.'

'I still don't buy it.'

'I'm not asking you to buy it,' she said. 'I'm asking you to carry out the orders you've been given.'

He stared at her, unblinking.

She sighed. 'Look, King, I don't understand either. This definitely shouldn't be our area of concern. But it is — for who-knows-what reason — and you need to do it. Poke around the village. Look for anything unusual. Do what you always do — improvise.'

'And if they really are gone? Disappeared without a trace?'

'Then find out what happened to them — by whatever means necessary — and get them back. You know how this works.'

'I don't know, Isla…'

'In all likelihood, they're all locked up in their HQ riding out a snowstorm or trying to patch up their communication equipment. Then you can turn around and head right back to Sweden. Okay?'

'Where's their HQ?'

'From what we know, they're using the town hall. You can't miss it.'

'You have the location?'

'Of course. You'll be supplied with everything you need.'

King felt the Lancer shudder underneath him and experienced a wave of unease as he contemplated just how far above ground they were cruising.

He imagined the oxygen mask clamped over his face, amplifying his panicked breaths, waiting for the bomb bay doors to shoot open and send him tumbling out into the freezing Russian sky.

Thirty thousand feet…

He shook it off, but couldn't help but consider the ridiculousness of what was about to happen. He was being forced to follow questionable orders and proceed with a HALO jump into a desolate wasteland. For a moment, he reconsidered his decision to sign on the dotted line back in New York and rejoin his old organisation…

He scolded himself for such thoughts. If he hadn't done so, a radical extremist from the slums of Cairo would have succeeded with his plan to obliterate a few hundred tourists at the Giza Pyramid Complex in order to turn a quick profit.

And more importantly, the WHO workers could be in serious danger.

He couldn't picture a scenario where all of their communication equipment — including backups — would fail at once for such an extended period of time.

He feared the worst.

That's because all you're used to is the worst, he thought.

Nevertheless, he calmed his heart rate and rested his head against the cold metal headrest behind him.

'How long's the flight?' he said, eyes closed.

'Only a couple of hours,' Isla said. 'This bird is fast.'

'Great.'

In the back of his mind, the fear threatened to break out. He didn't let it. The atmosphere of the cramped cockpit added to the unease. Cold steel and confined spaces — and below, tens of thousands of feet of nothingness. He wouldn't have batted an eyelid if he didn't have to leave the plane at the same altitude in just a few short hours.

He kept his eyes shut.

It would be a tumultuous plane ride for his emotions.

Transforming into the Jason King of operational ability was not as simple as flicking a switch.

He always prepared to enact savage violence, even though it might not come.

But something told him it would.

CHAPTER 8

Some time later, a hand seized his shoulder.

King's eyes shot open and he wrenched the arm away with lightning quickness. The frail wrist spun away from him and the owner let out a sharp gasp of air.

He blinked twice and saw Isla staring at him, shocked by the sudden outburst.

He calmed himself. 'Sorry.'

She shook it off. 'On edge?'

'A little. I need to be before this sort of thing.'

'Half an hour until drop,' she said.

'Half an hour?'

'You've been asleep.'

King shook his head to gather his senses. The run through Stockholm must have sapped his energy. 'Jesus…'

'You need to be briefed properly. Follow me.'

She led him through a narrow doorway into a claustrophobic corridor packed with all kinds of electronics. To his inexperienced eye, it looked like a systems bay. They moved past the flashing lights and shimmied down a hatch into the forward fuselage bomb bay.

King gulped back apprehension as he stepped into the space.

The floor consisted of the two bay doors, pressed together seamlessly along the centre line of the empty space. When they parted, it would expose the thirty thousand feet of sky between the Lancer and the mountainous Russian terrain.

A long way to fall, he thought.

The bay was dimly illuminated by several lengths of weak artificial lighting dotting the ceiling. Thick olive wires snaked along the steel walls, arranged neatly into rows. The air felt artificial and stank of aviation fuel and grime.

The space where the payload usually rested lay empty — save for a rudimentary plank that had been stretched across the bay at chest height.

'What's that for?' King said.

'That's where you sit.'

'Great.'

He walked tentatively across the bay floor, acutely aware that it would only take one flick of a switch to send the doors dropping away beneath him.

It would be a long and terrifying fall to his death.

He followed Isla to the plank, where an array of gear was sprawled across the metal underneath. He cast his eyes over

HALO jump gear, an oxygen mask, distress flares, an M4A1 carbine assault rifle, and finally a thick all-weather pack designed to strap on one's front during a skydive. The pack seemed loaded to the brim, likely filled with all kinds of survival gear in case King got caught in the middle of nowhere without viable backup.

He gestured to the duffel pack. 'What's in that?'

'Thought you might ask,' Isla said. 'A few changes of clothes — all top-of-the-line gear. Ration packs and water in case you get trapped in the middle of nowhere. And a Glock-22 — for good measure.'

King ran his hands over the M4A1 carbine.

'That rifle is standard,' she said. 'Three modes. Safe, semi-automatic, fully-automatic. But you knew that already. I heard it's your favourite.'

'Been a while since I've used one.'

'Yeah,' she said. 'You didn't get the chance in Egypt. Lord knows what would have happened if you were fully armed.'

'You know there's likely nothing down there, right?'

She nodded. 'This is all just precautionary.'

With one hand, she reached back and extracted a small syringe — capped for protection — from her jacket pocket. She slid the plastic cap off and flicked the thin needle twice.

'Hold out your arm,' she said.

'What the hell is that?'

68

'I'm not a doctor,' she said. 'I was told to give it to you. It'll act as a temporary barrier against a group of diseases. They were treating tuberculosis, remember.'

'Great.'

He rolled up his shirt and offered his arm. Isla sunk the needle into his skin — just above his bicep — and injected him with the contents of the syringe.

'Not targeting a vein?' King said through clenched teeth.

'Intramuscular injection is what I've been told,' Isla said. 'Once again — I'm not a doctor. Just following instructions.'

'Neither am I, so I'll take your word for it,' he said, rolling his sleeve back down. 'So what happens now?'

'Get dressed,' Isla said. 'Obviously I can't be in the bay when we hit our destination. The green light above the door we came through will turn on, and three seconds later the floor will open up. Then you drop.'

King suddenly felt a sharp wave of vertigo wash over him. It reminded him that the ground he stood on was really just a thin metal door, ready to thrust him into below freezing temperatures.

Isla handed him a thin chrome earpiece.

'Stick that to the inside of your ear,' she said. 'It's basically a miniature satellite phone. Contact me at any time by touching a finger to it. Got it?'

King nodded and wedged the device into his ear canal. It felt odd for a minute, but he soon acclimatised. It lent him an air of security. He had backup on standby at any moment. 'Anything else?'

Isla shrugged. 'Good luck. But I know you won't need it. I assume you know how to get this gear on?'

He cocked his head. 'I think I can handle it, Isla.'

Before she left, her expression changed.

King noticed it only for a split second, but it was enough to understand that she hadn't revealed everything to him. The facade of grittiness fell away and she looked at him like he hadn't ever seen before. There was vulnerability in her eyes.

'King,' she said, her tone wavering. 'Please find them.'

Then she turned on her heel and strode out of the bay before he had a chance to quiz her on the odd statement.

Alone in the empty bay, he set himself into a methodical trance-like state, checking and re-checking his weapon and gear until he was certain that everything would work. He undressed, shivering in the freezing air, and donned the tactical gear Isla had provided.

First came a layer of skin-tight thermal compression wear. Next he slipped on thick navy khakis, heavy black combat boots, several layers of dark upper-body protective clothing and finally a bulletproof vest made of Spectra instead of Kevlar. King had long been a fan of Spectra for operations such as these, where he was inserted into unknown territory and forced to carry all his gear with him. The material was lighter and more efficient than its better-known counterpart.

He secured the all-weather pack to the front of his torso, limiting his movement. When he hit solid ground, he would shed the parachute and its container — freeing him of the majority of the weight. Black Force had the budget to spare a parachute.

He stepped into the harness at his feet and shimmied it up his legs, tightening the leather straps around his thighs. He reached back and shrugged on the main container, heavy to compensate for his bulk. Next came the oxygen mask, which he slipped over his face and secured tight.

The visor dropped down over his eyes, tinting his vision. He connected the mask to the small oxygen bottle fixed into the side of his chute and checked the gauge.

Full.

He waited until the oxygen began to flow from the tank before breathing a sigh of relief. The last thing he wanted was a desperate scramble for the exit as he realised there was a malfunction, just as the floor fell away…

Finally he knotted the M4A1 to the pack pressed against his chest and stomach. The sheer amount of gear attached to him weighed him down, causing his quads and hamstrings to activate.

With a grunt of exertion, he heaved himself onto the plank, scrambling against the cold metal until he dropped onto the thin surface on his rear.

Then he waited.

He felt a pang of claustrophobia deep in his chest, listening to the sound of his own heavy breathing as oxygen flowed from the tank into his mouth. It tasted sterile.

The visor dulled his surroundings, to the point where they felt artificial. He experienced a certain disconnect from his reality, like the jump wasn't actually about to happen.

Five minutes later, the warning light above the exit door blinked on.

King stared at it.

Here we go.

He soaked in the relative silence while he had the chance.

The doors parted and unrelenting wind howled in, circling around the empty bay, pummelling his clothing, threatening to throw him off the ledge.

He gripped a nearby column tight. Below, gargantuan storm clouds roiled across a dark sky.

The ground was so far below that he couldn't see an inch of it.

He gulped once, tightened his gut, and fell forward.

Carried by the momentum of all the weight strapped to his chest, he toppled off the ledge and dropped like a deadweight away from the bomber.

CHAPTER 9

Chaos.

King entered an uncontrollable spin the second he fell into thin air.

Only a couple of seconds after dropping from the bomb bay, he caught a fleeting glimpse of the B-1 Lancer far overhead, nothing but a speck in the distance. Then the massive storm clouds swallowed him up, and he lost all sight of the aircraft.

He arched his back and splayed his limbs, maximising his surface area, but it proved futile. Carrying this much weight was disastrous. His vision blurred as he tore through hundreds of feet of thick grey clouds in the blink of an eye.

He twisted and spun in the air.

He knew that from thirty thousand feet, free fall was supposed to last a full two minutes.

He had one-hundred-and-twenty seconds to right himself, or he would fail to deploy his chute and hit the mountains at terminal velocity.

Still surrounded by cloud, his vision proved useless.

The ground was invisible.

He forced himself not to panic. With his senses overloading, any kind of descent into full-blown terror would inhibit his fine motor skills and cause him to sink deeper into the spin. He ignored his heart, pounding so hard against his chest wall that he thought it might burst.

He focused on the factors he could control.

Maintaining the arched back was paramount. He spread his arms and legs as wide as they could go, but the weight of the gear strapped across his body wrenched him downward at an incredible speed.

He needed to slow himself.

The drogue chute, you idiot.

Scolding himself for such foolishness, he reached back and yanked the drogue parachute out of its holster. The small stretch of canvas acted as a stabiliser to trail behind heavy skydivers and slow their descent by a few dozen miles per hour. It was often utilised by tandem skydivers to control the novice strapped to their front.

King had completely forgotten of its existence.

It had been a while.

He didn't see the drogue chute open, but he felt its effect. Almost instantly, the rapid spin corrected itself. It still felt like he was hurtling to the ground at terminal velocity — which he was — but the slightly reduced speed allowed him to stabilise more effectively.

Slowly, his vision came back to him.

Darkness. All around. Freefalling at night into enemy territory never failed to instil terror in even the most hardened veterans. The surrounding black conjured all kinds of imaginings in the mind.

He checked the altimeter strapped to his wrist.

Fifteen thousand feet.

He would pull the main parachute at three thousand feet. An incredibly low opening by normal safety standards, but the last thing he wanted was to open too high and find himself spotted by…

By who?

By a party of international relief workers, in all likelihood. Probably wondering why a Special Forces operative armed to the teeth had been sent to confirm their wellbeing.

You and me both, he thought.

At eight thousand feet he burst through the lowest layer of clouds and the Russian Far East revealed itself far below. Through his visor, he stared out at sweeping plains and massive volcanoes sprawled across the barren land. From this height, they looked like pimples on the surface of the Earth.

There was just enough moonlight to make out the features of the Kamchatka Peninsula. Without it, King wouldn't have been able to see a thing. He noted the complete absence of artificial light below. The region was almost entirely uninhabited.

Powering toward the peninsula at one-hundred-and-twenty miles per hour, King felt a chill arc down his spine. Decent infrastructure didn't exist out here. Barely populated, the Kamchatka Peninsula was effectively lawless. He wondered if there really was something sinister lurking amongst the volcanoes.

The altimeter's needle passed below four thousand feet. On either side of him, the mountains loomed.

King reached back and tugged the pilot chute free.

It took a couple of seconds to halt his descent. For a fleeting moment he thought there had been a malfunction and his stomach twisted. He reached instinctively for the handle that activated the reserve chute.

Then the straps under his armpits and around his thighs constricted, yanked up by the wind catching the vast canopy above his head.

The pack against his chest slammed into him, knocking the breath from his lungs. He hadn't secured it as tightly as he would have hoped. He checked the M4A1 carbine hadn't dislodged in the process.

Satisfied, he peeled off his oxygen mask before reaching up and taking hold of the toggles on either side of his head.

The darkness enveloped him. He didn't dare light a flare or use the LED light attached to the underside of the rifle against his stomach. He had undertaken enough skydives in his lifetime to know the correct manoeuvres like they were second nature.

Any kind of artificial light would only attract the attention of undesirables.

If they existed.

He scrutinised the landing area — at least, the parts he could see from this height. Below his feet lay a relatively flat section of the peninsula, complete with great swathes of forested area and snowy plains stretching toward the horizon.

If he peered hard enough, he could make out a smattering of thin unkempt roads twisting and turning through the desolate land. It was the first sign of any kind of civilisation he had seen since exiting the Lancer. Other than that, it felt as if he were landing on an alien planet.

Gazing around, he realised that if he had exited the bomber a dozen miles in any other direction he would have landed among steep and dangerous terrain. He spotted ravines running between sheer cliff-faces and unimaginably steep mountainsides dipping into tree-covered valleys. A layer of snow covered everything in sight.

Carter and his co-pilot had certainly done their homework on the ideal drop zone.

The ground rushed up to meet him, deceptively fast. He gently guided the canopy toward the patch of land covered in the least amount of snow. It was best to avoid any area where the depth wasn't ascertainable.

He flared the parachute periodically, expertly guiding his bulk onto a field of dead undergrowth. As his boots hit the rocky ground he let the tension go from his knees, folding with the impact. With so much weight strapped to his upper body, it would prove disastrous to land awkwardly on an ankle and tear ligaments.

He rolled along his back, skirting to a stop just a few feet from where he first hit the rock. The empty parachute container absorbed most of the impact, but it was still jarring.

Unfazed, he loosened the leg straps, unbuckled the chest strap, shrugged off the container and rose to his feet.

Surrounded by uninhabited terrain.

He took a moment to compose himself, then touched a finger to the small device inside his ear canal. Only a second or two later, a voice crackled to life.

'King?' Isla sounded like she was standing across from him.

'I'm on the ground. Don't think anyone spotted me. At least, not yet.'

'Good.'

'Do you know where I am?'

A pause. 'Yeah. We've got you.'

King peered up at the gloomy night sky. The sweeping cumulonimbus cloud he had passed through moments earlier rumbled overhead, like something out of an apocalyptic science-fiction movie. There was no sign of the B-1 Lancer, cruising at high altitude far above. 'How?'

'State-of-the-art GPS at the bottom of your pack.'

King glanced at the thick duffel strapped to his front. 'Glad to know I've got eyes on me at all times.'

'I hope you understand that we don't have back-up easily available. This situation came out of nowhere. For now, you're on your own.'

'You know,' King said, his breath misting in front of his face as the cold began to seep into his gear, 'I never did ask. How's the hunt for new recruits going?'

'It's painstaking,' Isla said. 'The two men you killed in Egypt were our hottest prospects. But that's none of your concern. Your sole focus right now is on the WHO workers.'

'Got it.'

'You landed exactly where we intended. If our planning is accurate, then you're roughly two miles from the village. See that road behind you?'

King looked out over sloping plains of tundra, devoid of forest. The land was covered in thick shrubs, craggy rock formations and brilliant white snow. He turned around to see a long expanse of deciduous trees trailing away in either direction. The Russian Far East had a number of different biomes, apparently.

Beyond the trees, King narrowed his eyes and made out a shoddy dirt road, barely illuminated by the faint moonlight. Even from this distance, the track clearly hadn't been tended to in over a decade. He struggled to comprehend how an ordinary vehicle could traverse the roads around here and remain in one piece.

'I'd say that barely qualifies as a road,' he said quietly.

'Good thing you're not driving on it,' Isla said. 'Get onto it and turn right. You'll hit the village before long. Stay low, stay quiet. Do your best not to get spotted. The town hall is at the far end. Check if it's populated.'

'And if it's not?'

Silence. 'We'll worry about that when you get there.'

King undid the two thick straps tying the duffel bag to his front and slung it onto his back, replacing the parachute container which now lay discarded on the rocky ground. He left the container and its ejected canopy where they rested, and made for the road.

Somewhere in the distance — miles away from his location — an ominous rumble whispered across the plains. King stopped in his tracks and listened intently, his heart rate increasing involuntarily. He activated his earpiece once again.

'Isla.'

'Yes?'

'Is this region prone to earthquakes?'

'Not that I know of. Why?'

'I heard something…'

'There's over a hundred volcanoes along the peninsula,' Isla said. 'Some of them are still active. You'll probably hear a lot of the effects of volcanic phenomena.'

King shrugged off a slight tremor in his hands. 'That's reassuring.'

'Just ignore it. You're not close enough to any particular volcano to get hit by a freak eruption.'

'Great.'

He pressed on.

CHAPTER 10

Utterly alone on the Kamchatka Peninsula, King had to avoid flinching at every footfall. The sound of his boots crunching against the flimsy bark dotting the forest floor seemed to echo across the plains, even though he knew there was no-one around to hear.

He darted between the vast trunks of the deciduous trees, one finger resting firmly against the trigger guard of the M4A1 carbine. He had the weapon set to semi-automatic, and was ready to fire at a moment's notice.

In all likelihood, he was the only armed combatant in the entire region.

But he would never drop his guard on an operation.

It wasn't in his nature.

His eyes grew accustomed to the darkness soon enough. He made out the road twisting and turning away into the plains, and the looming mountains on the horizon. The tallest mountains — or volcanoes — broke through the storm clouds trailing along the Russian sky. King gripped the carbine a little tighter and stepped out of the thin stretch of forest onto the dirt track.

His combat boots made less noise on this surface. He moved like a wraith, ghosting along the side of the track, sticking to the shadows on the off chance that a vehicle decided to come barrelling around one of the bends.

That outcome seemed just as likely as making alien contact this far out from civilisation.

The two-mile trek gave him time to think — which he could do rather effectively when in such a heightened state of awareness. He weighed up everything he had been told by Isla over the course of the day.

It certainly didn't bring him confidence.

Despite the fact that he had always been detached from the inner workings of Black Force and the finer details of high-level Special Forces government planning, something about this situation bothered him. He knew nothing about why such importance had been placed on these health workers — or even who had authorised the operation.

Now, he considered the potential for politicians to use him for their own bidding.

He had to follow orders. Isla was the link between the faceless members of Command and Black Force's operatives.

Perhaps he should request to be more involved in the behind-the-scenes workings in future.

He scoffed. That had never been of interest to him. He doubted it would in future. He shrugged off the uneasy feeling plaguing him and concentrated on the road ahead.

He was meant to operate.

Not bureaucratise.

Two miles along the trail, the dense forest on either side opened out and a smattering of traditional Russian dwellings began to appear. King shrunk further into the tree line, preferring to completely mask his presence from any prying eyes that might potentially be watching.

A noticeably vicious blast of wind howled through the trees. The accompanying wailing set King's nerves on edge. He raised the M4A1 to his shoulder and swept the barrel over the road ahead.

Nothing.

The village seemed like a ghost town.

Fearing the worst, he snuck along the edge of the forest, scouting the land ahead for any sign of unusual activity. He passed behind one of the small wooden huts and skirted around a cluster of chopped wood in the clearing behind the property.

In one of the windows, he saw a flash of light and movement.

He continued on, unwilling to make any form of contact with the villagers themselves. The fewer people that knew of his presence in the region, the better.

The wind whistling between the trees battered the side of his face. His cheeks tingled and he began to lose feeling in the exposed skin. His face was turning numb from the unrelenting cold.

Pausing behind one of the huts, he dropped his duffel pack silently to the forest floor and unclipped the top. He rummaged around inside the bag until he found a thick black balaclava. He tugged it over his head and slung the pack across his shoulders.

If anyone came across him now, it would be a terrifying sight. A two-hundred-and-twenty pound giant in dark combat gear, armed with an automatic weapon, his face masked by a balaclava.

He continued.

Several hundred feet later, the small neighbourhood of dwellings ended abruptly and the trees closed in on the trail once more. King wondered if that was the entire stretch of village, or if the populated area was made up of several clusters of huts.

In the distance, between the tree trunks, he spotted artificial light.

His heart rate quickened. With gloved hands he gripped the M4A1 a little tighter and carefully slotted himself into the shadows as he approached.

If Isla's instructions had been correct, the town hall lay ahead.

And someone was home.

He kept the barrel of his weapon low and his vision trained on the source of the light. From this distance, it was nothing but a soft glow emanating from the dead space between the trees.

As he grew closer, he noticed the glow changing colours in a predetermined pattern.

Flashing lights.

Red and blue.

Police.

King hunched over, constricting his large frame into as narrow a window as he could, doing his best to stay out of sight.

He rounded a narrow bend and dropped to the icy forest floor, squinting in the sudden flood of light. He scrutinised what he could see from this position.

A pair of police sedans were parked out the front of the town hall. The building was smaller than he had anticipated. It appeared derelict from the exterior, with paint flaking away and wooden planks rotting in their slots. Significant portions of the roof had caved in.

The vehicles themselves were empty.

The entire building had been cordoned off with rudimentary yellow tape, signifying an active crime scene. Its entrance doors lay wide open. Pale yellow light spilled out of the hallway within, adding to the flashing of the police lights outside.

King glimpsed a blurry figure pass through the hallway and disappear into an open doorway.

From here, nothing else was visible.

He kept his stomach pressed against the frozen grass and considered the ramifications of what he was seeing.

Something had certainly happened to the health workers. What that was would be difficult to ascertain unless he came to a decision shortly. The police would likely be as clueless as he was about their whereabouts if they truly had vanished, but King knew he wouldn't get anywhere by ghosting around the village and keeping to the shadows.

Despite that, his alertness remained high. The improvisational part of his mind made a suggestion, and he ignored it.

Then it grew on him.

He wasn't supposed to be here. If he wanted to interact with anyone, he would have to disguise his true intentions.

He knew exactly how to do that.

He peeled the balaclava off and slung the duffel bag off his back once again. He dug his hand through the cold-weather gear and extra supplies within until he came across the hard metal object in the centre of the pack, insulated by clothing.

The Glock-22.

He checked the magazine was fully loaded before slotting the pistol into the allocated holster at his waist. He tucked his undershirt over the weapon, concealing it from prying eyes.

Its fully automatic safety system ensured that in the off chance of confrontation, the pistol would be ready to fire as long as he depressed the trigger safety correctly.

King left the carbine rifle, the duffel bag and the balaclava in the snow and staggered toward the town hall with wide eyes and a perplexed expression on his face.

CHAPTER 11

A hundred feet away from the building, he spotted a Russian policeman step out of the entranceway and light up a cigarette in the freezing night air. A thin trail of smoke wafted away from him as he inhaled deeply.

Then the man noticed King stumbling up to the building and the cigarette fell from his mouth.

'*Stop,*' he commanded.

King hesitated, wondering if the man spoke English and how the hell he knew to use it. Then he recalled that the word *stop* was exactly the same in Russian as it was in English, and he settled.

He raised both hands in the air, indicating that he was unarmed. 'Please help.'

The policeman cocked his head. He had been in the process of reaching for the firearm at his waist, likely shocked by King's massive form trundling toward him. As the man heard the tone of King's voice he visibly relaxed. What at first sight appeared to be a dangerous mystery man now seemed like a terrified traveller…

King sauntered up to the policeman, lackadaisical in his movements. He took caution not to display any kind of outward threat. The officer was young — in his twenties, more than likely — with short hair and a pronounced jawline.

King pointed at the town hall. 'Where are my friends? I'm a health worker.'

The policeman gazed at him blankly, not registering what was being said.

He doesn't speak English.

'*Iosif!*' the policeman yelled, turning to face the entrance doors.

Ten seconds later, two more men dressed in identical garb strode out of the hallway. They both seemed older, more experienced, sporting similar haircuts to the first policeman. No-one else emerged from the hall.

Three of them.

King thought he could handle that.

The man on the left — sporting a permanent scowl and heavy, thickset eyebrows — stepped forward and looked inquisitively at the new arrival.

King raised both his hands again, in a gesture of compliance. 'I'm looking for my friends. Do you speak English?'

Iosif raised a hand and tilted it from side to side. 'Some. Who are you?'

'I'm with the World Health Organisation,' King said. 'I had to stay overnight in the village after I lost my way. I can't get into contact with all the other workers. What's going on?'

He talked fast, feigning unease and panic. The three policemen watched him squirm with deadpan expressions. The two who didn't speak English looked at each other briefly, weighing up what to do.

King got the general sense that they hadn't expected to be disturbed.

But why?

He noticed the body language of the trio. They were standing equidistant from one another, forming a rudimentary barrier between King and the entrance to the town hall. Like they were subconsciously protecting whatever lay inside.

'I am sorry,' Iosif said. 'Your friends are missing. We do not know where.'

King let his face fall and his eyes widen. '*What?!*'

'Yes. I am sorry.'

There was a palpable shift in the air as the subsequent silence stretched into a considerable length. King knew that there were proper procedures to adhere too — a crucial person to the development of the case had just turned up. The policemen should have been scrambling to take statements, or comforting him after the news that his entire party of co-workers had gone missing.

Instead, they stood awkwardly on the spot, shifting back and forth, trying to figure out what to do.

It couldn't have been more obvious that they were hiding something.

King had intruded on some kind of cover-up. He couldn't put anything together yet, but it was a start.

The soft touch of the Glock-22's holster at his waist became more noticeable.

His pulse quickened, and he got the sense that he might have to use the weapon before the night was over.

Iosif's beady eyes flicked across to his two comrades. They said nothing, but their eyes said everything.

They were nervous as hell.

King continued the facade of innocence and confusion. 'What could have happened to them? I need to contact my superiors…'

Iosif blanched. 'I do not know. Come to car over here. We will sort it out.'

King twitched nervously — a fake act — and went to move past them. 'My gear…'

Before either of the three could react he had scurried between them and was heading straight for the entrance to the hall. His instincts heightened, to the point where he was ready to react to the slightest hostile action.

But the trio of officers were too surprised.

They hesitated, letting him through, probably wondering just what the hell to do with him.

King strode into the dimly-lit hallway and made for the open doorway at the end.

He came out into the main area, which took up ninety percent of the space within the hall. He had made the brash move of powering into the building because he needed confirmation that the three policemen really did have something to do with the disappearance of the workers.

He wanted a clear conscience if he needed to act.

Instantly, alarm bells rang in his head. Fluorescent lights shone overhead, revealing the bare wooden floor of the room. There wasn't a single piece of furniture or identifiable equipment in the space.

It had all been cleared out.

More importantly, the floor was covered in soap suds. A pair of mops lay near the entrance, abandoned when the first policeman had called to his friends.

King spotted patches of soap in various areas that were tinged pale red.

They were mopping up blood.

Wiping down the scene.

Eliminating all evidence of a scuffle.

As soon as King registered what he was seeing, he knew the three policemen would not let him out of the hall alive.

They probably figured they had cornered him by letting him into the town hall.

In one fluid motion, King lifted his thermal shirt up and wrenched the Glock-22 out of its holster. He took one measured step to the right, away from the doorway, and slipped a finger inside the trigger guard.

Then he waited for the three men to storm into the building with guns blazing.

CHAPTER 12

It took mere seconds.

Like the amateurs they were, the trio hurried into the vast room single-file, standard-issue firearms aimed at the space in front of them, searching for a target but moving through each other's crossfire in the process.

The first man to enter — and the first man that King met — didn't stand a chance.

King glimpsed the automatic pistol in his hand and registered the officer's intentions.

He didn't hold back.

He pumped the trigger three times in quick succession, cutting a vertical line down the front of the man. The unsuppressed reports were so loud in the confined space that the other two men flinched hard, not used to a genuine firefight. King didn't imagine they experienced much resistance in the Russian Far East.

The first .40 S&W round smashed through the delicate bone between the policeman's eyes and blasted through into his brain, killing him instantly.

The other two shots were just for good measure.

One punched through his chest wall, sinking into his heart, and the other smashed through the guy's ribcage. Blood spurted from three separate exit wounds and the sheer force behind the bullets sent him twisting away.

His limp corpse slapped the floor loud enough to seize the attention of the other two officers.

They couldn't help it.

They had probably spent half their life working with the dead man in front of them, and the shock of his violent death caused them both to hesitate.

King revelled in foolish hesitation.

Close enough to touch the other two, he darted forward and shot Iosif through the side of the skull. He twisted on the spot and thundered a combat boot into the third man's solar plexus, sending him sprawling across the wet floor.

The third guy's head whiplashed against the soapy wood just as Iosif's lifeless body tumbled to the ground beside King.

King ignored the dead man. He was no threat.

He raised the Glock-22 and put three rounds through the last policeman's heart in quick succession.

Tap-tap-tap.

The guy died before he had even realised what was happening. Previously scrambling for purchase on the floor, his limbs went slack and he sprawled onto his back, a thin trail of blood leaking down the front of his uniform.

Clinical.

Precise.

Efficient.

King ejected the Glock-22's 15-round magazine and confirmed how many bullets he had used in the firefight. He nodded in satisfaction when he realised his count had been accurate.

Seven rounds. Three corpses.

Not bad.

He wondered if the locals had heard the commotion. More than likely, he figured. There was such little activity in these parts of the world that the sound of a gunshot would resonate for a mile in any direction.

He glanced at the three dead officers bleeding profusely all around him. The fluids pumping out of their wounds mixed with the soapy residue on the floor, turning it crimson.

King shook his head in disappointment.

It shouldn't have come to that. He felt nothing over killing the three of them. After all, they had been intent on finishing him off when they had stormed into the hall with weapons raised.

An eye for an eye.

But above that came a sinister feeling, a deep knot in his stomach that made him grimace with unease.

The **WHO** workers hadn't been riding out a snowstorm. They hadn't been dealing with malfunctions of their communication equipment.

They really were gone.

And King had three dead policemen on his hands who had been directly involved with the cover-up.

Instinctively, he touched a finger to his ear.

'Isla,' he said.

'What is it?' she said almost instantaneously. 'You're at the hall, I see.'

'I was with a group of police officers,' he said. 'The scene's been cordoned off.'

There was urgency in her tone. 'What are they saying?'

'*Was* being the crucial word.'

Silence. 'King…'

'They were halfway through covering something up. There's blood on the floor — I mean, apart from theirs. They were in the process of mopping it up.'

'Jesus Christ,' Isla muttered. 'I'm sure you understand that this is exclusively up to you now? If there's any link between dead officers of the law and an American operative there'll be hell to pay. We're going to deny all knowledge of your existence if you get caught.'

'I thought that was always the case. I won't talk, don't worry.'

'You won't get caught, I hope.'

'Of course not.'

'Then start—'

Something in the front pocket of Iosif's uniform crackled to life. King jolted at the sudden noise and raised his Glock out of instinct. He had the sights trained on the man's lifeless body in half a second.

But it wasn't Iosif in his death throes.

It was some kind of radio in his breast pocket.

King walked over, his boots squelching under the soap and the blood, and lifted the device out of the man's pocket. It was a standard-issue police radio, set to a certain frequency.

A deep voice blurted out a string of Russian, some kind of question judging by the inflection of his tone. The sharp and distorted vocals echoed off the walls.

King realised he still had his earpiece on.

'Did you get that?' he asked. 'My Russian's patchy.'

Isla hesitated. 'He asked if the worker was dead yet, and if they needed assistance. What does that mean?'

'I told them I was a health worker. They must have radioed their boss when I came in here…'

King froze as another few sentences were blurted out by the man on the other end. 'And that?'

'He says that if he doesn't hear a response, they'll come charging in. He said they're only a couple of minutes away.'

'Fuck,' King said. 'Gotta go, Isla.'

He dropped the radio, switched the earpiece off with the tap of a finger and gripped the Glock-22 tight. He listened intently for anything that resembled reinforcements. The only audible sounds were the wind buffering against the exterior of the town hall and the far-off rumblings of volcanoes and thunder.

Then a different kind of rumbling started to grow in volume.

He realised what it was almost instantly. It sounded exactly like the Otokar Cobra he had commandeered back in Venezuela — a behemoth of an armoured vehicle designed to resist bomb blasts and take part in urban warfare.

And it was headed straight for the town hall.

He turned on his heel and sprinted away from the entranceway, wondering just what the hell was about to unfold.

The answer came a second later.

With an ear-splitting shriek, some kind of gargantuan vehicle obliterated the front of the town hall and careered into the main room amidst a wave of demolished wood and plaster.

CHAPTER 13

The first thing King noticed was the intense brightness. The massive truck's twin headlights lit up the inside of the town hall, burning white light seeping into everything.

He made it to the other side of the room and dove into an adjacent doorway just as a hail of machine gun fire tore up the floor behind him.

Judging by the heavy reverberations King felt underneath his feet and the sheer noise of the gunfire, the weapon had to be an incredibly high caliber. A single wound from one of the rounds would likely take a limb off.

He crashed into a narrow hallway and sprinted further into the back of the hall, darting past a number of cramped offices — all unfurnished and abandoned.

He shouldered a flimsy door aside and ducked into the rearmost room of the entire building.

It was a bare rectangular space, just an empty area with flaking white walls and identical wooden flooring to the rest of the building. More importantly, two old-fashioned glass windows faced out over the rear of the property — a flat expanse of empty land covered in a thick layer of snow.

King destroyed the old pane of the left-hand window with an adrenalin-charged front kick. Wind howled into the room, loud enough to draw the attention of the yet-unidentified hostiles.

King stopped in his tracks.

He heard raucous commotion from the main room — boots slamming onto flat ground, magazines sliding into rifles, debris raining into the hall from the demolished front of the building.

There was a sizeable force coming for him.

It would do him good to eliminate a couple now.

He assumed at least one of them would have heard him shatter the window. He stayed frozen in place, waiting for someone to charge into the room in desperate pursuit.

The first man to enter was dressed differently to the policeman. He wore an outfit much similar to King's — tactical all-weather gear and a thick woollen mask covering his features.

Standard attire for a mercenary.

The guy stormed into the room and made a beeline for the broken window, not bothering to look in either direction for potential hostiles.

King lined the Glock's sight up with the back of his head in clinical fashion and pumped the trigger once.

With a .40 round embedded deep in the back of his skull, the guy slumped forward, carried by the momentum of his run. He toppled and his chin cracked against the bare windowsill, breaking his neck in grotesque fashion.

He wouldn't have felt it.

King charged forward and leapfrogged the corpse, satisfied with picking off one of their group. He vaulted through the window frame and crashed into the ground outside, skidding uncontrollably on a hidden patch of ice.

He lost his footing and slammed into the snow.

Just in time.

Muzzle flashes roared from the room he had leapt out of and bullets passed through the air above his head. His heart rate skyrocketed as he experienced the closeness to death.

Nothing paralleled that feeling.

King scrambled like a madman along the side of the town hall, putting cover between himself and the gunmen. He was overwhelmingly underprepared. He didn't know how many men had come with the armoured truck, or what level of firepower they possessed, or how talented they were.

He had a Glock-22 and his instincts.

And — if he could make it back to his duffel bag without dying — a carbine assault rifle.

That would certainly be useful.

The gunfire ceased as the men inside the town hall searched for a target. King pictured them sweeping their weapons over the land outside the window, hunting for his head. They wouldn't find it. He pressed his back to the brick exterior and crept around to the front of the building, keeping low and clasping the Glock two-handed.

Ten feet away from the front lot, one of the gunmen rounded the corner and came face-to-face with King.

It came down to a matter of reflexes.

He heard the scuffing of the guy's boots on the soft ground a moment before he came into view. Because of that, King had his sights trained on the dead space ahead a few milliseconds before he saw anything.

It saved his life and ended the gunman's.

He fired three times, blisteringly loud in the relative silence that had settled over the town hall. It was too dark to make out exactly where the .40 rounds struck home, but amidst the trio of muzzle flashes he saw the man jerk unnaturally and twist on the spot.

His body thumped lifelessly to the snow.

King dove for the assault rifle that the guy dropped from dead fingers, scooping up the weapon before it hit the ground. He expected an AK-74 or some kind of Kalashnikov at least, given the region and the firearm's popularity.

Glancing down at the rifle in his hands, he found himself pleasantly surprised.

These men were equipped with the very best.

It was an AK-15 with a digital-style snow camouflage wrap and attached suppressor. The AK-15 was one of the newest Kalashnikov's available to the Russian Armed Forces and an incredibly versatile weapon, with a firing rate of five hundred rounds per minute. They carried 7.62mm rounds, which caused massive internal damage to anyone unlucky enough to be penetrated by the bullets.

King yanked the magazine free and confirmed that it was fully loaded. He glimpsed a full stack of thirty rounds before slamming it back home.

The man hadn't had a chance to pull the trigger before he met his demise.

King discarded the Glock, its magazine almost empty and its firepower minuscule in comparison to the AK-15. He inched around the corner, sweeping the thick barrel left and right.

Two hostiles. Straight ahead.

Neither were prepared.

Positioned side-by-side, the pair stepped out of the gaping hole in the front of the town hall, surrounded by splintered wood and crushed brick and piles of debris. Their attention had been drawn to the other side of the building.

The wrong side.

He moved to take advantage of their unpreparedness.

Before he fired, he scrutinised their appearances. They wore similar garb to the man he had shot down in the back room, dressed head-to-toe in expensive tactical attire.

These weren't cops.

These were hired guns.

Soldiers of fortune.

King tasted something acrid and tangy in the back of his throat, a slight reflex that set him on edge. He hadn't just stumbled across a small group of crooked policemen here…

This was something larger.

The two mercenaries carried themselves with the measured pace and sharp reflexes of trained professionals. Yet there were still serious flaws in their tactics, as evidenced by King gaining the upper hand so quickly.

He touched the AK-15's stock to his shoulder, took careful aim, and squeezed off two separate bursts of fully-automatic 7.62mm rounds.

Three per man.

More than enough.

The pair were in the process of sweeping their gun barrels over King's position when the bullets struck. They jerked like marionettes on strings in the low light, blood spurting out of freshly formed wounds.

King spent a patient few seconds staring at the aftermath of his shots, confirming the two men in front of him were well and truly dead.

Their guns clattered away and they lay still on the gravel.

He nodded — reassured — and pressed on.

His ears rang from the automatic gunfire, in such close proximity to his eardrums that he experienced some temporary hearing loss.

Then the mechanical roar of an engine sounded inside the town hall, shockingly loud even with his impaired hearing. He froze in his tracks, one finger delicately resting on the AK-15's trigger. Normally he would employ trigger discipline when he wasn't confronted with a visible enemy, but it was clear that everyone in the area wanted him dead.

He heard tyres screaming against the wooden flooring inside.

The armoured vehicle was reversing.

CHAPTER 14

King turned and bolted for the corner he had rounded moments earlier. Realising he wouldn't make it in time, he dove into the snow and spun like a scrambling lunatic, yanking the AK-15's barrel to aim at the vast hole in the front of the building.

The massive truck came tearing out of the town hall a second later. He glimpsed the heavy machine gun mounted on a turret on the roof of the vehicle, the same machine gun that had almost torn him to shreds earlier.

It was his first proper look at the truck. He quickly identified it as an Otokar Kaya II. The tank-on-wheels was a full two feet taller than him, raised up on gargantuan bulletproof tyres and painted dark camouflage to blend in with the night.

Instantly, his attention snapped to the visible enemies. There was one man behind the turret, hastily searching for a target, swinging the thick barrel of the heavy machine gun in a wide arc.

There was no-one else visible.

King forced his mind to go entirely blank, zoning in on the man ahead. Most of the guy's body mass was protected by an impenetrable metal shield fixed into the turret. He must have been tall, because the top of his head poked out above the barrier, barely visible in the darkness. The Kaya's headlights flooded into the town hall, lighting it up in exquisite detail.

King had a half-second to act before the gunman found his target and opened fire. He lay out in the open, completely exposed, milliseconds away from being torn to shreds by rounds the length of his forearm.

He let his hands go still and his eyes laser in on the top of the man's head. As soon as he pulled the trigger, they would see him...

He opened fire.

The first four or five bullets hit steel. King heard them ricochet off the shield, sending sparks flying. The noise of the magazine unloading from his prone position drowned out everything else. He clenched his teeth, watching the gunman recoil in shock and start to swing the giant barrel of the heavy machine gun around.

Come on...

He tightened his aim. For a split second, terror shot through his bones. The man finished correcting his aim and

King stared down the barrel of the machine gun, waiting for the rounds to pulverise his exposed mass…

A vicious burst of crimson sprayed off the top of the gunman's head, backlit by the glow emanating from the Kaya's headlights. King saw the grisly cloud, and a moment later the guy disappeared from sight.

He let go of the trigger and tuned into the sudden silence.

Nothing. The Kaya froze in its tracks, motionless, surrounded by the dead. King imagined the dead gunman had slumped inside the vehicle, causing the driver to hesitate.

As the chaos settled, he quickly realised that the driver was the last man left alive.

One man in the back room. One on the side of the building. Two out the front. One manning the turret.

Five down.

One left.

King had decimated their forces without so much as a scratch to show for it.

In the heat of the moment, it never felt that way. He considered himself an inch from death at all times. It was only as the dust settled that he realised what he had done.

The odds he had overcome…

But it wasn't over yet. King heard the engines roar once more. The Kaya screamed as it rotated ninety degrees, completing the wild manoeuvre by pointing its nose at King's prone form.

Blinded by the headlights, he went pale and scrambled to his feet.

He knew exactly what the driver intended to do.

With a deafening growl, the armoured vehicle surged forward.

Thirty thousand pounds of steel, heading straight for King.

He kept the AK-15 clenched in one hand and sprinted away from the truck. The roaring of its engine grew louder. He felt the sheer weight bearing down on him.

At the last moment he threw himself to the side, taking a faceful of snow as he rolled away from the Kaya's trajectory. His blood ran cold as he felt the ground reverberate all around him. Freezing air blasted his cheeks. He opened his eyes to see the enormous tyres pass him by, only half a foot from crushing him to death.

The Kaya slammed on the brakes and spun in a tight circle, readying itself for another charge. King got back to his feet, snow cascading off his cold-weather gear. He snatched up the AK-15 — aware that it would be useless unless he could somehow find his way inside the vehicle — and took off across the parking lot.

A particularly vicious blast of wind turned his exposed face to ice. He threw a glance over his shoulder and saw the Kaya shoot off the mark, powering toward him.

His stomach twisted into a knot.

He knew he couldn't keep this deadly game up for much longer. Sooner or later his reflexes would fail him and the Kaya would crush him like a twig.

It had almost happened the first time.

Across the road, he spotted his duffel bag resting in the snow, propped up against the M4A1 carbine. Beyond that, the ground disappeared into shadow, plunged into darkness by the forest.

The trees.

He quickened his pace, pushing his limbs as fast as they would go. The roar of the engine filled his eardrums.

He powered across the road — almost slipping on a handful of icy patches spread across the dirt — and sprawled into the snowbank on the other side. He snatched up the duffel and his carbine, discarding the AK-15 onto the ground.

Then he sprinted full-pelt between two thick deciduous trees, passing between their trunks with inches to spare.

And milliseconds to spare.

The Kaya didn't slow down. Whoever sat behind the wheel possessed unimaginable determination, because the next thing King heard was the sound of steel crunching against wood.

With so much weight behind the collision, the ground shook and his surroundings vibrated.

King threw his possessions away and dove with every ounce of effort in his body. He was so close to the impact behind him that for a moment he thought he had been struck.

Then he smashed into the hard ground and rolled to a halt ten feet from where he had first leapt.

He spun on his back to see both tree trunks tear from the ground in twin explosions of dirt and roots. They moaned as they fell, slamming into the ground where King had stood moments previously.

Something sliced across his face, hard enough to make him recoil. He tumbled backward, away from the pain. When he righted himself, he realised that a mass of branches had clattered to the ground all around him, knocked off one of the trees as it fell. He tasted warm blood and realised he had been cut.

What came next sent shivers down his spine.

The Kaya, disabled by the massive blunt force of the collision, rolled against one of the fallen trunks and lurched sideways. King realised the act had been a last-ditch effort. The driver had sacrificed the integrity of his vehicle to crush King under the fallen trees.

It toppled just far enough to get carried by its own momentum.

The Kaya smashed roof-first onto the hard forest floor, its steel frame bending under the weight bearing down on it. It skidded a few feet, then its front end crunched against another tree trunk hard enough to rattle the ground again.

It came to rest upside-down, enormous tyres still spinning in thin air.

King slumped against the ground and let out his nerves in a single, long exhale.

The Kaya's crash had been so brutal that he knew the driver would at the very least have been knocked unconscious. Nevertheless, he wouldn't feel safe until every last threat had been dealt with.

He clambered to his feet and tugged the M4A1 out of a mass of branches. He double-checked the weapon was still set to fully-automatic before hurrying over to the motionless vehicle.

The dented steel door swung open.

King's heart rate skyrocketed as he levelled the barrel of his carbine, awaiting a blaze of gunfire in return.

When the driver of the Kaya tumbled out of the doorway in a semi-conscious state, he relaxed.

The guy's face was a bloodied mess. He sprawled on his back into the snow, landing hard on a tangle of branches. A rivulet of blood ran off the side of his head and tinged the snow around his head crimson. He sucked in deep breaths and stared up at the night sky.

The crash had knocked him senseless.

King strode up to the man and planted a combat boot against his chest, ensuring he stayed put. He touched the M4A1's barrel to his throat, pinning him to the ground.

'You want to live?' King said.

The man stared up at him with a vacant expression plastered across his face. He coughed viciously, and wiped a hand across his mouth. King didn't flinch. He knew the man was unarmed. He wasn't reaching for a weapon.

'I need some information,' King said. 'Or I'll kill you right here.'

His voice faltered unintentionally. Truth was, if this man died, then the last shred of hope King had of finding the missing workers died with him. It would leave him amidst a dozen corpses with nothing to show for it.

The workers could very well be hundreds of miles away by this point.

The driver seemed to know that.

With his eyes still glassy, the man reached for King's gun barrel — slowly, tentatively. He gripped the metal tight and shifted King's aim from his throat to his forehead. Then he raised the same hand and beckoned in King's face.

The guy smiled, exposing bloodstained teeth.

'Do it,' he spat in thickly-accented English.

King grimaced. He had few options. The longer he spent trying to prise the answer out of the driver underneath him was more time that the guy's comrades had to respond to the carnage. Spending unnecessary time around this village would prove disastrous.

He sensed that there were many more enemies to deal with.

It took significant manpower to wipe a ten-person party of health workers off the face of the planet.

Whatever this operation was, King knew he had stumbled on something serious.

He looked into the eyes of the driver. The guy's features were covered in blood. His pupils were hard and cold.

Soulless.

This man would not talk.

As soon as the realisation struck King, he slipped a finger into the trigger guard and fired. One shot was all it took. The hard ground behind the man's head masked the grisly exit wound that blew out the back of his head.

King turned away from the corpse and gathered his belongings.

No time for contemplation.

Not out here.

A simple decision, followed by immediate action. That was how he would make it through whatever came next.

He had no idea what that might be.

As he scooped up the duffel bag and slung it over one shoulder, bearing the full brunt of its weight, he noted the sheer silence of his surroundings. Before the conflict, even the slightest noise amidst the forest set his nerves on edge. Now he heard nothing. After dozens of discharged rifle rounds and the madness of the Kaya roaring towards him, the aftermath felt like a graveyard.

It is, he thought.

He strode past the Kaya, still overturned against the forest floor. Surrounded by destruction. He glanced at the enormous vehicle and sighed as he imagined charging headlong into enemy territory at the wheel of such a ride.

But it would take an industrial-sized crane to overturn the truck.

This far from civilisation, he had nothing.

With the mountain winds whispering against his cold-weather gear, he stepped out onto the same gravel trail. Then he sensed it. The tingling against the back of his neck, like he was being observed. After years upon years in similar situations, he had honed the sensation down to a tee.

He wasn't wrong often.

He glanced up and met the gaze of a sole figure, standing on the other side of the road, silhouetted against the forest behind.

Watching.

Waiting.

CHAPTER 15

King reacted instinctively, bringing the barrel of his M4A1 up like a rocket. He had the weapon trained on the figure in the blink of an eye. His index finger acted of its own accord, slicing into the trigger guard and hovering a hair above the mechanism that would set the gun blazing at the twitch of a muscle.

As the situation became clearer, he relaxed.

It was a woman.

An elderly woman.

Unarmed.

Hands crossed against her chest.

The sight unnerved him almost more than a mercenary would have. Sure, this lady didn't seem to want him dead, but something about her unblinking stare set him on edge.

'Hello,' he called above the wind.

The woman said nothing.

She looked to be in her early eighties — although if she was a resident of the village, she could very well be sixty. King imagined the weather and isolation took all kinds of tolls. She was wrapped in a simple woollen shawl. A rough beanie covered her wispy grey hair. Deep lines were creased into her forehead and cheeks.

'English?' King said.

She shook her head. As if to reassure him, she unfolded her arms and held them by her sides. Palms out, fingers splayed.

King lowered the carbine.

He walked across the road, almost checking for passing cars before shrugging off such a foolish gesture. He peered up the road at the town hall, once again shrouded in darkness. The only light came from the pair of deserted police sedans parked equidistant across the entrance. The Kaya had flattened the rear half of one of the vehicles on its mad chase. Both pairs of headlights still shone, illuminating the gaping hole in the front of the building.

The entranceway no longer existed.

King spotted a limb or two spread across the snow at the front of the building. A hand here, the side of a torso there.

The dead.

He hated spending time lingering around them.

He reached the old lady and slung his rifle over one shoulder, indicating that he had no intention of using the weapon. He could tell from her face that she meant no harm either.

Like she had been expecting to talk to him.

Like she had wanted him to kill the others.

King caught his breath, then pointed at the town hall. 'My friends.'

She cocked her head.

He gesticulated to the building in the distance, then pointed hard at himself. 'Them. Me. Together.'

She nodded understandingly, and bowed her head. Slowly, she rolled up one sleeve of her thick jumper, revealing a maze of puncture marks dotted around her protruding veins. She pointed to where she had received the injections, then at the town hall.

King nodded. 'They were treating you. Now they're gone.'

The woman lifted her chin, and King saw sadness in her eyes. He imagined she had formed a wordless bond with the foreigners sent to nurse her back to health.

Tuberculosis, he recalled Isla saying.

'Do you know—?' he started, taking his time to properly articulate the point he wanted to get across.

The woman cut him off with a raised hand. She used the same hand to hover two fingers above her eyes. Then she pointed those same fingers at the hall.

King raised his eyebrows. 'You saw it happen?'

She said nothing.

'You saw?' he said, mimicking her gesture. He mimed wrestling with a captive, dragging them away.

The woman nodded grimly. She turned and silently pointed down the road, where the trail twisted away into the forest. The Kamchatka Peninsula lay beyond. From here, it looked treacherous as all hell. The mountains arced into the storm clouds, surrounded by narrow valleys and vast sweeping plains of rock and snow.

'Along the road?' King said, following her gaze. 'That way?'

She gestured to the ground beneath them, then made a rising and falling motion with her hand. She thrust a finger in the direction of the looming mountains.

'Off-road? The peninsula?'

A nod.

King grimaced. He had feared as much. The workers had been abducted and taken into one of the most inhospitable regions on the planet. King had no familiarity with the area, and no idea what he would be heading into.

Yet he had to persevere.

This battle had unfolded at lightning speed, a confrontation so fast and vicious that the dead men around him would have failed to communicate King's presence to their superiors. No-one in the vicinity had tales to tell.

King still had the element of surprise on his side.

It seemed back-up wouldn't make it in time. This was a highly volatile and extremely sensitive operation, as evidenced by Isla's panic. King had doubted the validity of her concerns — which had now been confirmed in drastic fashion.

He looked at the elderly woman and smiled reassuringly. He pointed to himself, then to the peninsula.

I'll get them.

Worry creased her features. She shook her head, tightening her lips into a scowl. Then she drew a finger across her throat, still shaking her head.

They will kill you.

He tapped the M4A1 carbine at his side, then spread his arms wide, highlighting their surroundings.

Highlighting the dead mercenaries.

'You probably won't understand this,' he said, 'but this happens a lot. I'm used to it. I'll get them, don't worry.'

Then he rested a hand on her frail shoulder and nodded again.

Confident.

Brazen, even.

With a gesture of farewell, he turned and made for the abandoned police sedans in front of the town hall. He planned to drive one of the beat-up vehicles until it could go no further — and then he would cover the rest of the distance on foot.

Where to, though?

He didn't know. For as long as he could remember, he had focused on constant motion. It always seemed to provide results.

He assumed it would not fail him this time.

A thin hand seized his elbow, halting him in his tracks. He spun back to see the elderly woman shaking her head in vigorous fashion.

'*Nyet, nyet, nyet,*' she muttered disapprovingly. '*Sledovat.*'

He thought that meant *follow.*

He followed.

She led him down the trail, back into the village. Away from the swathe of destruction he had left amidst the now-empty town hall.

Clearly the sedan would not suffice.

He wondered what she would lead him to.

For cautionary purposes, he touched a hand to the carbine rifle at his side. Experience had taught him never to assume good intentions where there were none. For all he knew, the old lady could be a decoy leading him to a waiting ambush. A dozen new mercenaries, weapons at the ready, waiting for King to stumble around the corner and take him out for good.

That didn't turn out to be the case.

Half a mile down the road — at which point the town hall disappeared behind them — the old woman hobbled down the makeshift driveway of a traditional Russian dwelling. King considered himself worldly, but he couldn't recall the name for the huts.

She led him into the back of the property. He stepped out into a grassy field covered in a thick layer of snow. A thin wire fence trailed around sections of the perimeter, the metal rusting and jagged. Entire portions of the fence were missing. The land beyond was barren — sweeping plains of snow interspersed with a handful of dead trees.

Miles in the distance, he saw the land melt into the peninsula.

The woman shuffled over to a large patch of dirt directly behind the hut. The snow had been cleared to make way for a handful of items — a rusting stovetop over a cluster of dead coals, the burnt-out shell of an old car, and something the size of a refrigerator covered in a ragged tarpaulin sheet.

King motioned to the sheet. He thought he knew what lay underneath. 'This?'

She nodded and stepped back, too old and frail to assist with the grunt work. King wrenched the tarpaulin away and stared at the half-battered Taiga-551 snowmobile that lay underneath.

Its front skis were rusting and jagged, with flecks of their material having snapped off long ago. The grip on the handlebars had peeled away and the tracks on the rear looked like they could use some maintenance.

King noted the khaki paint covering half the exterior. The rest had flaked away.

Russian military, he thought.

'Where'd you get this?' he said, staring at the woman.

She gave him a vacant stare, followed by an expressionless shrug. King realised she wouldn't be able to communicate. Gestures and nods only got them so far. Maybe a late husband had scrounged it out of the post-Soviet leftovers and used it to travel from village to village for supplies.

He went with that theory.

Clearly, she thought it would prove more use than a car would.

He traced a path with his hand through the terrain out the back of the property, finishing at the base of the nearest mountains. A thin snow-covered valley led between them, curving away into shadow. He raised an eyebrow to ascertain whether he had the right idea.

The woman gave a solemn nod.

He sensed her hesitation. Maybe she had seen countless people taken by these forces. Packed up and carted off into the peninsula. Never to be seen again.

He would never know.

All he knew was movement.

So he strapped the duffel bag tight around his chest and clambered onto the worn seat of the snowmobile, feeling the chassis underneath him sag as it took the full brunt of his weight. He wondered how long it had been since the snowmobile had seen use.

He flicked the kill switch into the upward position, ensuring the motor would start, then yanked the pull cord until the engine coughed into life. It settled into a throaty chugging after a few moments of spluttering.

King met the gaze of the elderly woman across from him. He didn't know her name. She had no idea who he was. She had watched him massacre a small army of thugs, and for some reason had decided to trust him with her life.

More than that, she had assisted him.

He would never be able to put into words how grateful he was.

They exchanged a knowing nod that transcended language barriers.

Thank you, King thought.

You're welcome, she probably thought back.

He gripped the handlebars and set off, guiding the snowmobile across the small field and through a dozen-foot gap in the wire fence. The surroundings began to blur as he picked up speed. A thin smattering of trees passed by, and then he shot out into the plains.

Surrounded by nothingness.

He threw a glance back over his shoulder, squinting against the icy powder kicked up from the front skis. He saw the small hut and the surrounding forest fading into the horizon. He thought he could make out the shadowy form of the elderly lady, watching him just as intently as she had when he had first come across her.

He turned away from the scene.

Leaving behind almost a dozen dead bodies.

He didn't care who found them. He didn't care what official protocols were in place for such a discovery.

Hiding the dead would help nobody. Three of them were crooked cops. Sooner or later their co-workers would investigate their lack of contact and come across their bodies amongst a group of armed combatants.

A mob deal gone wrong, possibly.

King was unperturbed. By then, he was hoping to be off the continent.

He pushed the snowmobile's motor to its maximum capacity, hunched low over the handlebars, and shot toward the looming mountains in the distance.

Toward war.

CHAPTER 16

Sarah Grasso surfaced from unconsciousness all at once, like tearing her head out of murky waters. Sight and sound and smell came back to her in an overwhelming jolt of sensation.

She lifted her eyelids and scrambled against cold hard concrete, fingernails scraping against the ground's surface.

She had shaky memories. Like flashes of distorted stills.

The cramped metal interior of a vehicle.

Her shoulder pressed up against another motionless body.

A building tucked into the alcove of a cliff.

Stern men murmuring back and forth in Russian.

Then they had noticed her watching them from inside the vehicle...

...and one of them had moved in again with the rag.

Sweat dripped off her forehead as she cast a panicked look at her surroundings. She couldn't make out much. The only light came trickling in through two stained windows. Cracks were spread across the glass like spiderwebs. There was no illumination in this room itself.

The room was a tiny box with a concrete floor and tin walls. Rectangular in shape. It stank of fuel and rot and rust. Some kind of storage shed.

She lay on her back in the centre of the room, her hands and feet bound together with tight leather straps. With a heave of effort she sat up, activating her abdominals in the process.

The cold hit her next. It seeped through her parka and leeched into her bones, so biting that her teeth began to chatter almost instantly. The sound was deafeningly loud in the silent space.

Someone stirred nearby.

'*Sarah?*' a confused voice whispered.

She turned her head — which took a considerable amount of effort — and saw Jessica sprawled across the concrete in the corner of the room. Her limbs were bound with the same straps as Sarah's. She had shimmied along the floor and propped herself up against the far wall. One eye was swollen shut. The skin around the socket had turned an ugly shade of purple.

'Fuck,' Sarah coughed. 'Are you okay?'

'I think so,' Jessica said. 'Just drowsy.'

'Oh my God,' a third female voice whimpered.

Both women whipped their heads around to search for the source of the noise. Sarah spotted a figure tucked into the space between two sets of wooden shelving. The shelving was entirely bare, perhaps cleared out to restrict their access to anything they could use to cut the straps.

The third woman leant forward into the sliver of light arcing in through one of the grimy windows. Oily hair fell in strands on either side of her face. Her features were pale and terrified.

Carmen, Sarah thought.

The third female member of their party.

'Are you hurt, Carmen?' Sarah said.

'Yes.'

'Where?'

Confused silence. Carmen stared at her dirty clothing with wide eyes, searching for an injury. 'I don't know...'

'You're in shock,' Sarah said. 'But I don't think any of us are hurt.'

'We were drugged,' Jessica muttered.

Sarah nodded. 'What happened to you all? Léo picked me up at the end of the shift. We got back... it was like we walked into a war zone.'

Jessica grimaced. 'I ... can't really remember. Everything was fine. Then the lights went out all at once. Someone got up to check it out, and all these men flooded in...'

Carmen gulped back apprehension. 'There was fighting. Screaming.'

'My memory is awful,' Jessica said. 'I can only remember fragments.'

'Do you remember a building?' Sarah said.

The other women gazed at her blankly.

'Not this one,' she said. 'A massive warehouse. Like a … I think it was a mine.'

The mental image of a vast cage covering some kind of elevator came back to her. Descending into the depths of the earth.

She shivered involuntarily.

Carmen's eyes went wider still. 'Is that where we are? Are we underground?'

Sarah heard her breaths quicken. She sensed the panic and the claustrophobia in her tone. Carmen thought that if they were miles underground, there would be no hope of escape.

She was probably right…

Sarah bucked and rocked on the cold floor until she built up enough momentum to leap to her feet. She got the soles of her all-weather boots underneath her and sprung up in one fluid motion.

High-school gymnastics paid off, she thought.

From here, she could get a better look out the windows. She crossed to the nearest pane by hopping on both feet, taking care not to tumble off-balance in the process. At any moment she expected one of the men who had abducted them to thunder into the storage shed and strike her down.

With a racing heart, she made it to the window. The entire pane of reinforced glass had fogged up from the body heat within the storage shed. She raised both hands — still tied together — and swiped downwards with her sleeves, carving a vertical line through the condensation.

She gasped.

'What is it?' Jessica said.

Sarah stayed silent for a long moment, taking in the view. 'We're not underground. We're nowhere near a mine, that's for sure.'

'Where the fuck are we?' Carmen muttered.

'I ... don't know.'

Sarah stared out at a view that stretched for dozens of miles in every direction. The storage shed was on the outer limit of some kind of remote outpost, built into the side of a mountain. The ground sloped away almost immediately, descending at least half a mile to a forest far below. A narrow road wound treacherously down the side of the mountain, barely wide enough to fit a car.

'I don't think we're getting out of here easily,' she muttered.

Carmen and Jessica struggled to their feet and hopped over to her position. They both stared silently out at the terrain, mouths agape.

'Are you sure you saw some kind of mine?' Jessica said. 'The last thing I remember is being attacked in the hall…'

'Me too,' Carmen said.

Sarah nodded. 'I'm sure of it. The three of us have been moved.'

'That means…'

'All the men were taken underground,' Sarah said, connecting the dots. 'I have an awful feeling that I know what we're up here for.'

Their eyes turned to the door fixed into the wall nearby. It was made of the same tin as the walls, only discernible from the surrounding area by a thin line running the length of its perimeter. There was no handle on the inside.

On a whim, Sarah threw her frame against it, adding strength pent up from the terror of being held against her will.

It didn't budge an inch.

She tried again. Twice more. Just in case.

Nothing.

Just rattling — which probably alerted their abductors to the fact that they were awake.

Defeated, she slumped against the back of the door and squeezed her eyes shut, riding out a vicious wave of nausea. A single drop of sweat fell from her eyebrow, splattering on the concrete between her legs.

'Wait—!' Jessica yelped. 'What was that?'

'Fuck! I saw it too,' Carmen said.

Sarah leapt to her feet, renewed with a newfound vigour. There was a semblance of excitement in both women's voices. She shuffled to the same window and peered into the valley below.

'Something flashed,' Jessica muttered. 'Down there.'

Then Sarah saw it. A flicker of artificial light, at least a mile below them. Some kind of beam passing between trees, slicing through the forest. A vehicle, perhaps…

She scoffed. 'It's probably more of them. There's no-one else around here.'

She pressed her back against the wall and slid back to a sitting position, just as a monstrous headache sprouted to life behind her eyeballs.

Out of hope.

Out of energy.

She closed her eyes again and waited for them to come for her.

CHAPTER 17

A little over a mile away, Jason King clenched his teeth as he navigated a dangerous path through the forest.

The pass between the mountains had been nothing short of terrifying. All kinds of hidden drops and crevasses had only presented themselves as he passed them by, unnervingly close. It had taken him most of the journey to get used to the snowmobile, and just as he had mastered it the terrain had turned perilous.

The land beyond the pair of mountains was home to this forest, with trunks thicker than cars pressing in on all sides. He travelled as fast as he could without losing control. The sole headlight on the front of his snowmobile cut a thin white line through the forest ahead.

It only served to accentuate the shadows.

They pressed in from everywhere. In the early years of his career, the situation would have sent chills down his spine. Steering a borrowed snowmobile through dark, uninhabited forests in the most isolated section of Russia.

Now, it felt like another day at the office.

Not that he wasn't scared.

By this point, being scared was nothing short of a regular occurrence.

He kept on the lookout for something, anything, that signified manmade structures. It was a wild goose chase. After three full minutes of nothingness, he touched a finger to his ear and slowed the snowmobile in between two towering deciduous trees.

'Isla,' he said, keeping his voice low out of instinct.

She responded instantaneously. 'We thought you were dead for a moment. You didn't make contact, then suddenly you're speeding into the peninsula.'

'You thought they were carting my body back to their headquarters?'

'Who are *they?*'

'I know as much as you do,' King said. 'All I know is that they're well-equipped.'

'Not equipped enough, obviously. What happened in the village?'

'Three crooked cops and an armoured tanker full of armed hostiles in tactical gear.'

'All dead?'

'You bet.'

'This is serious shit,' Isla said. 'I'm sure you know that. An outfitted mercenary force? We all know the ramifications if this makes it public.'

'I'll make sure it doesn't go public.'

'Find them. Get them back. And don't let anyone except the health workers see your face.'

'Got it. I'll check in when I find something.'

He heard an audible click in his ear canal and switched the earpiece off. The typical background noise of forest life was non-existent. All kinds of animal cries and bird calls and rustling leaves were drowned out by the relentless wind, cutting through the trees and bombarding King's cold-weather gear.

Out of habit, he switched the snowmobile's sole headlight off, plunging his surroundings into darkness.

Observing.

Instantly, he noticed something out of the corner of his eye.

It was just a fleeting flash of light, but amidst the sheer isolation it was immediately visible. He peered up through a gap in the canopy of branches above his head. The nearest mountain rose away in the distance, a slope so large in magnitude that the peak was shrouded in storm clouds.

Halfway up the hill, he saw it.

There was a cluster of buildings scattered across a flat alcove in the mountainside. From this distance he couldn't make out all the features, but there seemed to be four buildings total. Some kind of multi-storey watchtower, a long low hall likely to be living quarters, a large garage with roller doors — and at the edge of the complex, a tiny tin shed shrouded in darkness.

Maybe an old military installation.

Maybe a pit stop for industrial workers contracted to stints this far out from civilisation.

Whatever the case, it was clearly inhabited. A dull lightbulb shone on the exterior of the low building, providing the slightest artificial glow that had attracted King's attention in the first place. Probably nothing. But there was no harm in checking it out.

No stone unturned, he thought.

He recalled Isla's voice in his head. *Don't let anyone see your face.*

Begrudgingly, he clambered off the snowmobile and dropped into the snow. His combat boots sunk fully into the forest floor, icy powder reaching up to his ankles. He tied the duffel to the handlebars and fished two spare magazines out of the top of the bag.

Thirty rounds each.

5.56mm NATO rounds.

Capable of decimating anyone in front of him.

Which was exactly what he intended to do if anyone pulled a gun on him.

No mercy out here.

He set off toward the base of the mountain, leaving the snowmobile in the forest. He kept one hand around the grip, index finger resting against the trigger guard. With the other he clenched the additional tactical grip on the front of the weapon. It would take him a second to line up his aim and fire if confronted with hostiles.

The gale-force wind iced his face as he reached the foot of the mountain and began his steady ascent. He followed a narrow trail intended for vehicles, which he assumed led up to the outpost's front door. He kept to the side of the road at all times, entirely shrouded in darkness. Each footfall turned cautious. The last thing he wanted was to turn over on his ankle halfway up the mountain and find himself stranded.

Conditioning wasn't an issue. His resting heart rate barely changed throughout the climb. Thousands and thousands of hours of cardio and weights and hardcore training paid off in situations like these, where his physical fitness barely crossed his mind. He welcomed it. It freed up his mind to concentrate on what really mattered.

Remaining undetected.

He didn't make contact with a living soul throughout the entire journey. Halfway to the outpost, he paused a beat to look out over the Kamchatka Peninsula. It was an awe-inspiring sight.

Thunder boomed far in the distance. On the horizon, he thought he saw a crack of lightning, arcing briefly through the black sky. His eyes had become accustomed to the night, and he made out the shadowy outlines of mountains and volcanoes stretching as far as the eye could see. Below, the forest sprawled out for a couple of miles before seemingly ending all at once.

From this viewpoint, he could see why.

The plains below dropped sharply away in a rigid line, at the edge of unimaginably-high cliff-faces. King couldn't make out the valley below that. It was too dark. Yet it created a tiered appearance to the landscape. The enormous valley cast in shadow, then a stretch of forest higher up, then the gargantuan mountain he was currently perched on.

Unfathomable scenery.

He couldn't imagine the sight during the day.

He pressed on. By the time he sensed the glow of artificial light becoming a little more apparent, his face had turned entirely numb from cold. He guessed he had been walking for a little over twenty minutes. Now the conditions were beginning to affect him. His lungs constricted in uncomfortable fashion, his chest tightening as he searched for breath amongst the altitude.

He crouched in the lee of a rock formation and took a moment to compose himself.

From what he could tell, the outpost lay directly above him. The mountain road curved around a bend just ahead, which he predicted would open out onto the land in front of the complex.

Time to get a better look.

He crept silently along the trail, buffeted by winds at least twice as strong as before. The U-bend came up faster than he anticipated. He stuck to the scrub, to the darkest corners of the uneven trail.

Silent.

Measured.

Ready.

Gripping the carbine rifle double-handed, he rounded the bend. Now was not the time for rapid movement. Charging like a living battering ram had its advantages, and had paid off well for King in the past.

Here, there were too many variables.

This outpost could be full of civilians with no knowledge of a group of missing health workers. Or — worse still — it could be populated by hostiles with live hostages at their disposal. He recognised the benefits of stealth in a situation like this.

He saw the complex ahead.

He slowed.

The long low building in the centre of the outpost resembled a ski-lodge up close. Warm light emanated from the wood-framed windows running the length of the property. The communications tower situated against the side of the building was dark, devoid of all life. Everyone was indoors at this time of the evening. The enormous garage off to one side of the complex was similarly unmanned. Its roller doors were shut.

No-one was watching. No-one kept lookout.

The whole outpost had a lackadaisical air about it, like it was home to shift workers protecting themselves from the extreme weather. There was no-one patrolling the perimeter, no-one keeping a lookout for intruders.

King relaxed his grip on the M4A1. He got the feeling it would not be needed. Whoever populated the outpost seemed to have no concern with the surrounding area.

Or they've grown lazy, he thought. *Their isolation has made them careless.*

On cue, the lodge's door burst open. King shrank into the dead vegetation on the outskirts of the complex, separated from the building by a vast snowy lot and a potholed mountain trail.

The man who stepped out of the lodge was dressed identically to the outfitted combatants back in the village. Heavy combat boots, pressed khakis, an expensive buffer jacket, a bandanna tied across the lower half of his face to protect his skin from the cold.

He looked to be a little over six foot tall — roughly King's height. The man filled out his clothing substantially. Likely packed with muscle.

Instantly, King's reflexes sharpened. He felt cortisol flood his veins.

This isn't a worker.

Then he spotted the faded MP-443 Grach pistol in the man's hand, confirming his suspicions all at once.

The guy didn't look once in King's direction. His gaze locked onto the small storage shed on the left-hand side of the property, directly ahead. He made straight for it, keeping the handgun at the ready.

King watched the man cross the complex. He stayed still as a statue, thinking twice about using the carbine so soon. He was entirely uninformed about the layout of the outpost. He didn't know how many hostiles were here, and what kind of firepower they had.

Besides, suppressor or not, any kind of automatic gunfire attracted attention. King knew one wrong move could leave him horrendously outnumbered.

So he stepped silently out of the shadows as soon as the man passed him by. He noticed a flash of movement in one of the shed's foggy windows, like a body passing briefly across the dead space behind.

He paused.

What's going on here?

The man strode up to the shed's rickety door and unlocked a thick steel padlock attached to the handle. It sent alarm bells ringing in King's head. The guy slid the bolt out of its latch and swung the thin door inwards. He raised the Grach and advanced into the shed.

King dropped low — crouching below the window level — and hustled across the open space. He pressed his back against the shed wall, only half a foot from the open doorway. He listened intently.

'*Fuck* off,' an angry female voice spat. 'Don't touch me.'

King heard a scurry of movement, then the unmistakeable strike of hand against flesh. A woman whimpered and the frantic movement stopped. The man who had entered the room scoffed loudly. King heard the rustle of clothing.

Then he had heard enough.

He spun on his heel and charged into the shed. What his imagination had conjured up was confirmed a half-second later. He saw three women — each sporting a variety of bloodstains and bruises, all bound at the limbs. They were spread across the claustrophobic confines of the shed's interior, helpless.

The man in the tactical gear was perched over one of the women, in the process of trying to remove her clothing. She was bucking and squirming with everything she had, one cheek reddened by the slap King had heard a second ago.

The guy had his back to the entrance.

Big mistake.

King kicked out with a heavy combat boot, aiming for the hand wrapped around the Grach. He connected hard enough to shatter a few fingers. The crunch of splintering bone resounded throughout the shed, drowning out all other noises. The guy shot up like he'd been struck by lightning, temporarily paralysed by the immense pain. The pistol dropped out of his shattered hand.

As soon as he knew the guy was disarmed, King dropped his rifle and lunged. In one motion he snatched a handful of the guy's jacket and hurled him to the side. Adrenalin and raw power lent him all kinds of abilities. The guy lost his footing and began to fall.

With his other arm, King twisted his entire body into a scything close-range elbow. As the man toppled backwards, the bony point of King's elbow smashed into his forehead hard enough to give him permanent brain damage.

The blow added extra momentum to the guy's fall.

Already unconscious, the back of his head hit the wall behind at unfathomable speed.

Crack.

The guy dropped, all tension gone from his limbs.

He slumped into an unconscious pile amidst a scattering of unused shovelling equipment, suffering from internal bleeding at best.

Two seconds after stepping into the shed, King ducked quickly below the line of sight and shut the door behind him.

CHAPTER 18

The three prisoners watched him in terrified silence, unsure who or what he was.

What his intentions were…

He looked at each of them in turn. 'You work for the World Health Organisation?'

They nodded in unison. The woman on the far right made to speak, but something stopped her. Her eyes flicked to the debilitated mercenary in the corner and she faltered.

King understood.

Savage violence was shocking at the best of times. Those who were unaccustomed to it had a hard time digesting its consequences. Especially the kind of violence that King dealt out.

'Is he…?' the woman finally muttered.

The one in the middle cut her off. 'Who gives a shit? You saw what he was about to do, Carmen. I hope he's dead.'

This woman had light brown hair and pale skin. Her accent was American — midwestern, if he had to guess. Despite the obvious tension and unease of the situation, she kept her chin held high, refusing to cave into the pressure. She spoke reassuringly.

King admired that.

'My name's Jason King,' he said. Slowly. Calmly. 'I'm a government operative. I'm here to help you.'

The woman nodded. 'I'm Sarah. We're all with the WHO.'

'Do you know how many men are at this outpost?'

Sarah shook her head. 'We all woke up here, in this shed. We were taken from the village — I know that much. They drugged us. I remember another location. Some kind of mine. We were there first. There are seven other people in our party — all men. I think they were kept at the first location. We were carted up here for … other reasons.'

King couldn't help but be impressed. For someone being held in captivity against their will for sadistic purposes, Sarah delivered all the information she could in clinical fashion. If King had been an ordinary civilian, he never would have held the same composure.

It set off some kind of memory in the back of his head. He ignored it and pressed on. 'They separated you based on gender?'

'I think so.'

'What makes you sure it was a mine?'

'We were driven into a huge warehouse. Like an empty airplane hangar. There was one of those cages in the corner — you know the ones with an elevator inside?'

King nodded. 'I think there's gold mines in this region.'

'But I can't be sure…'

'Did you see the men taken away?'

'No.'

'Just a guess?'

'Yes. Well, they're not here, are they?'

'They could be. Have you just been confined to this space?'

Sarah nodded. 'I feel like the mine had a purpose though.'

'Just a hunch?'

She bowed her head. 'Do you think I'm wrong?'

'Of course not. Half my career has been based off hunches. What else do you know?'

She shrugged, and for the first time her voice cracked as she spoke. 'I don't know. That's it. Everything's foggy…'

King held up a hand. 'You're doing incredible. All three of you, focus on your breathing. In and out. Slow and controlled. If we can avoid panic attacks until we're safe and sound, that would be best.'

'How did you find us so quickly…?' Sarah muttered.

'Our government is on the ball with things like this,' King said. 'You missed a check-in, apparently.'

Sarah flashed a glance to the other two women. 'No we didn't.'

King paused. 'What?'

'We weren't even scheduled to contact anyone until tomorrow morning. They're not that rigorous about things like that. Probably to our own detriment…'

The woman in the corner — Carmen — nodded. 'Generally we're left to our own devices.'

The third woman, who had yet to speak, piped up. 'There's no way anyone should have known about our dilemma.'

King didn't respond. Gears were whirring in his head.

Odd phrases, strange orders.

Puzzle pieces began to fall into place.

Sarah's mannerisms came to the forefront of his mind again. They reminded him of someone.

He turned to her. 'Do you all keep in contact with family while you're out here?'

She shrugged. 'Some of us do. We have the communication equipment for it. Satellite phones, that sort of thing.'

'Have you been talking to anyone?'

She hesitated. 'I'd prefer not to discuss that sort of thing if it's not necessary.'

'It's incredibly necessary.'

A pause. 'Yes, I have been.'

'Who?'

'My sister.'

With one hand, King balled a fist as tightly as he could, clenching his fingers together until his knuckles turned white, preparing for how he would react to the next answer. He had to maintain his composure at all times.

He wondered if he would…

'Tell me if I'm wrong,' he said, 'but your sister's name wouldn't happen to be Isla, would it?'

Sarah cocked her head to one side, confused. 'Yeah … how'd you know?'

King's vision went red. Insuppressible anger flooded his veins, hot and fiery. He held up a finger.

'Excuse me for a moment,' he said. 'I'll be back.'

He slipped out of the shed, taking care to ensure the coast was clear before stepping out onto open ground. No-one else had followed the mercenary out of the lodge.

The man had likely requested to be left alone while he took advantage of the prisoners…

Satisfied by the lack of hostiles, King scurried around to the rear of the shed, out of sight from the main buildings. He touched a finger to his ear, barely keeping his temper under control.

It felt like an eternity before Isla answered, even though it couldn't have been more than a couple of seconds.

'Yes?' she said.

'You think I'm fucking stupid?' King said.

'What?'

'Feel free to correct me if I'm making wild accusations —
but this isn't an official operation. Black Force has no
knowledge of it, do they?'

The silence went on for an uncomfortable length of time, to
the point where King wondered if Isla would ever respond.
Then she sucked in a breath, full of nerves and pent-up stress.

'No.'

CHAPTER 19

'This whole operation has felt off from the start,' King said. 'Now I know why.'

'I can't begin to tell you how sorry I am.'

'Doesn't change a thing.'

'I know.'

'Do you realise what you've done?'

'Yes.'

'You understand the ramifications this will have?'

'I acted out of impulse. It's family.'

'You broke every rule in the book. A hundred times over. I'm in the middle of Russia. I've killed a dozen people. None of it authorised in any sense of the word.'

Isla paused. 'It's never official. Black Force isn't on the books. You know that. You practically founded the division all those years ago.'

'And I work for the division.'

'I know.'

'You exploited the fact that I have no contact with any superiors other than you. You knew you could utilise that to make this feel like another routine assignment. You'd have me back in Sweden in time for an *actual* mission, and no-one would be any wiser. Myself included. Am I right?'

'You're right.'

'Consider me retired again.'

'Jason…'

'I'm done, Isla.'

He meant it. He never wanted to work for any kind of government body for the rest of his life. His blood boiled in that moment. He had never been so furious.

Angry that Isla would use him as a pawn for her own intentions.

Angry that Black Force's operational structure allowed room for such a gross miscarriage of procedure.

Angry that the true purpose for his presence in the Russian Far East had been covered up.

He'd put his life on the line for a lie.

'If you'd told me,' he said, 'I might have helped you. If you found me in that alley and opened up about how your sister hadn't contacted you and you feared the worst, I might have offered my services free of charge. Because I like you, Isla. Despite all the official bullshit, you mean well. At least I thought you did.'

'I do mean well.'

'Carter,' King said. 'Who's he?'

'He's who I said he was,' Isla said. 'Air Force. That's how I got the bomber.'

'Oh.'

'Yeah…'

'I assume your position allows you all kind of requests to be met immediately. They probably don't need official confirmation, either. Given what you managed to pull off…'

'I am the official confirmation. Black Force has clearance at the highest levels. We're designed to respond to threats by any means necessary.'

'So you used your position to deceptively take advantage of U.S. military resources? You contracted a bomber to fly over Russia without *anyone* in an actual position of government aware of it other than yourself?'

'I have a way with words. People seem to believe me when I'm demanding.'

'Won't do you much good in military prison, Isla.'

'King, I know what I've done. I know the consequences it'll have. I did that willingly. I took that risk.'

'You could have started World War Three if the plane was detected.'

'It wasn't detected,' Isla said. 'It never would have been. I ensured that. I always do my research.'

'Your sister is here,' he said after a pause. 'She's tied up in a remote outpost. A hostage for some kind of mercenary force. I haven't quite worked that out yet. I just saved her from being raped five minutes ago.'

'Sarah?'

'Sarah.'

Her voice turned raw. 'Jason, please…'

'Give me one reason not to leave right now.'

'You wouldn't.'

'You're right,' he said, teeth clenched, hands shaking. 'I wouldn't. And you know that. That's why you went through with this. You knew that even if I discovered the truth halfway through the operation, I'd see it out if they were truly in danger. You know how I am. And you used it.'

'I saw an opportunity and I took it,' she said. 'It's my career down the drain, I know. Probably my life, too. Everything I've worked for is fucked. But I don't care. Just get my sister back. Please.'

'I will,' King said. 'I'll sort this all out, and I'll bring them back. Then I'll have you fired, and I'll never step foot on U.S. soil again.'

He wrenched the tiny speaker out of his ear and tossed it off the side of the mountain.

CHAPTER 20

He stood frozen on the other side of the storage shed, looking out at the view. The winds blasting away at the side of the mountain drowned out everything else. They kept him rooted in place, taking the time to consider what had happened.

In the end, he had no choice but to soldier on.

Official or not, he had a job to do. Innocent lives were in danger, and by this point it was inarguable that something sinister was afoot in the Kamchatka Peninsula. If he packed up his gear and high-tailed it out of Russia, ten health workers would die.

Or worse.

Whatever the case, they would never be heard from again unless he acted.

He sympathised with Isla for a brief moment. He didn't know the exact details of her relationship with her sister, but it must be close. Some kind of check-in time must have been set-up, likely a precautionary measure influenced by Isla's government roots.

Sarah had missed it.

Isla, panicking, had used the resources she had available to send in a one-man hit team.

If it had proven to be nothing, she would have extracted King and had him back on home soil before anyone knew he'd been used. King would have carried on with his operations, unaware that no-one had ordered his visit to Russia.

But now he did know.

The bureaucracies and politics could be sorted out at a later date. Right now he was deep in enemy territory, responsible for the rescue of ten hostages.

He switched back to focus on the mission, shutting out all extraneous thoughts.

Compartmentalise, he thought. *There's time for everything else later.*

He circled back around the shed, staying low, watching the lodge like a hawk. A shadow passed briefly across one of the windows, indiscernible in the lowlight. King kept his barrel trained on the front door and counted out long beats.

One.

Two.

Three.

Nothing. He wanted to avoid confrontation at all costs. For all he knew, there could be an army of hired thugs inside the lodge, restless after long months of nothingness, itching for a firefight.

Just waiting for the opportunity to unleash an arsenal of weaponry.

He wouldn't give them the pleasure.

He ducked back into the storage shed and came face-to-face with the trio of health workers. They sported confused expressions — eyes wide, brows furled. He realised that in his haste to get answers out of Isla, he had left them to their own devices.

They might have thought he had abandoned them.

'Where'd you go?' Sarah said.

He tapped his ear. 'Just had to check in with my superiors. Let them know I found you three.'

'How did you know my sister's name?'

He paused. 'She was the one to let us know of your disappearance. We acted immediately.'

'I see.'

'Are you two close?'

Sarah nodded. 'She's going through a messy divorce, and work's been wearing her down lately. I think I'm the one keeping her sane. We've pretty much been in daily contact for the last couple of months. Hence her immediate response, I'd say.'

King cocked his head. *The more you know.*

'What does she do?' he said, innocently enough.

Sarah shrugged. 'Some kind of government office job. Maybe that's why she managed to get onto you so quickly. Are you Special Forces?'

'I am,' King said. 'And yeah, maybe that's why.'

He crouched by the door and stared at the ground, thinking hard.

Finally, Sarah interjected. 'What are you doing?'

'Thinking about the best way to handle this,' King said. 'You'd recognise the mine if you saw it again?'

'I'd say it's the only building around here. So, probably.'

'I only have a snowmobile,' King said. 'I can't fit the three of you on the back. And the trek down the mountain is going to be risky as hell. We're sitting ducks if they find the shed empty and spot us on the trail.'

No-one spoke.

'What are you saying?' Carmen whispered.

'I might have to deal with this,' he said. 'I can't see a feasible way of getting you three off the mountain safely otherwise.'

The trio went visibly pale.

'What are you going to do?' Sarah said.

King tapped his rifle. 'You three stay here. Keep your heads down. Okay?'

'No.'

King looked at her. 'Trust me.'

'You'll die. You don't know how many there are.'

'Doesn't matter how many there are,' King said. 'This is the right way to do it.'

'But—'

He rose and checked the lodge for signs of life. Its residents were firmly shut up inside. No-one else had emerged from the building.

'Coast is clear,' he muttered.

The woman named Carmen piped up. 'What's your plan, exactly?'

He glanced at her. 'To clear the lodge.'

'How do you propose to do that?' she said.

He held up the carbine rifle in one hand. 'With this.'

'With one gun? There could be a dozen of them.'

King patted the breast pocket of his vest. 'That's what the spare magazines are for.'

Astonished, she leant back against the wall and closed her eyes, shaking her head in disbelief. 'You're going to die, and then they'll kill us too.'

'*Carmen...*' Sarah muttered.

'What? You think this is a good idea?'

'I'm not sure we're in the position to tell him what a good idea is.'

'You're going to have to trust me,' King said. 'As much as you might doubt it, I value my own life. I wouldn't go through with this if I wasn't confident.'

'It's called being delusional,' Carmen said.

Sarah said, 'Ignore her.'

King shrugged. 'I'd feel the same if I was in your position. I probably look like a madman.'

'You sure do,' Sarah said. 'But you seem like you know what you're doing.'

'Sometimes I question that,' King muttered.

Then he threw the door open and stepped out into the howling night.

CHAPTER 21

He moved in on the lodge step-by-step.

Locked and loaded.

Ready for war.

It would be a matter of instincts. All combat was. But the few seconds after he smashed the front door in were vital. Those seconds spelled the difference between life and death. He would have to line up his targets in the blink of the eye and execute in devastating fashion.

No hesitation.

No mercy.

Thankfully, he had a lifetime of experience in similar situations.

They wouldn't know what hit them.

He stepped onto the rickety wooden deck running the length of the lodge's exterior, taking care to adjust his weight in order to silence his footsteps. He kept the M4A1 in a tight double-handed grip. His hands didn't waver. His heart rate barely rose.

He would need every sliver of concentration for what came next.

King took three sharp breaths — and entered a different zone.

He couldn't talk in this state, even if he wanted to. He was primed and ready to unleash. The energy and adrenalin and raw sensation built up in his chest until it felt set to explode.

He pressed one ear tentatively against the thin wooden door at the front of the lodge.

He listened.

Low voices inside. More than one. Less than five.

He could handle that.

He laid two fingers on the outside handle and lowered it inch-by-inch. It was unlocked, as he anticipated. This deep in the Russian Far East, security and awareness took a nose dive. Especially after what King expected was a lengthy period of uneventfulness.

As soon as the door clicked, he switched gears and shouldered it inwards. Dead-centre, two hundred and twenty pounds of muscle straight into the flimsy wood. It flew along its hinges like a rocket, opening in a half-second.

Then it hit something on the other side.

For a panicked beat King thought they had barricaded the door in anticipation of his arrival. That would pose problems. It meant there would likely be weapons aimed in his direction.

Then the object on the other side of the door let out a sharp breath and stumbled off-balance.

A man.

King charged into the room and flicked his eyes over its contents.

The lodge consisted of a single communal area stretching from one wall to the other. At the back of the space, a handful of doorways led into what he assumed were living quarters. The main area was furnished with a smattering of old couches and dusty coffee tables. A tiny kitchen had been jammed into one of the corners. Dirty plates and mugs were piled high in the sink.

But King didn't pay attention to any of that.

He focused on the living bodies in the room, assessing their hostility in the blink of an eye.

One man was in the process of leaping off a couch.

Another was sprawled on the floor in front of him, scrambling for purchase.

They were the room's only inhabitants.

King saw the man furthest from him diving for a gun resting on the nearest coffee table. He was a scrawny Russian, all bone and sinew and lean muscle. There was sheer panic in his eyes.

Not one of ours, he would be thinking.

King raised his M4A1 and fired a precise volley across the room. Four bullets total. Mostly muffled by the suppressor screwed onto the barrel, but the sound still punched through the cool night air.

Rat-a-tat-tat.

The man caught two rounds in the throat just as he got a hand on the pistol. King noted its make — an MP-443 Grach handgun. One of the standard issue sidearms in the Russian Armed Forces. These men must have secured a stash of them off the black market — or received a direct supply from a corrupt official.

So far, none of them had got the chance to use the weapons.

Arterial blood arced from the wounds in the man's neck and he cascaded to the wood-panelled floor, knocking over a lampshade in the process. King registered the glassy look in his eyes and knew instantly that the wounds were fatal.

He shifted his aim to the man on the floor.

Fuck.

The guy was fast. He had half-made it to his feet, wrenching a serrated combat blade from a sheath on his belt. He sliced it through the air, barely aiming, swinging for the fences. Nevertheless, a knife could do a world of damage if it even touched King.

He shot backwards, hearing the steel whistle through the dead space near his throat. The mercenary — another scrawny guy almost the same height as King — stumbled, thrown off-balance by the miss. He had put everything into the swing.

King planted his feet, switched the carbine to semi-automatic, and fired a single unwavering shot through the side of the man's head.

Just above the ear.

The guy hit the floor in equally brutal fashion. The tension dissipated out of his limbs before he dropped, which resulted in his corpse slapping the wood like a rag doll only a couple of seconds after his friend.

Twin thumps.

Two down.

King didn't move a muscle. He let the reverberations of the impacts fade away until the only audible sounds came from the wind outside and the soft creak of a rocking chair that had been disturbed by the first guy's face-plant.

No-one came tearing out of the adjacent rooms searching for a target. King was prepared for that. He swept the barrel of the M4A1 clinically from door to door, ready for any additional attackers.

After ten long seconds of inactivity, he moved to clear the lodge.

The bedrooms were empty. The bathrooms were empty. The toilet cubicles were empty.

Two men total, then.

Three, if you counted the guy that King had dispatched in the storage shed.

He ran the situation through his head. It made sense — three of the thugs had been sent off with the female prisoners, to keep them secure at this remote outpost while the real event took place elsewhere with the males. The women were obviously not needed for whatever their captors had in mind, so they had been locked up in a shed and left to the devices of this small detail.

An abandoned mine, he thought, recalling what Sarah had told him in the shed.

If he found it, the environment would suit him. He thrived in cramped spaces. Two hundred and twenty pounds could achieve vicious results in close quarters.

He hoped the rest of the thugs were ready.

Satisfied that all hostiles at the outpost had been eliminated, he made his way back out into the cold and opened the door to the storage shed. He was met with three terrified gazes.

He couldn't imagine the fear that would course through the trio if it had been one of the Russian thugs who entered instead of King. It would mean that their last hope of escape had been dispatched.

Then their faces flooded with relief.

'Come into the lodge,' King said. 'It's warmer in there.'

He led them across the flat land and ushered them onto the deck and through the open front door. He took one last look out into the howling night, then followed them inside.

Carmen and Sarah were the first to lay eyes on the bodies. Jessica trailed meekly behind, keeping her eyes fixed firmly on the floor, likely in preparation for what she knew she might see. The two women in front had vastly different reactions.

Carmen recoiled, astonished by the amount of blood spread across the floorboards. She turned away from the two dead men and made eye contact with King.

He saw something there. A kind of detachment. Like she didn't consider King human.

He didn't blame her. This world was nothing like the civilian world. He would have preferred if situations like this didn't exist, and he could spend his days in a relatively normal profession. Yet this seemed to be what he excelled in, and there would always be people across the globe with sinister intentions.

So he killed them like it was nothing.

He wondered if she considered him a cold-hearted murderer. Maybe he was. Maybe he had become so desensitised to the violence that it felt casual, like something that needed to happen regardless.

He looked past Carmen, to where Sarah stood frozen with her back to them.

Sarah had no visible reaction. She kept her gaze transfixed on the pair of dead men, almost trance-like in her lack of movement.

'Sarah,' King said, breaking the silence. 'You okay?'

She wheeled around. 'Yeah.'

Carmen stared blankly out the window. 'How can you look?'

'What do you mean?' Sarah said.

'This is horrendous.'

'You know what they were going to do to us. One of them almost did, in case you forgot. Why wouldn't I look? Why would I care that they're dead?'

'I *don't* care,' Carmen said, her voice faltering. 'But this is…'

King studied the room around them, and all of a sudden their voices faded away. He concentrated on particular details that he hadn't paid attention to before.

There were over ten plates in the sink.

There were eight dirty mugs spread across the countertop, each recently stained.

He doubted three men went through that much kitchenware.

He brushed past Sarah and Jessica, making for the bedrooms. Something had felt off while he'd swept their contents for hostiles, but he hadn't paid attention to it.

He stuck his head around the doorway and noted at least six hiking backpacks sprawled across the stained carpet.

That was all he needed to see.

There were others.

CHAPTER 22

The trio sensed his urgency as he stormed back into the communal area.

'Jason?' Sarah said.

He met her curious gaze. 'There's more of them. I don't know where, though.'

'What do you mean?'

'There's gear for at least six or seven men in these rooms. Possibly more.' He paused, thinking hard. 'Are you sure you three didn't see anything?'

Sarah and Carmen nodded in unison.

King stared past them to where Jessica stood, hunched over by the door, her face a pale sheet. 'Jessica…'

She looked up, eyes wide. 'I—'

She trailed off.

King strode across the room. 'You need to tell me, right now.'

'I'm so sorry,' she said, spluttering. 'I heard engines when I woke up. Heading away from here. Like three or four snowmobiles fading into the distance. I was too scared to tell you when you first asked. I thought I might sound stupid. I thought it was nothing.'

'Like a search party?' Carmen said.

Jessica shrugged, and shrank back into her shell. 'I don't know. That's just what I heard.'

'Most likely,' King said. 'Looking for me, I'd guess. Maybe news of the skirmish in the village made it up here…'

'But you would have passed them on the way up,' Sarah said. 'There's only one way down the mountain.'

'I know.'

A faint growl drifted in through the open doorway. It was barely perceptible, but King heard it. His blood ran cold and he hurried out onto the deck. He peered in the direction of the noise, past the garage and watchtower. Behind the properties, the mountain spiralled away into the sky. The landscape was a mass of sheer rock walls and snow-covered boulders.

He glimpsed a dark trail disappearing into the hillside, curving between rock formations on either side. He hadn't seen it the first time. It spelled the continuation of the trail he had ascended to reach the outpost, heading further up the mountain.

From the entrance to the trail a faint glow emanated, brightening with each passing second.

Headlights.

Coming down towards the outpost.

Not a search party. A search party would have headed straight down the mountain if they received word from the crew dispatched to the village. King didn't think anyone had got the message out. The skirmish had unfolded too fast.

So this was something else. Four or five of them had trekked up the mountain, ascending to the summit around an hour ago — given the timeframe that Jessica had provided.

Why?

It was inconsequential.

The trail was only wide enough to fit one snowmobile at a time. The first vehicle came tearing out into open space at full speed, engine screaming above the winds. King spotted the driver hunched over the handlebars, minimising the target space.

They knew he was here.

The crew must have spotted him from above. It was the only reasonable explanation for their awareness. The driver of the first snowmobile let go of one handlebar and reached back, grasping at something.

A weapon.

He started to bring the gun around.

King dropped to one knee, raised his carbine, lined up his aim and pumped the trigger.

Thwack.

One bullet spat out of the rifle, an isolated burst that ripped across the lot faster than he could see. No further shots followed, even though his finger stayed tight against the trigger, pressing it against the back of the guard.

Semi-automatic! a voice in his head screamed.

Foolish. He hadn't switched the weapon back to its full-auto setting before unloading on the approaching snowmobile. He fumbled desperately for the switch on the side of the rifle, fully aware that he was completely exposed to a barrage of gunfire.

In his peripheral vision, he saw the driver jolt backwards, taking a dead-on impact to the face. A puff of brain matter shot out as he tumbled off the seat. King watched his lifeless body drop in a heap to the snow while the snowmobile drifted on, carried by its own momentum.

In the end, the first shot had been the only bullet necessary.

Silently thanking the years of training that had allowed him such accuracy, he adjusted his aim to the mouth of the trail. His heart thrummed against his chest wall like a beating drum. The cortisol threatened to take over, scrambling his reflexes and fine motor skills. He forced it back down and waited for more hostiles to appear.

The combined roar of the group of engines came from a point several hundred feet in the distance.

King had a few moments to assess.

The first guy was a test.

The thought raced through his mind as he watched the now-empty snowmobile drift towards the lodge, coasting across the snow on its skis. Its ex-driver lay dead in the middle of the flat area. The snow around his head was quickly turning crimson.

There were four more coming, at least. Each on separate snowmobiles. Each armed. They would likely pour out of the opening nose-to-tail, ready for a firefight after witnessing their friend get shot down.

Their suspicions would have been confirmed.

They would not charge lightly into open ground.

King went pale as he realised this was a situation where he couldn't come out on top.

Hands shaking, he turned to face the open doorway of the lodge. The trio of workers peered out at him, curious and terrified all at once.

'Close the door,' he said. He motioned to the pair of corpses on the floor behind them. 'Fetch the guns off those two. If anyone walks in, shoot them dead. Don't stop to check whether it's me or not. I'll warn you if it is.'

'Where are you going?!' Sarah demanded, exasperated.

'There's too many coming. I need to draw them away from here.'

'How are you going to—?'

There wasn't time.

King stepped to the door and slammed it closed, sealing the three health workers in the lodge. If all went to plan, the approaching party wouldn't notice their presence. They would be too fixated on King's actions.

He spun and took off at a sprint, racing toward the driverless snowmobile that had now drifted past his position. It was headed for a collision course with the storage shed. King pushed himself faster, breath pounding in his throat, lungs heaving.

To his rear, he heard the engines grow louder.

Headlights lit up the outpost as the group of snowmobiles tore out the mouth of the trail and fanned out across the lot.

King didn't look.

No time.

He reached the back of the snowmobile ahead and leapt onto the seat, landing hard on the faded leather. He ignored the wind buffeting his clothes, numbing his hands and feet. He slung the carbine rifle over his back and used both hands to snatch control of the handlebars.

Ahead, the storage shed loomed.

King wrenched the snowmobile to the left, squinting to combat the icy breeze slicing across his face. He saw a flash of blurry movement as the tin walls of the shed passed him by at lightning speed.

He missed an impact by mere inches.

'Shit, shit, shit,' he muttered as he lurched in the direction of the descending mountain trail.

The path he had trekked up.

It was the only way back down.

As he was struck by the danger of the situation, he reconsidered. He caught a fleeting glimpse of the treacherous slope spiralling down to the forest below. There were all manner of sharp twists and turns along the way. It had been a tough trek up on foot. He couldn't imagine going down at speed on an unstable vehicle.

He began to falter.

One hand reached for the brake.

Then a cluster of bullets struck the back of the snowmobile. The sound of tearing metal filled his ears, sending jolts of panic through his chest. A half-second later, the report of the automatic gunfire reached his ears.

They were firing on him.

He threw a brief look over his shoulder. Four identical snowmobiles were converging on his position, each kicking up a geyser of snow behind their rear tracks. Each was manned by a balaclava-clad mercenary, dressed in tactical garb similar to the four men King had already killed.

Two of the drivers were fumbling with automatic weapons. One had squeezed off a barrage of shots, hoping to shoot King down before he could put distance between them.

King's stomach dropped as he spotted the party.

They were armed.

He was at a disadvantage.

He *hated* being at a disadvantage.

He thought of the forest at the base of the mountain, with its claustrophobic darkness and interspersed tree trunks. Tight spaces. Uneven ground.

There, he would have the upper hand.

But he had to reach it first.

Sucking in a lungful of air in an attempt to muster the courage, King shut out the part of his brain warning him not to act suicidal and rode his snowmobile off the lip of the trail.

CHAPTER 23

The wind tearing up the side of the mountain washed over him like a glacial storm.

At the same time, his stomach fell to his feet.

With his teeth clenched and his heart pounding, King felt the snowmobile's front skis slam onto the trail. It signalled the start of what would no doubt be a terrifying descent.

He wrestled with the handlebars, fighting for control. They vibrated uncontrollably in his grip, turning his fingers numb from exertion. He spotted the first bend ahead. It was a sharp U-turn that arced away from a sheer cliff-face.

One wrong move would spell a few hundred feet of free fall — followed by a gruesome death.

He applied the brakes at the last moment and felt the snowmobile slow under him. At the same time he twisted the handlebars with all his effort. His forearms burned from the intensity.

He shut the pain out.

With a stomach-lurching skid, the snowmobile swung round the bend at thirty miles an hour. A fountain of snow shot off the edge of the cliff, kicked up by the skis and the rear tracks.

For a horrifying instant, he lost control of the vehicle. He turned the handlebars again in an attempt to correct himself and the snowmobile swayed hard on the trail.

He glimpsed a look over the edge of the path. His muscles tightened and his heart leapt.

Then he fought the snowmobile back under control and continued tearing down the side of the mountain.

He heard the enemy vehicles following suit. With chaos and confusion swirling around him he had no time to catch a glimpse of the pursuing party, but the noise of whining engines tackling the steep trail drifted down from above.

King fought an internal battle, trying to get his instincts under control. Part of him wanted nothing more than to slow down and avoid a grisly fate. Yet if this was to work, he needed to put space between himself and the mercenaries.

So he shook the nerves away and yanked the right handlebar back, picking up even more speed as the throttle engaged.

The next two bends proved easier to tackle. King became accustomed to the relentless shaking and rattling of the seat under him. These sections of the trail were less steep, with wider corners with which to manoeuvre around. He handled them confidently, slicing the snowmobile around the turns.

Then it happened.

Something punched him in the back, so hard and vicious in its impact that he thought he might be thrown from the snowmobile. Pain seared his ribcage, which absorbed the brunt of the shockwave.

It took him a moment to realise he had been hit.

The round had been successfully stopped by the bulletproof Spectra vest under his jacket — otherwise he would have been in a whole new world of hurt. The shot would have killed him if it had struck bare skin. He would have bled out from the exit wound in his stomach.

Nevertheless, a bulletproof vest had limited capabilities. It didn't protect him from the breath being smashed out of his lungs, or the momentum that threw him forward in his seat. He crunched against the handlebars, recoiling away from the impact. His right hand slipped, dropping off one of the handlebars and knocking the throttle in the process.

The snowmobile accelerated violently.

King spotted the twist in the trail ahead. Nothing separated him from a sheer drop down a vertical rock face.

His stomach tightened into a knot.

His heart leapt into his throat.

He scrambled for the brake lever and tugged it, grinding the rear tracks against the snow under the vehicle. The back end of the snowmobile slid out, unable to handle the rapid change of direction in such a short space of time.

King saw the drop looming on the right-hand side. The skis were in the process of turning, but they wouldn't make it in time. Traction had been entirely lost. He would skid sideways off the edge of the trail if he did nothing.

In one motion he swung his right leg over the seat and leapt off the snowmobile, still gripping the handlebars as tight as his gloved hands would allow. His feet touched solid ground at the same time, planting into the snow and landing on the rock beneath.

He estimated that the snowmobile weighed five hundred pounds.

He could deadlift that amount of weight with ease.

He wondered if he could swing it around.

You'll find out, a voice said.

The snowmobile's right-hand ski and rear track lurched into open space, shooting off the cliff. King wrenched the handlebars in his direction with a primal heave, letting out a roar of exertion in the process.

The veins in his forearms and shoulders bulged.

The kind of strength that came from a life-or-death situation kicked in.

With a strain he had never felt before, he turned the front end of the snowmobile around and thrust it back on course, using its own momentum to help guide it in a rudimentary semi-circle.

As he corrected its trajectory, he felt the weight of the vehicle throw him off-balance. His feet slipped on the rock and he fell forwards, hands still wrapped around the handlebars.

With a final, desperate push off his back heel, he jumped.

The snowmobile carried him almost horizontally in the air, yanking him off the ground. He sprawled across the seat, hitting it stomach-first. The impact barely registered in his mind. Every ounce of his being was fighting for survival.

Suddenly — all at once — he got the situation under control.

He planted both boots in the footrests and slammed his rear against the leather seat. He corrected the path of the snowmobile and took off down a lengthy stretch of unwinding terrain. His sternum throbbed from the bullet's impact in the centre of his back, but apart from that he was unscathed.

Bruised.

Battered.

But functioning.

The distant *crack* of gunfire made his heart skip a beat. They were still firing on him. He hunched low over the handlebars and pushed the snowmobile faster, intent on entering the forest like a speeding bullet.

The foliage of the towering alpine trees would provide effective cover.

Then it would become a close-quarters skirmish.

Just what he wanted.

He covered the last stretch of the mountain trail at close to fifty miles per hour, utilising a combination of the downward momentum and the capacity of the 1,000cc engine under the hood.

The forest rose up to meet him. The sole headlight on the front of King's snowmobile cut a sharp beam of light into the depths of the woods. He glimpsed the shadows falling away. A path became illuminated between a cluster of trees. Behind him, the four pursuing vehicles whined as they began to close the gap.

With a twist of the throttle, King rocketed the snowmobile off the base of the mountain and into the forest.

CHAPTER 24

Sarah Grasso clutched the semi-automatic pistol with shaking fingers.

She crouched behind one of the couches — boxed in by Carmen and Jessica on either side — listening to the engines outside fade slowly into silence. The distant whining dropped lower and lower down the mountain with each passing second.

The party of thugs had taken King's bait.

They were pursuing him.

'Do you think it'll work?' Jessica muttered.

'Of course it fucking won't,' Carmen said. 'He's insane.'

Sarah looked at the dead man sprawled across the carpet a few feet away. 'He seems to know what he's doing.'

'We can't just stay here,' Carmen said. 'They're going to kill him eventually. Then they'll come back up here and see we're not in the shed. They'll kill us too.'

'We have guns now,' Sarah said.

'We have two pistols. And none of us have fired a weapon in our lives. You want to take your chances in a shootout with trained killers?'

'I guess not.'

'So we need to do something.'

'I agree,' Jessica said in a voice barely above a whisper.

Sarah shrugged. 'Yeah. You're right. But what do we do?'

'Run.'

'We'll freeze to death out there. We don't have any idea how far we are from help. It could be dozens of miles for all we know.'

Carmen got to her feet and crossed to a coat rack by the door. She snatched one of the expensive jackets off its hangar. 'We'll help ourselves to all their gear. We can check the garage for vehicles.'

'I'm not sur…' Sarah began.

Carmen glared at her. 'You're putting too much faith in that guy. His luck will run out eventually. We're doing our own thing, okay?'

Silence.

'Well,' Carmen said. 'At least I am. You two can stay here if you want. It's a death sentence.'

'No,' Sarah said. 'We'll come. You're right about not staying here. Nothing good can come of it unless Jason manages to kill them all.'

She rose and followed Jessica across the room. They fished through the coat rack until they found garments that fit. Sarah didn't take her hand off the gun in her hands for a second. She felt vulnerable amidst the corpses in the room — like they were sitting on a ticking time bomb.

She had never seen a dead body before.

Léo. Is he dead?

The thought flashed through her mind, and she scolded herself on not thinking of the others sooner. She had been so preoccupied on her own survival that she'd neglected considering what fate the rest of their group had suffered.

There was nothing she could do to help them. Her best chance at ensuring they remained unscathed would involve alerting the authorities and letting them do their thing.

Something sinister was afoot. She was sure of it.

The three of them heard the noise simultaneously.

Sarah snapped her head up in unison with Carmen and Jessica. Her eyes went wide as she discerned exactly what it was.

It was unmistakeable. The drone of a snowmobile's engine. Growing closer and closer.

Coming from the same trail that King had just descended.

The fight-or-flight mechanism kicked in, flooding her veins with adrenalin. Tremors ran through her fingers. The gun in her hands shook uncontrollably. Sweat from her palms turned the grip slippery.

'Is it King?' Jessica said.

'Back against the wall,' Sarah demanded. 'Carmen — your gun?'

'Got it.'

'Be ready.'

'He said he'd warn us if it was him,' Jessica whispered. 'It's only been five minutes since he left.'

They retreated to the far side of the communal area, putting a maze of furniture between themselves and the front door. Sarah heard the snowmobile pull up outside the front of the lodge. The driver killed the engine and the mechanical noise faded into oblivion, replaced by the elements.

Nothing happened for a prolonged period of time.

There were no sounds. No footsteps on the deck outside. No cocking of weapons.

Like the driver was observing the scene.

Considering how to proceed.

'It's not King, is it?' Jessica whispered, her face a pale sheet.

'Quiet,' Sarah muttered.

She raised the pistol in a double-handed grip and pointed the barrel at the flimsy door.

Sudden movement. All at once. She heard booming footsteps on the deck that reverberated through the silence.

Then a loud *crash* as someone thundered a boot into the door, snapping it off its weak hinges. The door crashed to the carpeted floor inside the lodge and a broad-shouldered figure stepped through into the room.

It wasn't King.

It was the man she had glimpsed hours previously in her semi-conscious state. She had peered out of the armoured vehicle at the hardened face, complete with a jagged scar running the length of one cheek. A face devoid of emotion or empathy.

Now she stared at the same face — still just as expressionless, just as cold.

'Hello,' the man said softly. His voice was deeper than Sarah expected, so low and monotone that it felt artificial. His frame was enormous, filling the doorway completely. He was even larger than King.

'Don't move,' Sarah demanded, but her voice faltered. She kept the gun raised. She didn't even know what model it was.

Or if it would fire…

The man in the doorway lifted a finger and pointed at the weapon. 'Your hands are shaking. You'd better hit me on the first try.'

'Shut up!' Carmen roared, attempting to intimidate, her own pistol trained on the man. 'Let us leave.'

'I came to check on my men,' the man said. 'It seems they are not here.'

'Just us,' Sarah said.

'Where are they?'

'They're gone.'

'Where?'

'We have a friend.'

The man raised an eyebrow sarcastically. 'A friend?'

'Yes. He came for us. A soldier.'

He feigned mock surprise. 'A soldier? How frightening.'

Sarah said nothing.

'And where is he now?'

She didn't respond. The tension turned palpable in the air. It seemed the man was waiting for one of them to make a move. He stood frozen in the doorway, hands by his sides, watching them like a predator observing its prey.

'He's not here,' he said. 'That's a shame.'

It sent a chill down Sarah's spine. Finally, the terror became too great. She had spent thirty seconds battling with her mind. One part of her told her to pull the trigger. Another raised all kinds of doubts.

What if you miss?

What if he doesn't die from the first shot?

They reached a crescendo, and then another voice drowned out all the others.

Now.

She pulled the trigger. Her legs tensed, ready to explode off her feet as soon as the shot was fired. She planned it out in her mind — first watch the man fall, then sprint straight past him. Out into the night. There, they could make their way off the mountain and look for help.

None of that happened.

The gun in her hands didn't make a sound.

Fear rolled over her in waves.

Panic set in.

The man in the doorway noticed her unease. Slowly, a wry smile spread over his face.

'That was a mistake,' he said. His eyes flickered over to Carmen. 'Would you like to try?'

She pulled her own trigger.

Same result.

The man scoffed and reached behind his back, withdrawing a sleek, matte black handgun from the holster at his waist. He brought it around to hover by his side.

'This is a MP-443 Grach,' he said. 'The same handgun you two are holding. I equip all my men with them. We have a limitless supply from the Russian Armed Forces. There is a manual safety catch on both sides of the weapon. It's a pity you didn't know that.'

He raised the weapon.

CHAPTER 25

King reached his old snowmobile less than a minute after entering the forest.

He slowed just long enough to snatch the duffel off the handlebars. Nothing else was necessary. Then he gave the throttle of his new ride a brief twist. The engine screamed and he shot off the mark, heading away from the dormant vehicle.

Hopefully it would confuse his assailants. They might think he had abandoned his ride and chosen to flee on foot.

Whatever slows them down...

He powered through dense and claustrophobic terrain, surrounded on all sides by sheer darkness. At one point the ground crested and fell in a small mound. The handlebars rattled underneath him. One of his legs slipped out of its footrest. He corrected the vehicle's path and continued on.

The sounds of his pursuers echoed through the trees behind him. He heard intermittent bursts of noise — the revving of an engine, a sharp command in Russian, the brief flash of a headlight.

So far, they hadn't caught up.

He shifted in his seat, adjusting the duffel slung over one shoulder and the M4A1 hanging off the other. Losing either would spell disaster.

He remembered the view of the peninsula he had glimpsed from the outpost. The forest ended somewhere up ahead, dropping away into a sweeping valley. That was where he planned to make his stand.

His headlight revealed the drop first.

It sent a shiver down King's spine. The artificial light gleamed off the snow-covered ground between the tree trunks ahead, just as it had done for the last half-mile.

Then the snow vanished. A dark, seemingly endless void stretched out from where the ground fell away.

King coasted his snowmobile to a halt at the very precipice of the cliff.

He killed the engine. Silence enveloped his surroundings, amplifying the noise of the four pursuing vehicles. He fumbled for the headlight switch, flicking it off in the blink of an eye. The night wrapped around him.

He *sensed* the edge of the cliff behind him, even though it wasn't visible in the lowlight. There was a certain feeling that came with standing on the lip of a great chasm in the land. A sense of vertigo. A sense of awe. The wind howled through the forest ahead, sweeping off the cliff.

One wrong step, a voice told him.

He ignored it and leapt off the snowmobile, landing in the snow. It took half a minute for his eyes to grow used to the night. He dropped the duffel bag on the empty seat and stalked away from the idle vehicle, heading for the nearest trees.

If all went to plan, the skirmish would unfold so fast that the four hostiles wouldn't get a chance to fire a shot.

He saw them coming. A few hundred feet into the woods, white light poured from a cluster of sources. As he crouched beside a towering deciduous tree and peered into the gloom, he noticed two of the snowmobiles branch off, heading to the left.

The other two made straight for him.

They hadn't seen him. Not a chance. He had kept himself hidden in the darkness.

He gripped the carbine rifle in both hands and waited for them to ride straight past him.

It happened too fast for him to process fully — yet he was ready for that. A decade of combat had taught him to act out of instinct.

He did so…

…to devastating effect.

The first snowmobile bore down on him in a kaleidoscope of light and noise. King spotted the outline of the driver and let loose a three-round burst.

Clinical.

He knew the muzzle flare and subsequent discharge would attract the attention of all four of them.

Once he started, there would be no pause until the last man was dead.

The driver of the first snowmobile took all three rounds to the upper chest. One of them must have punched through his throat. Arterial blood fountained into the freezing night, illuminated for an instant by the muzzle flare. He tumbled off the seat and the snowmobile tore past King's position.

King heard it roar away, kicking up snow on either side until it dipped off the edge of the cliff and tumbled into oblivion. The driver's body disappeared amidst the churned snow, but King knew he was dead.

He swung his aim to line up with the second snowmobile.

This driver had impressive reflexes. He slammed on the brakes as soon as he saw his comrade fall. The snowmobile ground to a halt a dozen feet in front of King, sending a fresh burst of snow into the air. It temporarily obstructed King's vision.

As soon as the snow fell away, King saw the guy brandishing a high-powered assault rifle.

He ducked low and charged, zigzagging between trees. The headlight blinded him as he ran. His world turned to madness. A volley of bullets passed over his head. He returned fire with a sharp burst, hitting nothing but air.

He lifted his head and spotted the snowmobile only a couple of feet away. The driver stood up on the footrests, ass off the seat, trying to lock onto King with the Kalashnikov in his hands. King ducked again and sprinted the final stretch. He dropped his shoulder low and crash-tackled the man off the snowmobile.

They sprawled into the snow, hitting the ground hard enough to knock the breath from both their lungs.

But King came down on top.

That was all he needed.

He still had one hand clenching the grip of the M4A1. In one motion he rolled off the winded driver and swung the barrel around in an arc. As soon as it touched the guy's head, King pulled the trigger.

Two shots.

One would have been enough.

Panting, clawing for air, King sprung to his feet and stared around with wide eyes, assessing where the other two snowmobiles had disappeared to.

Shit!

An explosion of light sliced through the trees to his left. He spun around just in time to see a third snowmobile screaming across the terrain. It shot between a pair of trees and bore down on King like a freight train.

Between him and the approaching snowmobile, the second snowmobile rested idle.

Driverless.

A barricade of sorts.

The driver of the third snowmobile noticed it. He reacted fast, leaping off his own ride and hitting the ground in an expertly-timed tumble roll.

King had no time to move.

The third snowmobile crashed into the second in brutal fashion. It knocked the second away like a child's toy…

…straight into King.

He took most of the impact to his left-hand side, turning away from the six-hundred-pound battering ram. Pain flared across his side and he twisted in the air, thrown off his feet by the sheer momentum. A dull throbbing sprouted behind his eyeballs as his head rattled from the collision.

He smashed into the snow head-first, tumbling and turning, desperate to get his bearings.

When he finally rolled to his feet a few feet away from where he had been struck, he found himself weaponless. The carbine rifle had been knocked out of his grip from the force of the blow.

Everything hurt, all at once. But there were still two men breathing in these woods who wanted him dead — which meant as long as nothing was broken, he would continue.

Suddenly vulnerable, his vision blurry and his hands empty, he searched for where the third man had landed.

He spotted him — just over a dozen feet away — scrambling to his feet.

Also unarmed.

I can handle that, he thought.

They stared at each other in the lowlight, separated by a stretch of land home to a sea of churned snow and a pair of destroyed snowmobiles. King heard a distant rumble to his left.

He turned to see the edge of the cliff only ten feet away.

That's not good…

The driver charged at him.

CHAPTER 26

King sized the guy up as he approached.

He was shorter — probably just under six foot, if he had to guess — but built like a tank. Muscles bulged under the cold-weather gear. The man's face was mostly covered by a balaclava stretched over his nose and mouth. His eyes were hard and cruel.

King saw the first blow coming from a mile away. The thug sprinted up to him and swung a wild haymaker with everything he had. If it connected, it would knock King dead — or at the very least caused massive neurological damage.

The guy had experience, for sure. Not many people could throw a punch like that.

But it was sloppy. King assumed the extent of the man's training had been exacted on stationary heavy-bags.

King jerked back a few inches — a risky manoeuvre, all things considered. He needed to be in range for what came next. The haymaker sliced through empty space, horrendously close to his chin. He heard the air whistling away from the missed punch.

He dropped low — now only a foot away from the guy — and threw a savage uppercut, electing to sacrifice accuracy for power due to the proximity. His fist smashed into the guy's ribcage hard enough to break bones.

A devastating shot.

The guy backed up a step, which was where King made a mistake. He didn't follow up with another blow immediately. He hesitated, trying to work out exactly how much damage the uppercut had dealt.

Not enough.

The guy ignored the pain that would no doubt be burning through his torso and twisted at the waist, again putting maximum effort into a strike.

This time, it was a scything roundhouse kick, aimed at King's stomach.

This time, it connected.

King felt the burly shin crunch into his abdomen almost before he saw the kick coming. It had years of martial arts training behind it. The guy had utilised the opportunity to its fullest.

Agony flared through his stomach. The pain was so intense that for a brief instant he felt his legs buckle. His body threatened to collapse into the snow, which would line him up perfectly for another kick to the side of the head.

That would put him out for good.

Mentally, he battled tooth and nail for control of his motor functions. As soon as he found them, he exploded into action. He knew he only had a few seconds of life-and-death adrenalin before the pain caught up to him.

He snatched a handful of the guy's khaki jacket and tugged him into range. With his other hand, he jabbed a straight right into his face. He'd thrown the punch with half his usual power, but he knew the importance of accuracy when it was needed.

He felt the guy's septum shatter under the punch.

With the same arm, he smashed an elbow across the guy's jaw. A sharp *crack* echoed off the nearest trees. Something was broken — indiscernible exactly what in the chaos, but it signified damage dealt.

Stunned by the two blows, the guy stumbled.

King darted out of range, taking a half-step back to line up for the final blow. He sucked in a breath and launched a scything front-kick. His boot crunched into the same rib he had injured earlier.

Due to a combination of momentum and the act of recoiling from such a painful blow, the mercenary lost his footing.

He slipped desperately, knowing fully well how disastrous losing his balance would be in this situation.

Too late.

King sprinted forward, wrapped two hands around the back of his jacket and hurled him off the edge of the cliff.

The guy let out a noise somewhere between a grunt and a yell. He fell head-first, tumbling away into the darkness. King lost sight of him within a couple of seconds.

He turned away from the cliff and peered back into the forest, searching for the fourth and final mercenary.

Nothing.

Both sets of headlights fixed into the two unmanned snowmobiles had flickered out. They had been destroyed in the collision, plunging the surrounding area into darkness. King tried to make out the faint glow that signified where the fourth snowmobile would be located.

He couldn't make out a thing.

The guy's disembarked, he thought.

Smart.

After taking the glare of a headlight directly in the eyes moments previously, his eyes weren't used to the night. The fourth man could be anywhere amidst the trees. King crouched low, his heart pounding, blood boiling in his ears.

Exposed to whoever may be approaching.

There was a flash of movement to his right, near the area where he had parked his own snowmobile. He dropped to the ground, minimising the target area that the mercenary had to hit.

But the guy wasn't heading for King.

The distinctive sound of a pull-start echoed through the forest. King recognised the noise, but stayed frozen in place, trying to ascertain what was happening.

Another tug of a cord and an engine spluttered to life.

His own engine.

He began to make out the outline of the man hunched over his snowmobile, reaching for one of the handlebars. Before he could do anything, the guy steered the vehicle in the direction of the cliff and tugged the throttle.

King could simply watch as his snowmobile — along with the duffel bag containing all his supplies — accelerated over the short stretch of land and dipped nose-first into empty space.

Five seconds later, he heard the six-hundred-pound vehicle obliterate against the bottom of the valley.

'I hope you needed that bag,' the final mercenary roared in stunted English. 'You are a dead man.'

King spotted his M4A1 rifle ahead, wedged into the snow at the base of a tree. He scrambled through the freezing powder and snatched it up, checking the weapon was set to fully-automatic out of instinct. He wouldn't make the same mistake twice.

A ripple of discomfort spread through his abdomen as he straightened. He hoped the muscles weren't torn. Anything that impeded his movement would cause grave problems down the line.

The last man came stumbling out of the tree line with the barrel of his automatic rifle sweeping in all directions.

The guy hadn't a clue where his enemy was.

King took his time lining up the shot. He didn't want to expend a single bullet that wasn't necessary — especially given what had just transpired.

The mercenary stalked along the edge of the drop, crouching low as if that would protect him from being exposed. He hadn't spotted anything yet.

King put a single round through his throat.

The grisly result was masked by the darkness. King heard the slump of a body against the powdery ground and then a sharp *whisk* as the guy tumbled off the cliff-face, tipping the wrong way in his death throes.

King wondered if the man would feel the impact far below.

Probably not.

The bullet would have killed him.

A particularly vicious gust of wind whistled through the forest, adding to the unease that ran through King. He always felt this way in the aftermath of brutal conflict. There was a silence that resonated more than usual, a sudden quiet, in direct contrast to the violence that had just unfolded.

He lowered his weapon and scrutinised the two remaining snowmobiles. They were in bad shape. Dented plastic hung off each chassis and both had snapped skis and twisted rear tracks.

Not drivable.

It took him two minutes to find the fourth man's snowmobile. The guy had disembarked a few dozen feet into the woods, parking the vehicle behind a tree in an attempt to employ stealth. King started the engine with a few vicious tugs of the ripcord. He switched the headlight on, lighting up his surroundings.

He started the journey back to the outpost, carrying the M4A1 on his back and a couple of extra magazines in various pockets of his jacket.

All the rest of his gear was smashed across the rocks hundreds of feet below.

CHAPTER 27

King knew something was wrong the second he arrived at the outpost.

The wind had all but disappeared, replaced by something close to serenity. It was too quiet. The door to the storage shed swung back and forth on its hinges, creaking. All the lights across the four buildings had been shut off.

The lodge's door lay on the carpet within, forced off its hinges.

He parked the snowmobile by the front deck and stepped down onto flat ground. His boots crunched against the fresh powder. Somewhere in the distance, thunder boomed, resonating softly across the outpost.

King checked the M4A1 had ammunition in the magazine and was ready to fire.

He crept onto the front deck, trying to cause as little noise as possible. If there were hostiles here, they would have heard him coming anyway.

They would be ready.

Staying low, he darted in through the open doorway and slapped his hand against the inside wall — where he remembered glimpsing a panel of light switches.

He hit a switch, and a group of the pale light tubes running along the ceiling came to life.

There were no mercenaries lying in wait. There wasn't a living soul inside the lodge.

But the three health workers were still here.

King bowed his head as boiling anger threatened to take hold.

Sarah. Carmen. Jessica.

The trio lay on the far side of the room. The carpet around their heads was stained with blood — three identical pools of crimson soaked into the light grey flooring.

Each sported a cylindrical hole in the centre of their foreheads. Their skin had turned pale and clammy when they had been killed. Based on the freshness of their corpses, King guessed they had been murdered less than ten minutes previously.

Gunned down. All at once.

He didn't let his gaze linger on them any longer than he needed to. He spun on the spot and put an enormous hole through the plaster wall with a single, furious kick.

'*Fuck!*' he roared to no-one in particular.

The syllable sliced through the silent air, echoing through the outpost. No-one heard it. Whoever had done the job was long gone. Not part of the search party. King knew he had drawn all the men stationed at the outpost away from the mountain.

Someone else…

He grimaced, suddenly dejected. He begrudgingly anticipated the conversation with Isla that was sure to follow.

I'm sorry.

I tried my best.

Briefly, he wondered if he really did. Maybe if he had done things differently…

He shrugged it off. If he had stayed at the lodge, they all would have died. He needed the trees and the tight spaces and the confusion to gain the upper hand.

One assault rifle against four on open ground could only achieve so much.

Contemplating his next move, he noticed a soft blinking light on the edge of his vision. He turned to the source.

There was a small translucent dome fixed into the upper corner of the room by two chunky screws. Bchind thc glass, a tiny red light flashed on and off — King counted a full second between each blink.

'Security camera,' he muttered.

He left the lodge and crossed the empty field of snow, heading for the watchtower. If his best guess was accurate, the footage might be collected on a bank of computers in the tower. He couldn't see any other use for the building. The camera would also likely be linked to the mine Sarah had briefly talked about — so that the leaders could keep an eye on the remote locations under their control.

On the way there, he considered the scope of his issues. He had no idea why the workers had been taken, or who had taken them. They were heavily armed and had over a dozen men at their disposal. If King was lucky, he had taken out most of their forces.

If not...

There were seven WHO workers left unaccounted for. All men, apparently. King was yet to find out what purpose they were serving.

He reached the tower and shimmied up a thin steel ladder that had been frozen over by the elements. It led to a narrow balcony with grated metal flooring running around the length of the room within. He found the nearest door — made of wood, thankfully — and smashed it open with three well-placed kicks to the space around the lock.

He stepped into a freezing cramped space packed with banks of electronic equipment. Cable management had been ignored entirely. Wires sprawled across the flimsy desks, twisted and knotted at random. Various power switches glowed softly in the lowlight.

Communications equipment, King guessed. So they could keep in touch with the others.

Whoever the others were…

He crossed to the nearest computer and booted it up. Electronics weren't his forte, but he thought he could manage.

He was presented with a home screen and set to work attempting to locate the security footage.

CHAPTER 28

Vadim Mikhailov arrived back at the gold mine in a fuming rage.

He jumped the snowmobile through the open warehouse door and ground it to a halt on the concrete floor. He ignored the skis grating against the ground underneath.

The vehicle could implode for all he cared.

He leapt off onto solid ground, heading for the elevator at breakneck speed.

If there's even the slightest chance that we're compromised…

The satellite phone at his waist started to vibrate, an incident which could only spell trouble given the nature of the individuals who had access to it. With fury tearing through him like liquid fire, he pulled the phone free and stared at the incoming number.

Shit, was all he could manage to think.

He answered, ensuring his voice remained neutral. 'Yes?'

'How are things proceeding?' a stern voice said.

'We're almost ready.'

'You were supposed to go live half an hour ago.'

'I know that.'

'I have heard that some of my colleagues are growing impatient. They need some entertainment.'

'And that's what we provide,' Mikhailov said. 'Now give us a moment. We'll have everything up and running shortly.'

'Why the delay?'

'I had to check on one of our outposts,' he said. 'They're responsible for maintaining the satellite dish on top of the mountain. So you can all tune in.'

'And?'

'Everything is good,' he lied. 'No problems at all.'

Mikhailov recalled watching each of the three women fall in turn. His pulse quickened in anger. He couldn't let word get out that an intruder was stalking the peninsula.

It would spell the death of him and everyone he knew.

'Then get moving,' the voice said. 'You know who's watching.'

'On it,' Mikhailov said.

He shut the phone off and slammed the door to the elevator cage open, letting it rattle on its hinges. His temple throbbed and his hands shook. He had selected the Kamchatka Peninsula as the location for this endeavour because of its sheer isolation. The fact that some kind of soldier had found their way into the region spelled disaster.

215

And located an outpost…

He still hadn't heard from the task force he'd sent to clean up the village. Twice he had tried to contact them, to no avail.

If the mystery man had truly taken them all out — and finished off his crew at the outpost — then he would be difficult to deal with.

He snatched up a rusty electronic remote attached to the side of the elevator and thumbed a large black button. An engine whirred and the steel cable suspending the elevator in the mine shaft began to unspool.

The warehouse disappeared as Mikhailov sunk into the earth.

As he paced back and forth impatiently across the cage — waiting to reach the sub-levels — an inkling of his past reared its head.

He knew what it was.

The concept of an enemy warrior in the region excited him, despite his best efforts to ignore the sensation.

It was a challenge.

He had not been challenged in quite some time.

This was what he was born to do. The business ventures that currently took up most of his waking hours did nothing to get his blood rushing. He missed the thrill of combat. He missed the feeling of beating another man into submission. He missed the sheer power and dominance that came from such a feat.

When the elevator slammed home at its first stop, Mikhailov shuffled out with a single resolution on his mind.

Let him come.

He hurried down a dark tunnel, passing uneven walls of sheer rock. The only light came from the other end of the path — a faint glow that emanated from somewhere far in the distance.

Mikhailov pulled up short of the tunnel's end, ducking into a side passage that ran through man-made corridors. He spotted a circular space that had been converted into a makeshift office and stepped inside.

Two men in khaki gear greeted him with silent nods. They sat at opposite ends of a cluster of trestle tables that had been erected in the centre of the room. Atop the workspace rested a spread of high-technology gadgetry that provided a wired landline connection to the warehouse above, which in turn connected to the satellite dish that Mikhailov's team had erected above the outpost a dozen miles away.

It gave them high-speed internet access six thousand feet below the surface. It had been incredibly costly, but paramount to his operation.

One of the men piped up. 'Boss, he's still there.'

'At the outpost?' Mikhailov said.

The guy nodded.

'So he really did kill all of them…'

'He's looking at the security footage as we speak.'

Mikhailov smiled. 'Good. That might anger him. I want to get inside his head. I was hoping he'd find it.'

'He's a big guy.'

'Do you have a live feed?'

The man nodded and gestured to the monitor in front of him. 'See for yourself.'

Mikhailov crossed the room and stopped behind the man's chair. He peered at the screen.

The enemy soldier sat in the outpost's watchtower, hunched over one of the desktop monitors, scrolling through a list of folders. An assault rifle rested against his chair. He seemed fixated on the task at hand.

'Does he know we're watching him?' Mikhailov said.

The man shook his head. 'Not a clue. It's taking him a long time to find the footage.'

'I made a gesture to the camera. Hopefully it provokes him.'

On the screen, Mikhailov noticed a landline phone resting on the desk near the soldier. He pointed to it. 'We have access to that?'

'Of course.'

'Wait for him to watch the footage,' Mikhailov said. 'Then I'll give him a call. The quicker we can goad him into coming after us, the better.'

The man threw a questioning glance over his shoulder. 'Are you sure? You've seen what he's done.'

'That's exactly why I want him here,' Mikhailov said. 'Consider it a personal challenge.'

'To take him out?'

'I want to break him.'

CHAPTER 29

It took King seven minutes.

He spent the majority of the time trawling through directories and sub-folders, all of which were labelled with a random combination of letters and numbers. When he finally stumbled across a folder of neatly-organised video logs, he opened several files until he found a grainy feed of the lodge's interior — timestamped to today's date.

He fast-forwarded through hours of the eight occupants sitting around playing card games and flicking through television channels. Around half an hour before he arrived at the outpost, five of the men abruptly left.

That was the search party, heading up the mountain to complete whatever task they had been delegated to carry out.

King realised he had stormed the outpost at the most opportune time possible.

Eight on one all at once would not have favoured him.

He saw himself on the screen. The two mercenaries died in a blaze of gunfire, and King watched himself shepherd the three women into the lodge in fast-motion.

Then he disappeared, and the trio were left alone in the room.

A pit formed in King's stomach. He knew what was coming.

He took his finger off fast-forward.

Even though the resolution left much to be desired and the footage had been recorded without audio, the fear was palpable. He watched Sarah and Carmen gather the handguns off the dead men. They both stared at the weapons like they were foreign objects.

The trio retreated to the back of the room and fidgeted restlessly. Their eyes were trained on the door.

A few minutes later, the door crashed off its hinges. A man stepped into the room — roughly the same size as King, measured in his movements. They had a noiseless conversation. King was oblivious to the topic.

Then Sarah raised her weapon and attempted to fire.

King bowed his head. She'd left the safety on. Carmen tried in turn, with equally dismal results.

The man in the doorway — hovering directly below the security camera — withdrew a handgun. He levelled the barrel at the three women and delivered a trio of clinical shots, one after the other.

All headshots.

All fatal.

First Sarah dropped, then Carmen, then Jessica. The man noted his handiwork and tucked the gun back into its holster. He turned and stared up at the camera.

As if he was aware that King was watching.

The face was sharply defined, with high cheekbones and a straight hairline. The man's hair was cut close to the skull — jet black in colour. The skin underneath one eye was twisted and mangled horrifically — an old scar, uncared for. His eyes were cold.

He sported a knowing smirk, keeping his gaze locked onto the security camera for a significant length of time. The man raised a hand toward the lens, palm facing away from it.

He beckoned with four fingers, inviting King to pursue him.

Then he left the lodge as abruptly as he had arrived, storming out into the night.

King sat in stunned silence, fully aware of the bait that the man had set. The guy knew the emotional reaction King was likely to have to the footage. He had preyed on that.

Staring into space, King tried to keep a level head. Objectively, he had no obligation to continue. Isla had sent him on a personal endeavour that had gone horrendously wrong. The reason for his presence in Russia — Isla's sister — was no longer a factor. Any action he took from this point onward would be entirely voluntary, which meant he would be acting as a rogue operative. If word got out of his actions, there would be hell to pay.

He now had full knowledge that the mission had no ties to the government he worked for.

If he continued, it was on him.

The landline phone on the desk beside him shrilled in its holder.

King jolted out of his stupor, shocked by the sudden burst of noise. He stared at the shrieking device. It couldn't be a coincidence.

Someone wanted to talk…

He lifted the phone to his ear, keeping his mouth shut. Despite his best efforts, his hand shook from a combination of anger and unease.

'I see you got my message,' a male voice said in accented English, deep and sinister in its tone.

'You're the one that killed them?' King said.

'Yes.'

'You know why I'm here?'

'I can guess. I've been trying to contact a few of my men. I'm having trouble.'

'They're dead. They're all dead. Every man you sent to the village, the three cops, all the people at this outpost.'

'I see.'

'You're trying to coax me into coming for you,' King said. 'Trying to get me to make mistakes. I see it.'

'I think I've succeeded,' the man said. 'I could hang up this phone right now and you would come after me. I can hear it in your voice. You're furious. And you are not very good at hiding it.'

King didn't respond.

'You are American. Did your government send you?'

King stayed quiet.

'You don't know who I work for,' the man said. 'This could have serious ramifications. An American should not be sniffing around in places he's not wanted.'

'Too bad.'

'You should have seen the looks on their faces when I killed them.'

King's fingers gripped the receiver tighter. His knuckles ran white. He ground his teeth together, riding out the wave of suppressed rage.

'So you want me to come after you?' he said. 'You'll have your men ready? That's what this is?'

The man laughed cruelly. 'It appears my men aren't very effective against you. I'll deal with you myself. It's been a while since I've been provoked.'

'I'm provoking you?'

'You've set me back, I won't lie. Over a dozen of my men are dead. Hard-working opportunists with combat experience. They busted their asses to make a good wage. So I'll take pleasure in killing you myself.'

'Where are you?'

'Head down to the forest and continue north. You'll pass between another pair of mountains. The mine is in the shadow of Shiveluch Volcano. You will not miss it.'

'What if I leave? I could send an entire battalion to clean things up.'

'You know the consequences of that,' the man said. 'You and I both do not want to start a third World War. That doesn't benefit anyone. You want to deal with this quietly. Get your men back and leave without anyone knowing. You think you can, too. I can tell. You're confident.'

'See you soon,' King said.

He slammed the phone back into its cradle and gathered up the carbine rifle by his side. There was nothing left to achieve at the outpost.

He had two options.

He could head south and organise a rendezvous with Isla to inform her of the devastating news and forget he had ever set foot in the Russian Far East. They would leave the disappearance of the health workers to the proper authorities, waiting until alarms were raised naturally.

But by then, he couldn't imagine what fate the remaining seven workers would have suffered.

Or he could head north, knowingly walking into the trap that had no doubt been set for him.

It was an easy decision. He had never willingly left innocent people to suffer. He would rather be dead than live with the knowledge that he'd abandoned them. So King clambered down the watchtower's ladder and headed for the same snowmobile he'd arrived on.

No duffel bag.

No supplies.

A M4A1 carbine assault rifle slung across one shoulder and two spare magazines in his breast pockets.

He swung a leg over the snowmobile and fired it up. He stared at the lodge one final time, where the three health workers lay dead.

They'd never provoked anyone.

He let the anger fuel him. Then he twisted the handlebars and began the precarious journey down the side of the mountain.

CHAPTER 30

By the time he made it to the forest floor, a storm had blown in from the east.

The canopy of branches above his head protected him from the worst of the weather. Torrential rain lashed against the treetops. It was the first downpour he had experienced in the region.

Isla had warned him of the weather's severity.

Water poured off the trees around him, soaking him to the bone in seconds. Lightning flashed intermittently in the sky above, followed by sharp cracks of thunder.

He steered the snowmobile through the darkness, squinting against the rainwater pouring down his face. He began to shiver uncontrollably. Tremors ran down his spine. He lost most of the feeling in his hands as they chilled underneath his gloves.

He went numb to the elements.

Teeth chattering, he burst out of the forest after five minutes of claustrophobic travel. The man on the other end of the phone had not been lying. Two mountains of similar height lay directly ahead. The valley between them was devoid of trees or vegetation. Rock formations dotted the landscape. The snowmobile's headlight pierced across the ground for a hundred feet, then faded into nothingness.

The dark landscape beckoned.

King felt real fear course through him. He grew hesitant, slowing the snowmobile to a crawl. Either his surroundings had unnerved him, or the sheer scale of the task at hand had begun to set in. It didn't matter either way. His own emotions had little to do with his actions. He had always managed to achieve that balance.

Selective attention to his own feelings.

An intense focus on what needed to be achieved.

He applied the throttle and pressed on, speeding across the open plain with icy wind buffeting his face and sheets of heavy rain flowing off him in rivulets.

Tune it out, he thought. *None of it matters.*

The mountains swallowed him up, filling his peripheral vision with two giant slopes ascending into the clouds.

The front skis hit a deep layer of rainwater that had flowed down from a nearby slope of rock. The rear tracks slid out, biting for purchase. King blanched as he fought for control, knowing that one wrong turn could prove fatal.

He made it through to the land beyond the mountains, growing acutely aware of his distance from civilisation. There was no-one to help him out here. Isla had no idea of his location. She had been tracking him via the GPS in the duffel bag — which now lay at the bottom of a cliff amongst the wreckage of a snowmobile.

He began to regret tossing the earpiece away with each passing second.

He roared out onto another desolate plain, this one dotted with patches of forest. It was too dark to make out exactly what lay ahead. In a landscape of this size, the sole headlight on the front of his vehicle showed just how insignificant he was amidst the peninsula.

A ripple of lightning flared on the horizon, silhouetting a mountain so enormous that King had trouble processing what he could see.

Shiveluch Volcano.

'Jesus Christ,' he whispered as the scale of the volcano dawned on him.

At its peak, it soared at least ten thousand feet into the air. Another lightning strike arced through the night sky and King realised the volcano was at least thirty miles in the distance. It dwarfed everything in sight, so gargantuan that King felt a distinct sense of panic in his chest. He pressed it down, ignoring the sensation.

He kept his eyes peeled for anything resembling a mine.

Twenty minutes later he came across the warehouse, constructed in the shadow of a towering cliff-face. It had clearly been abandoned years ago by those looking for resources in the earth. King couldn't imagine why anyone would construct a mine in such close proximity to an active volcano — which had likely been the reason for its desertion.

Greed, he thought.

He had seen enough of it for one lifetime. Men and women careless for their own safety or the safety of others. Those who were only interested in dollar signs. He reminisced to a brief period of his life he had spent in the backwoods of Australia.

Then Venezuela.

Then Corsica.

Then Egypt.

The adversaries he'd faced in each region all had one thing in common.

Greed.

A lust for money or power.

It came in many forms.

King approached the warehouse at a crawl, taking care not to rev his engine too hard at risk of attracting attention.

Not that it mattered — the storm drowned out all noises. There could be a horde of mercenaries firing on him and he would be none the wiser.

He disembarked the vehicle a few hundred feet away from the reinforced tin building, killing the engine between a cluster of trees. He landed in a thick layer of sludge — millions of gallons of falling rainwater had coagulated the snow, turning it to mush.

Approaching with stealth would not be on the agenda.

Another resonating *boom* of thunder tore through the sky, making him flinch. He powered through the muck, sloshing it away from him. There were a hundred feet of open space between his snowmobile and the warehouse. He kept low, running in a crouch across the flat stretch. He zigzagged wildly from left to right along the way.

Just in case they had night vision optics trained on him.

But he doubted it — for a number of reasons.

If his memory was correct, he had killed fourteen men — excluding the three corrupt police officers that had likely been paid off. Six at the town hall. Eight at the outpost. He couldn't imagine there would be dozens more to deal with. If there was, he would handle it, but even a mercenary force funded to the eyeballs had its limits. Employing more than twenty hired guns to stand around and do nothing was impractical and incredibly costly.

In a region this desolate, King guessed there were less than ten men left in the mine.

At least, he hoped.

The second factor was the man on the phone. The guy's tone had been laced with something close to excitement, something palpable and tangible. He wanted to deal with King himself. He had been invigorated by the challenge. Maybe the man had previously held a career very similar to King's. Spending his time holed up in an abandoned mine might have motivated him to seek out competition.

Or not.

Maybe they had fifteen weapons trained on him and all these thoughts bubbling in his head would soon cease to exist.

Heart pounding, he reached the front of the warehouse. A vast sliding door made of tin rested on weathered tracks.

Unlocked.

King gripped the handle with one hand and wrenched the door along its tracks, taking care to stay in its shadow. As soon as the door picked up momentum — grating as it slid — he let go and swept the barrel of the M4A1 around the corner.

He sliced the sights from left to right, clearing the space.

Empty.

He ducked inside the vast concrete space. Immediately the torrential downpour ceased, bombarding the roof of the warehouse instead. Water poured off him as he strode across the floor, running from his weapon, his clothing, his hair.

The chills set in.

The space was eerily quiet. Aside from an elevator shaft in the corner of the room, all the machinery had been stripped from the warehouse. The grooves and dents in the concrete floor signified heavy equipment that had rested in place for years.

'Where is everyone?' King muttered.

Still soaked to the core, he crossed to the mine cage and scrutinised it. It consisted of a rickety elevator made of steel, surrounded by a protective mesh cage. Beside the elevator, an enormous metal drum was fixed into the floor, connecting a thick suspension cable to the top of the elevator. He leant over the slim gap between the cage and the warehouse floor and peered straight down the mine shaft.

It descended into sheer blackness.

King wasn't one to get claustrophobic. If he did, he never would have been able to continue.

He stepped across the gap and dropped to one knee inside the elevator. It swayed slightly as he entered, which sent a bolt of terror down his spine. He wondered how long since it had received proper maintenance…

A chunky control remote dangled from a cord near the cage's entrance. King snatched it up and clutched it in a sweaty palm. There were only two buttons on the device. It had likely been installed for ease of use after the mining operation had ceased.

He stared at it. This was the point of no return. Whatever awaited below would not be pleasant. He still had the option to walk away. Once he was down there, there would be no turning back.

With the warehouse around him groaning as it was buffeted by howling winds and lashed by sheets of rain, King thumbed one of the buttons.

Gears whirred, and the cable unspooled.

With a jolt of motion, he descended into hell.

CHAPTER 31

The journey down felt like it would go on forever.

King kept the same position the entire time — his back pressed up to the opposite end of the elevator, his M4A1 trained directly on the cage doors ahead. As soon as he hit the bottom, the doors would fly open and it was anyone's guess what he would be faced with.

He was prepared for war.

He planned it out in his head. If he spotted hostiles waiting for him he would throw himself to the elevator floor, letting off three-round bursts until either he or his enemies died in a blaze of gunfire.

He fully expected for it to come down to a matter of milliseconds.

As the elevator sank further and further into the earth, the darkness wrapped around him. The only light came from a tiny flickering lightbulb swinging back and forth on the roof of the cage. King reversed the grip on his rifle and slammed the stock into the bulb, shattering the glass. It died out.

He had never experienced such sheer darkness. It was like going blind. He couldn't see his own hand in front of his face. The pressure in his ears built as he dropped thousands of feet below ground. They popped simultaneously after a few beats of sharp pain.

He retreated to the same position and lay in wait. It would prove an advantage when it came time for combat.

Then the cage shuddered. A moment later, it ground to a halt.

King heard the doors swing open.

He saw nothing. He heard nothing.

Sheer silence, and total darkness.

His heart felt like it would burst out of his chest at any second.

He let the silence reach an uncomfortable length. It unnerved him that there was no-one waiting for him. The mine was too quiet. This deep into the earth, all sounds of nature were non-existent.

No wind.

No rain.

No sun.

No wildlife.

Just rock and darkness.

He breathed as quietly as he could — yet even that felt like a freight train echoing off the walls. He shifted his hand on the rifle's trigger guard, which he swore he could hear echo off his surroundings.

Eventually, his eyes became accustomed to the dark. He picked up the faintest source of light somewhere far in the distance. Nothing visible, but there was a slightest glow emanating off rock walls a hundred feet ahead.

It was a tunnel.

That much he could make out.

The rest was a mystery.

It took him what felt like an hour to make any sort of movement. Time after time he psyched himself up to hurry forward, but the tension kept him from action. He feared that any sort of noise would blow his cover.

What cover?

He had been invited into the mine. He was charging into a slaughterhouse, relying on instincts and the enemy's underestimation of his skill-set to keep himself alive.

King scrambled to his feet. His footsteps felt like bombs going off in the tunnel, so loud and piercing against the silence that he flinched involuntarily, anticipating gunfire at any moment.

None came.

It felt like a horror-style video game — treading slowly down a dark path in search of hostiles, waiting for a jump scare. His heart thumped hard against his chest wall. Sweat broke out across his brow despite the chill.

He stepped out of the elevator cage and advanced into the mine.

His boots clattered against the rock, despite his best efforts to stay silent. After a moment of consideration, he decided to light the way ahead. He couldn't see a thing, and one wrong step could send him tumbling down a mine shaft.

In the darkness, his mind conjured all kinds of chilling images. Reaching out with a foot. Finding nothing but thin air. Overbalancing. Falling to a grisly death in the depths of the Russian Far East.

He shivered involuntarily and reached for the flashlight on the underside of his rifle's barrel.

It flooded the tunnel with artificial light, overwhelming in its intensity. It took a moment for his eyes to adjust — time which he spent acutely aware of the fact that he was impaired. Now was the opportunity to put a bullet through his skull.

Then he regained his vision and scouted the ground ahead for signs of life.

It was a narrow tunnel with uneven walls of sheer rock, spiralling away into the darkness. There were no secret hiding places that he could see. He took a deep breath, switched the light off, and plunged himself back into darkness.

He set off, moving fast.

The tunnel ran for at least two hundred feet, twisting and turning through the earth. King imagined the hard labour involved in creating it.

Greed knows no boundaries, he thought again.

The glow grew stronger. Ahead he spotted the tunnel opening out into some kind of cavernous area. This far away, it was hard to ascertain exactly what he was looking at.

He pressed on.

Crouching low, he realised what it was.

The ore zone that had been excavated in search of minerals was the size of a small office building. Six or seven storeys high, it was the centre point to a plethora of similar tunnels at different levels. A grated metal walkway met this particular tunnel, running around the cavern walls. The entire space was illuminated by harsh spotlights fixed into the ceiling.

From his position a dozen feet inside the tunnel, King couldn't see the majority of the space without exposing himself completely. He edged toward the walkway, barrel up, aiming at the space ahead.

Ready to react to the slightest sign of movement.

He heard something.

A whisper of movement.

Behind him.

So quiet and unnoticeable that he hesitated, unsure if his mind was playing tricks on him.

Then a sharp barrage of movement, all at once.

Rapid steps toward him.

He twisted at the waist, swinging the M4A1 one-hundred-and-eighty degrees, searching desperately for whatever had made the sound.

Too late.

CHAPTER 32

Powerful arms wrapped around him, spiking his heart rate. They squeezed tight in a crushing bear hug.

King bucked and writhed, to no avail. His arms were pinned to his side.

To do that to a man of his size and strength took considerable power.

He was lifted off his feet. One moment his boots were touching rock — the next they were suspended in mid-air.

He was helpless.

His attacker took two massive strides — carrying King's weight the entire time — then dropped him face-first towards the metal walkway outside the tunnel. King saw the grated flooring rushing at him.

He crashed into the steel.

Pain exploded across his face. He took the majority of the blow to his forehead, trying to avoid shattering his nose, knowing the consequences of such a debilitating injury. The result was his entire bodyweight — plus his attacker's —

driving into the floor. His chest hit the walkway next, wrenching the breath from his lungs.

Dealing with several waves of agony at the same time, King snatched for his rifle. It had been pinned awkwardly against his side by the crushing squeeze, and the impact with the walkway had knocked it away.

As he touched a finger to the stock, an enormous combat boot slammed down on the gun. In one motion the man kicked it off the edge of the walkway.

'*No weapons*,' he barked.

King scrambled desperately away from the man, putting distance between himself and another crushing blow. He righted himself, vision spinning.

Eyes blurring.

Head pounding.

The impact had done damage. He would find out shortly exactly how much.

His legs and arms felt weak. He stumbled to his feet, snatching at the thin railing running the length of the walkway. The other side was home to sheer rock wall. He got his boots underneath him and stared across the few feet of space between them.

'I didn't think it would be that easy,' the man said.

It was the guy on the phone. The same man King had seen on the security footage. He was far bigger in person, at least an inch taller than King and roughly twenty pounds heavier.

All muscle.

Zero fat to be seen.

He was dressed in a tight-fitting, long-sleeved compression shirt and loose khaki pants tucked into heavy combat boots similar to King's.

'I'm Vadim Mikhailov,' the guy said.

'Jason King.'

'Nice to know. Why did you come?'

'You took some people that I'm responsible for.'

'I did.'

'I need them back.'

'You're not getting them back.'

'Then I'll keep killing your men.'

'Oh...?'

With savage speed, Mikhailov covered the distance between them in a bull-rush, charging straight at King.

This time, King was ready.

He side-stepped, balling his right hand into a fist and slicing round with a right hook to the jaw. As soon as it connected against Mikhailov's chin, King followed up with a devastating knee to the solar plexus. Both blows slammed home hard enough to turn his limbs numb. The two impacts echoed off the surrounding walls.

Mikhailov rolled with the force of the strikes. He stumbled backwards and slammed into the rock wall.

King hesitated.

Then Mikhailov bounced off the wall like it was nothing and threw a right uppercut with unimaginable speed.

King saw the blur of movement and suddenly knuckles crashed against his chin. He barely had time to tense up before the punch connected. It took him off his feet. For the second time in the space of twenty seconds, he sprawled to the metal in a tangle of limbs, reeling from the blow.

The lower half of his face went numb from the power behind the shot. King quickly realised he had bitten his tongue in the process. He spat a glob of blood onto the walkway and clambered to his feet.

'This is good,' Mikhailov said, rolling his wrists in small circles, his fists balled. 'I haven't felt this in some time. I missed it.'

'You were a soldier?' King said, panting for breath.

He was buying time. He wondered if Mikhailov realised. The pain in his neck and jaw threatened to buckle him at the knees. He needed a moment to compose himself.

Thankfully, Mikhailov took the bait.

He shook his head. 'No. I worked for the government. But not a soldier.'

'A killer?'

'That's more like it. A one-man wrecking machine. I dealt with the trickiest problems. Took care of the most brutal tasks.'

Wonder who that reminds me of, King thought.

'It seems you are this man, too,' Mikhailov said, echoing his sentiments.

King shrugged. 'I think our governments are slightly different in the tasks we're elected to carry out.'

'I don't think so,' Mikhailov said. 'We are all murderers. It is all death.'

'It's not as black and white as that.'

Mikhailov raised an eyebrow. 'Ah, you think you are a noble man?'

'Not exactly.'

'You are nothing. If you think you are doing good, you don't know anything.'

'You're kidnapping health workers just trying to do their job,' King said. 'So you can take your advice and go fuck yourself with it.'

Mikhailov's eyes flared and he charged.

King braced for impact.

He rolled with the first blow, taking a staggering kick to the mid-section. It knocked the wind out of him but he caught

Mikhailov's shin and wrenched him forwards, pulling him into range.

Before he could throw a single punch in retaliation, Mikhailov snatched two handfuls of his jacket and head-butted him square in the nose.

King recoiled backwards as needles of fire punched into his brain. He didn't hear an audible crack. Best case scenario — nothing was broken. But the pain was undeniable, causing him to falter and release Mikhailov's leg.

The big brute capitalised on it.

A fist thundered into King's stomach, cracking against his skin like a whip. He spluttered. The next punch hit him in the throat with pinpoint accuracy just as he went for a breath of air. He recoiled again, now completely on the defensive, stumbling in a blur of agony away from Mikhailov.

He couldn't come back from this.

He knew that.

Fear shot through him — the kind of fear that didn't strike him often. It was the realisation that nothing he could do would get him out of this situation. He had to run if he wanted to survive. He couldn't beat this man in combat.

He had to level the playing field.

He surged down the walkway, ready to take off at a sprint.

Just before he was about to run, a powerful hand seized him by the side of the neck. It wrenched him back, playing with him like he was nothing.

Panic struck him.

'Where do you think you're going?' Mikhailov said. 'Trying to give up already?'

King had no more time for words. He wasn't even sure if they would come out properly — given the strikes he had taken to the torso. Instead he scrambled for air. He twisted at the waist and thundered a fist into Mikhailov's side.

The man swatted it away like it was an irritating fly.

He seized King by the collar and tugged him forward so they were face-to-face. King saw rage in the man's eyes. Anger that he would still bother to attempt more punches.

'You throw one more strike and I'll—'

King pushed away and kicked out, sending the heel of his combat boot scything through the air. It crashed into Mikhailov's stomach hard enough to wind him. The big man doubled over, clearly in significant pain.

It was the first external response King had seen to his own strikes.

It lent him a burst of motivation.

In hindsight, he should have realised it had provided him with a window of opportunity. He could have fled down one of the tunnels, retreating into the depths of the mine to regroup and recharge.

But he didn't.

He couldn't remember the last time he had come up short in a hand-to-hand fight — apart from a brawl in a Corsican airport with none other than Will Slater.

Surely you're just off your game…

So he surged into Mikhailov's range, taking advantage of the pain the man was suffering.

As soon as he closed the distance he understood the gravity of his mistake.

Mikhailov lurched up, teeth bared like a rabid dog, angrier than King had ever seen a man. He bundled King into the wall and locked two hands behind his head, embracing him in a traditional Muay Thai clinch. King was trapped in place by Mikhailov's grip strength. He couldn't move.

He sucked in a sharp breath of air and prepared himself for what would inevitably follow.

Muay Thai fighters specialised in delivering vicious knees to the body and head while keeping their opponents locked in a clinch. Mikhailov obviously had years of training in the martial art, because he snapped three knees into King's mid-section in rapid fashion. Each had technique and accuracy and horrendous raw power behind them.

The knees felt like baseball bats slamming into him.

King buckled under the first strike. The second sent unimaginable pain tearing through his body. He crossed his arms over his stomach to protect from the third.

Big mistake.

The point of Mikhailov's kneecap crunched into King's left wrist hard enough to break it. He heard the clear *snap* above the chaos of the fight. Instantly, he went pale.

Mikhailov heard it too. He let go of the clinch and darted out of range, intent on assessing the damage. He eyed King's left hand, now dangling uselessly by his side.

King began to hyperventilate, shocked by the intensity of the agony. Hot liquid fire arced up his forearm and through his shoulder, incapacitating his entire range of movement.

'I think we're done here,' Mikhailov said.

He snatched two handfuls of King's jacket and hauled him to the edge of the walkway. King's stomach dropped in terror, but there was nothing he could do. Mikhailov manhandled him like a child. The pain had paralysed him. From his nose, his wrist, his stomach, his lungs, his neck.

Everything burnt.

And it seemed it was about to get a whole lot worse.

He threw a last-ditch punch, swinging for the fences, throwing technique out the window. He knew that if he put all his power into it, he could shut Mikhailov's lights out. He had to connect in just the right place.

His fist scythed through the air.

Mikhailov leant away from the blow, almost nonchalant in his demeanour.

The punch went whistling past his throat.

The man smirked, impressed by King's attempts.

'You're trying so hard,' he said. 'It's almost sad.'

He continued dragging King over to the railing. King stumbled along, trying to keep his balance in the process. They stopped by the edge of the walkway and he got his first proper look at the cavern.

Similar walkways were fixed into the rock at various heights across the space. King spotted one a couple of dozen feet directly below, connecting to a handful of tunnels — all identical to the one he had come through.

The cavern floor stretched at least a hundred feet deeper into the earth. It was well-lit. It seemed every floodlight in the space was aimed at the ground. The surface had been smoothed completely flat.

King thought he saw blood smeared on the rock…

'Like the place?' Mikhailov said. 'Pity you won't get to see what we do here. You're going over in three seconds.'

King mumbled something through bloody teeth.

Mikhailov inclined his head ever so slightly. 'What?'

'I said…' King muttered. 'I know I am.'

He threw a head-butt with such intensity that he briefly considered the ramifications of knocking himself unconscious with it. His forehead hit Mikhailov's chin in *exactly* the right place. Blood spurted from his mouth. A couple of the man's teeth were knocked loose.

King followed it up with a brutal kick to the groin, planting the toe of his boot square between Mikhailov's legs.

He knew the strikes would not put the man down. Mikhailov was seemingly made of titanium, immune to even King's most devastating shots.

But it bought him a second.

Mikhailov shrank away, startled by his injured jaw and the emasculating blow to his privates. King felt the energy leeching from his bones. He had put everything into the actions. He couldn't attack with anything else.

There was nothing left in the tank.

So he threw caution to the wind and dove over the railing — into a hundred feet of empty space.

CHAPTER 33

King's stomach fell into his feet for a tenth of a second.

Then he snatched out and gripped the edge of the walkway at the last second. At two hundred and twenty pounds, he would never have been able to hold on for an extended period of time with a couple of fingers — but he used the momentum of the brief grip to change his direction slightly in the air.

He swung like a monkey, letting go after a half-second of effort.

He dropped — now falling towards the walkway below.

He grimaced. It would come down to a matter of inches.

He landed feet-first on the thin sliver of railing at the very edge of the lower walkway, crashing into the metal at breakneck speed. He teetered backwards. Momentum threatened to tip him over the edge. Then all his effort would have been for nothing.

At the last second he reversed direction, toppling forwards onto the walkway.

'*Kill him!*' Mikhailov roared from above.

King landed in a heap on the metal. He kept his broken wrist pinned against his stomach, absorbing the landing with the rest of his body. Any further aggravation to the snapped bone would make his legs buckle. He couldn't afford that.

A piercing *clang* resonated near his head, shockingly loud. It was accompanied by the striking flare of metal against metal. His heart leapt and he rolled away from the source.

Bullets.

He continued the barrel roll, aiming for the mouth of the tunnel drilled into the rock. A volley of bullets lit up the walkway around him. Several struck the railing nearby. But he remained a moving target, never staying stationary, always on the move. He reached the tunnel and threw himself undercover, his pulse pounding with each new round of ammunition that struck around him.

He couldn't have been on the walkway for more than a couple of seconds.

When under enemy fire, time always seemed to slow down.

More rounds slammed into the metal grating in front of him as he scooted back into darkness. When he was sure that he had retreated far enough into the tunnel, he slumped back against the wall and forced his breathing back under control.

It wouldn't take much to induce a panic attack. He was somewhere in the sub-levels of an abandoned gold mine, unarmed, badly injured, with no light source of any kind to direct him.

Worse, he was surrounded on all sides by Mikhailov's thugs, all of who were heavily armed.

You've been in worse situations, his subconscious told him.

The gunfire ceased. King heard movement on the walkways above. Loud footsteps echoing off the metal. Everything went quiet.

'Come out, King,' Mikhailov called, his deep voice resonating through the cavern. 'You're only drawing this out.'

Clutching his useless left hand to stabilise it, King got to his feet and strode down the tunnel, heading away from the walkway. His surroundings grew steadily darker, until the same blackness enveloped him. He reached out with his right hand and drifted it along the smooth rock wall, guiding himself by touch alone. All sounds of commotion from the cavern faded away.

The lack of vision concentrated all his focus on the pain — something he had been struggling to suppress. It rolled over him in increasingly nauseating waves, twisting his stomach. He paused in the middle of the tunnel as his gag reflex triggered. He vomited what little food he had left in his stomach, taking care to keep as quiet as possible.

A cold sweat broke out across his brow, and his hands began to tremble. He battled the sensations down and pressed on.

The tunnel ended after roughly a hundred feet, coming to a T-junction. He opted to head left, keeping his paces measured and his right hand pressed firmly against the wall at all times.

He walked for what felt like an eternity. In the darkness he lost all sense of time, focusing on nothing but putting his feet in front of him and tuning out the crippling agony in his wrist and neck. The rock floor began to slope steadily downwards. He had no other way to head, so he continued, concentrating hard on keeping his balance.

Finally, he sensed a shift in his vision. The same faint glow of artificial light glimmered somewhere in the distance.

He was heading back to the cavern.

He kept low, listening out for any sign of one of Mikhailov's men. Barely audible echoes drifted down from far above. As far as he could tell, there was no-one nearby.

He dropped — lying prone — and crawled to the source of light.

This tunnel ended in empty space. There was no walkway to exit onto — just a sheer drop to the cavern floor below. Thankfully the mouth of the tunnel was shrouded in shadow, so King could inch up to the edge without being spotted by any onlookers.

He scanned the walkways on the opposite side of the cavern, and realised there were none.

He peered out at what he could see.

From here, he had an unobstructed view over the cavern floor. Floodlights far above were trained on the flat stretch of rock. Above and below, walkways twisted around the uneven rock walls. The entire cavern was shaped like a cylinder, like a viewing platform for whatever took place on the ground.

Then King noticed the cameras.

There were at least five of them, fixed into the curved walls at different heights. None were more than twenty feet off the ground. They were high-end setups, all aimed directly at the cavern floor. Thick cables snaked up the rock behind them.

There was movement below, at the edge of King's peripheral vision. He wheeled his gaze off the cameras and saw Mikhailov stride through an open steel door at ground level. He had cleaned up — the blood around his mouth had vanished and he had clearly splashed his face with water. He looked as good as new.

A man in ripped jeans and a black hooded sweatshirt followed him. He had thin receding hair and a pale complexion. The guy stood out in contrast to the beefed-up mercenaries in tactical gear.

They spoke in low tones, but the sound carried in the dead quiet.

The man in the jumper spoke first, his accent distinctly British. 'We're incredibly late.'

'I know,' Mikhailov muttered. 'We're dealing with a problem, in case you didn't notice.'

'Why didn't you just shoot him?'

'I will now.'

'Do they know of the problem?'

'The viewers?'

The other man nodded slowly.

Mikhailov shook his head. 'They would kill me if they knew there was the slightest chance of being compromised.'

'So what do we do?'

Mikhailov lifted his gaze, sweeping it across the cavern. King shrank into the shadows, hoping he wasn't spotted.

'We get on with the show,' Mikhailov said. 'My men are dealing with the problem. He's hurt bad — I broke his wrist and knocked him semi-conscious. He won't be in any condition to interfere.'

'Okay,' the guy said, cracking his neck by rolling his head from side to side. 'Stream's going live in thirty seconds, then. You ready?'

'We've done this enough times,' Mikhailov said. 'I know how it works.'

'You don't get nervous? You know who's watching.'

Mikhailov turned and regarded the man with contempt. 'I used to kill people for a living. Get the fucking stream going before we make them even angrier.'

The hooded guy scurried back through the steel door. Mikhailov stood patiently in the centre of the floor, hands clasped behind his back, unblinking. King noticed the intense calm of his demeanour. It seemed as if nothing would faze him. It was unnoticeable that he had been in a life-or-death fistfight minutes previously.

King lay on the cold rock, his heart thumping, waiting for the cameras to go live.

For what? he thought.

An audible alarm blasted out of hidden speakers, harsh and digital.

Mikhailov turned to face the cameras.

The stream had begun.

CHAPTER 34

'Welcome,' Mikhailov said.

He wasn't yelling, but his voice seemed to amplify effortlessly, resonating through the cavern like it was coming from an artificial source. King grimaced as a particularly intense needle of pain sliced through his wrist. He wiped sweat off his brow and focused on the scene below.

'As always, I'm speaking in English upon request of the highest-paying party,' Mikhailov said. 'We provide translations into seven different languages along the menu bar. Switch audio feeds at your own leisure.'

He paused for effect, allowing time for the viewers to adjust. As he spoke, he turned methodically from camera to camera, focusing on each lens for an interval of time.

He's a professional, King noted.

'We have three events tonight with the typical tiered pricing structure in place. You have all browsed the catalogue and made your purchases. Before we get things underway, I'll recommend the final event to you once again. We don't often get seven young, healthy men at the same time. There will be two preliminary bouts, then a five-man free-for-all with the three remaining contestants and the winners of the two early bouts.'

'Oh, no,' King whispered. 'No, no, no. *Fuck...*'

'I apologise for the late start tonight,' Mikhailov said. 'I know you're all eagerly anticipating some bloodshed. I won't delay it any longer.'

King went pale. He hadn't anticipated such a brutal situation. An underground fight ring, where innocent hostages were pitted against each other to satiate the needs of the viewers. Hence the remote location. Hence the outpost halfway up the side of a mountain — likely responsible for maintaining a secure connection for the live stream.

But he feared there was more to the operation than just a fight...

Mikhailov turned to the cameras again. 'Now, I know much of the appeal comes from the fear. So — as usual — none of the participants know what they're in for. You can follow along as I enlighten them.'

He spun on his heel.

'Bring the first two in,' he commanded.

Two mercenaries in balaclavas and khaki tactical gear herded two of the health workers through the steel door.

It was the first time King had seen them.

They were in bad shape — and rightfully so. Fear was eating them alive. They were both deathly pale and gaunt, with hollow, sunken eyes and chattering teeth. Their gazes flicked around the cavern at an incredible rate, trying to take in everything at once. They both raised a hand in unison to shield their eyes from the stark lighting.

The mercenaries slapped their arms away and threw them to the floor.

The pair of thugs retreated back the way they had come.

Mikhailov smirked knowingly at the cameras, then crouched between the two civilians. He turned to the man on the left — a tall, lanky man with thick blond hair and an athletic build.

'This is Eli,' Mikhailov roared.

Eli jolted, shocked by the volume of his tone. He stared up at Mikhailov with wide eyes. 'Please, man…'

Australian, King noted.

'Eli looks like he has a mean streak,' Mikhailov said. 'He could be the favourite here.'

He turned to the second man — shorter, chubbier, with a long flowing mane of black hair spilling down his back. This guy was equally terrified.

'I'm told this is Seth,' Mikhailov yelled. 'They work for the World Health Organisation. We snatched them not too far from here, as it happened. What a stroke of luck.'

Mikhailov looked away from the cameras and focused on the man on either side of him. He dropped to one knee, bringing himself closer to them.

'Eli and Seth,' Mikhailov said. 'You are both scared. You both want to go home.'

The pair slowly nodded, as if cautious of being baited.

'Well, good news!' Mikhailov said. 'One of you gets to go home. Can you imagine it? Leaving this terrible place behind. Returning to your families. Hugging them tight. Promising to never find yourself in a situation like this again. To take greater care when you wander into places you're not wanted. That would be nice, wouldn't it?'

Neither man responded, but even from three storeys above King could see the glint in their eyes. The hope. They had probably never been in trouble in their lives. Good people with good intentions, focused on making the world a better place by helping those who needed it the most.

Health workers.

Decent humans.

Good men who now lay shivering on the cold floor of a deserted gold mine, held against their will by a party of Russian mercenaries.

King couldn't imagine how badly they wanted to put it all behind them.

Mikhailov got to his feet. He pointed at each man in turn.

'The only person stopping you from going home is the one across from you,' he said. 'You two will fight to the death. When I'm sure that one of you no longer has a pulse, the other will be released.'

Neither man responded.

'No-one will ever know what you did.'

Silence.

'If you refuse, I will kill you both right now.'

Mikhailov took a sleek, jet-black handgun out of its holster and held it at the ready, poised by one side. King recognised the make. It was a MP-443 Grach.

Mikhailov took a step back and waited.

Seth and Eli let their gaze settle on each other. They were both shell-shocked. A tense silence settled over the cavern. King heard a creak above him. He glanced up to see a group of mercenaries on the walkway directly above, watching the scene below intently.

'Seth, no…' Eli muttered.

Seth said nothing. He stared at Mikhailov, then at Eli. Back and forth. Again and again. Frozen like a deer in headlights.

Seth's fingers twitched. He started to move.

'*Don't,*' Eli said. 'Don't make me fight back, man. We're better than this.'

All the colour had drained from both their faces. Seth got to his feet. He balled his fists and clenched his teeth.

King had seen enough.

It didn't matter what the extent of his injuries were. He had to put a stop to this before one man lay dead and the other was scarred for life. He didn't care if he died in the process.

He couldn't let this unfold.

It was so sick and twisted that he felt like fainting.

He shrank a step back into the mine, wondering how he could throw Mikhailov off.

Then he had an idea. The man been terrified of his audience discovering that there was trouble afoot. Perhaps there were personal details stored on hard drives in the mine. Details that would cost careers and lives. If a rogue agent managed to get his hands on them…

'*Mikhailov!*' King roared at the top of his lungs. It tore through the cavern, freezing everyone in place. He kept to the shadows and put on his best Russian accent. 'All our men are dead! The American killed them! He's looking through the computers!'

Mikhailov would identify the ruse in an instant.

But his viewers wouldn't.

As it was a live stream, King imagined there was no tape delay. The audio would have reached them — whoever they were. They would know that something was awry.

Hidden inside the mouth of the tunnel, King had no view of Mikhailov's reaction. Hopefully, the man was shitting his pants.

King turned and sprinted back into the depths of the sub-levels.

CHAPTER 35

This time, the blind fumbling proved easier to stomach. King had spent enough time without vision in the claustrophobic tunnels to have grown somewhat used to the sensation.

He followed a trail through the maze of sub-levels, ignoring the voice in the back of his head that warned him not to get lost.

Dying of starvation, unable to find his bearings, clawing at the walls.

The idea sent shivers down his spine.

He moved methodically, retreating when he noticed the ground ascending. Reaching the ground floor was top priority. There, he could improvise.

They were storing the prisoners somewhere on that level.

That was all he needed to know.

Some time later, just when he thought he might have to backtrack and concede defeat for now, his right hand struck something fixed into the wall.

A door.

He ran his hand silently along the steel. It was the first man-made structure he had come across inside the mine, having grown so accustomed to the smooth rock against his palm that the texture made him jolt in surprise. A thin line of yellow light filtered underneath the door, barely perceptible.

He paused and listened.

Nothing audible came from the other side. For all he knew, he could be walking into a death trap. He fully expected to meet a cluster of automatic weapons on the other side, all aimed at his head.

Instincts.

He reached for the handle, wrenched the door open and powered into the room.

His eyes adjusted to the light faster, now used to alternating between total darkness and harsh artificial bulbs. He had entered some kind of production room at ground level, dimly lit by overhead LEDs. Across one wall, a long pane of one-way bulletproof glass faced out across the cavern floor, providing an unimpeded view of what took place in the makeshift arena.

The production room housed an array of slim computer monitors — each connected to a separate camera feed. Papers and folders were strewn across the desks. It was a mess.

There were two men in the room. A bald tattooed mercenary in a tattered singlet faced away from the door, in the process of opening a cabinet. The British guy with the receding hair that King had seen earlier was hunched over the monitors, scrutinising the different camera feeds. He had obviously been taken by surprise by the pause in the action after King's outburst.

This would take him by surprise even more.

King darted around the cluster of tables in the centre of the room and smashed a boot into the small of the mercenary's back. The guy hadn't been expecting anything. He careered into the metal cabinet face-first, breaking his nose on the hard surface.

King followed up immediately with a right hook from behind. His fist swung around the side of the mercenary's head and crunched his chin, snapping his neck around.

Lights out.

The guy dropped, taking out one of the flimsy tables in the process. The explosion of noise caused the British guy to scramble out of his seat, terrified into action by the commotion.

King imagined the man was there as a production assistant as opposed to muscle. In fact, it seemed like the guy had never been in a fight in his life. He froze like a deer in the headlights when he saw King.

King despised him immediately.

The guy was a coward — only used to watching the terror from afar.

King noticed an identical MP-443 Grach handgun on the table between them.

'That yours?' he said.

The British guy faltered.

'For your own protection?' King said.

No response.

'You were probably too distracted by what was going on out there,' King said. 'Weren't expecting me to come charging in. Thought you were safe?'

The provocation got to the man. He squirmed on the spot, visibly sweating. His face had turned pale. A thin sheen of perspiration coated his features.

'Do it,' King said. 'Give it your best shot.'

The guy took the bait. He tensed up like a coiled spring, his intentions so obvious that he might as well have held up a sign announcing his next move. He made a dive for the pistol, feet slipping on the cold floor as he did so.

King pounced, snatching the gun off the table a moment before the British guy got to it. As soon as he had control of the weapon the man dropped to his knees. He spread his palms wide and tucked them behind his head, effectively surrendering before King could shoot him.

King didn't care.

The thought of the man organising dozens of fights to the death and watching in glee from this sheltered production room made him sick. He evidently had no concern for the lives he had ruined. Mikhailov was likely paying him a large salary to ensure the live stream operated smoothly.

King flicked the safety off the weapon and shot the man through the top of the head.

A quick death.

The guy had been staring at the floor, unaware of what was coming. Merciful, all things considered. The guy deserved to suffer the same fate as the innocent civilians he had watched beat each other to a bloody pulp for however long this operation had been going on for.

Consider yourself lucky, King thought.

Now alone in the production room, he looked through the pane of one-way glass for the first time, taking in the view of the cavern floor.

His stomach fell.

There was no sign of Mikhailov. Instead, two bodies lay motionless in the centre of the space. Their heads rested in bloody pools, sharply illuminated by the floodlights trained on the ground.

Seth and Eli.

Mikhailov had opted to gun them down instead of letting the fight play out. King's attempt at an intervention must have unnerved the man. Instead of shepherding the two prisoners into a locked room and saving their fight for later, he had disposed of them. Mikhailov was likely stalking the tunnels of the mine with his thugs, searching desperately for King before he could ruin their production any more.

King didn't move. He watched the pair of corpses for a long time, hoping for some sign of life. The floodlights infuriated him. Their bright glow stripped the dead men of their dignity, exposing them in stark detail to the viewers on the other end of the cameras.

Unable to suppress it, King felt anger rising in his chest. He hoped Mikhailov came for him. Even with a broken wrist and a spinning head, he wanted nothing more than to get his hands on the man. Mikhailov was ruthless.

King would do whatever it took to eliminate him before he could lay a finger on the other five hostages.

He would not let this operation become a total failure.

Charged with a newfound energy, he turned his attention to the bank of monitors in front of him. Each displayed a different angle of the two corpses — some had wider lenses, some were zoomed right up to their bloody features. King spotted the cylindrical bullet hole in the side of each man's skull.

He hoped they hadn't started to fight before Mikhailov shot them down. He hoped they had kept their dignity. The dehumanisation of being forced to kill a friend would have been horrendous.

He heard something.

A footstep.

The scuffle of heel on rock.

It echoed faintly in through the open doorway, floating down from the tunnel beyond. King saw the faint white shimmer of a distant flashlight. He skirted to the doorway and pressed himself against the rock wall, listening intently.

The shuffle of bodies became clearer. There was a search party heading for the production room. They were trying to stay silent, but King heard everything.

They would have been drawn to the sound of unsuppressed gunshots.

Surprisingly, King's heart rate calmed.

He was outnumbered, with no idea as to how many men were approaching, or how heavily armed they were. One of his arms was completely useless, and his vision swam from a pounding headache behind his eyes.

But none of that mattered. He glanced down at the MP-443 Grach in his hand.

He had a gun.

CHAPTER 36

Determination took over. His veins turned to ice. The fog of incoherence lifted momentarily as his reflexes sharpened and his instincts heightened.

He adjusted his grip on the handgun and held his breath.

There were three men approaching. He singled out their footsteps in turn, paying attention to every sliver of audible noise. Two of them advanced rapidly, hustling towards his position. There was the faint scuffle of a third man a few feet behind, taking up the rear of the party.

An inverted triangle, all with their guns trained on the door, no doubt.

King glanced at the lifeless body of the British tech guy. He was slim, and short. King estimated his bodyweight at somewhere around one-hundred-and-sixty pounds.

Manageable.

Taking care not to grunt from the pain, he switched hands with the MP-443, cradling it delicately in his swollen left palm. Ignoring the throbbing, he silently crept over to the corpse and wrapped the fingers of his good hand around the back of the guy's shirt.

With two bounding steps and a heave of exertion, he tossed the limp body through the open doorway.

Having only died minutes previously, rigor mortis had yet to set in. The corpse slapped into the opposite wall of the tunnel in a tangle of gangly limbs. King heard two sharp intakes of breath in unison, followed by a barrage of unsuppressed gunfire a half-second later. As he suspected, the reaction speed and professionalism of the mercenaries had dulled after so much time spent in isolation, without regular training.

They'd twitched and jumped at the first sign of life.

King switched the Grach back to his good hand and leant round the doorway, using the muzzle flare from the panicked rifle bursts to identify the two silhouettes in the dark tunnel. He spotted the pair of hulking forms, which was all that was required in the confined space.

As the tunnel plunged back into darkness he fired four shots, clinical and measured.

Tap-tap, tap-tap.

Then he ducked back into the production room, avoiding any potential retaliation.

He heard two bodies thump into the hard rock.

If his hearing was correct, there was still one man left to dispatch. He crouched low — heart now pounding in his chest — training the MP-443 Grach on the doorway. He hoped the last man would come charging in foolishly. He'd lost count of the number of times his enemies had let their adrenalin take over, which always culminated in mistakes.

That turned out not to be the case.

'*Jason,*' a deep voice boomed, resonating in from the tunnel. 'You're causing me a lot of trouble.'

Mikhailov.

The man's tone had been affected by his damaged jaw, which he had covered up impeccably whilst hosting the live stream. Now his voice sounded stuffy and laboured. Perhaps his mouth was beginning to swell.

'I'm giving you five seconds to give yourself up,' Mikhailov said. 'Or I'll leave and murder the other five men — just like I did to Seth and Eli. You don't want that, do you?'

King stayed quiet.

His mind whirred, racing through the options available. Without a doubt, Mikhailov had an automatic weapon fixed on the doorway, ready to fire the second King stepped through. He quickly crossed off a list of ideas.

He would lose a stand-off — that much was certain. Mikhailov had more than proven himself as an elite combat operative, and King imagined that the man had retained all the weapons training of his past. That put them on roughly equal footing — and in that case, an automatic rifle beat a handgun nine times out of ten.

'Five,' Mikhailov said, initiating a countdown.

King turned, surveying the room. There were no other weapons visible — nothing to give him the advantage he so desperately needed. Aside from erecting a barricade of overturned furniture, he couldn't figure out a way to gain the upper hand.

Perhaps it would have to come down to a matter of reflexes.

'Four.'

Ordinarily, he had full faith in his ability to react faster than anyone else.

Here, he wasn't so sure.

The beating he had suffered on the walkway made him hesitate. It was a mental barrier, plaguing him with doubt. He felt slow. Sluggish.

'Three.'

By the cabinet on the opposite wall, King picked up a tremor of movement. It was barely noticeable, but his eyes darted to it.

The thug he'd knocked unconscious had stirred. King knew a devastating concussion when he saw one, and this man had been on the receiving end of an expertly-placed strike. He would have a headache for the next few days, and long-term effects for up to six months. One of his hands resting on the rock floor twitched slightly, the muscles seizing as he surfaced from unconsciousness.

Then the man's head lifted off the ground.

His eyes were half-closed and his head dipped and rose with each breath. He wasn't fully aware of his surroundings, locked in a semi-conscious state as his senses returned.

'Two.'

King sensed an opportunity.

He skirted across the room, keeping low, making as little noise as he possibly could. Without a word he hauled the mercenary to his feet. The guy obeyed silently, too disoriented to be fully aware of his surroundings. King looped an arm around the guy's back to stabilise him and helped him stumble towards the doorway.

'One.'

'Coming out now,' King said. 'Just don't hurt my friends.'

Mikhailov laughed cruelly. 'I'll do whatever I want to them. Two of them are lying dead in the arena. I'm sure you saw that. How did that make you—?'

At that moment, King disentangled himself from the mercenary and thrust the guy forward. Barely conscious, the man stumbled through into the tunnel beyond. He hadn't a clue as to his location. The guy swayed off-balance and walked blindly in the direction of Mikhailov's voice.

King followed him out.

In the lowlight, confusion reigned. Mikhailov would see the man stumble out of the doorway, but it would take him a second to register his identity. With the only artificial light coming from the production room, everyone who exited was backlit by the glow.

Just a black silhouette against a bright background.

King sprawled stomach-first across the ground behind the mercenary. He raised the MP-443 Grach to aim between the semi-conscious guy's legs and fired six times down the tunnel, unloading the clip. He only had a second or two of hesitation to capitalise on, so he opted to use all the ammunition he had in hopes of succeeding.

All or nothing.

Mikhailov grunted audibly and King heard his boots slide out on the rock. He had been thrown backwards by whichever rounds had slammed home.

King wasted no time. If Mikhailov wasn't dead, he was still dangerous.

King scrambled to his feet and charged down the tunnel. The mercenary had ducked his head as the gunfire tore through the space around him. He'd frozen in place, still not cognitive, terrified by the loud outburst of light and sound.

King dropped his shoulder and smashed into the back of the guy, throwing him forward off his feet. The man came down awkwardly on top of Mikhailov. King couldn't see much, but he heard a low curse as Mikhailov found himself pinned to the tunnel floor.

King followed the mercenary down, crushing Mikhailov's weight under another body. The point of the manoeuvre was to pin the man's arms down, preventing any last-ditch efforts to squeeze off return fire. King heard Mikhailov struggling against the deadweight on top of him, desperately trying to wrench his weapon free.

By sound alone, King located Mikhailov's rifle.

He reached down, letting go of his handgun and tossing it behind him in the process. Suddenly vulnerable, he snatched at the assault rifle, wrapping his good hand around the gun's stock. He wrenched with primal energy, tearing it free from Mikhailov's grip.

He threw that behind him too, eliminating all weapons from the equation.

Silence settled over the tunnel.

King got to his feet and hurled the mercenary aside. The dazed man collapsed in a heap on one side of the tunnel, unmoving.

Mikhailov lay on the tunnel floor, panting heavily. The extent of his wounds were unclear. King couldn't see much in the lowlight. He hauled Mikhailov to his feet and hustled him into the production room.

With a single heave, he dumped the man onto the cluster of tables in the centre of the room. Mikhailov offered no resistance. The big man slammed onto the table back-first and lay still, his chest rising and falling in rasping gasps of air.

King slammed the door behind him and breathed a sigh of relief.

He had succeeded.

CHAPTER 37

In the stark lighting of the production room, King had a clear view of Mikhailov's injures.

The 9mm Parabellum bullets had riddled his body. King had fired six shots in total. Two were embedded in the bulletproof vest draped over the man's long-sleeved shirt — clearly a precautionary measure thrown on by Mikhailov before he set off in search of King. These rounds would have winded him, possibly breaking a rib if they struck in the right place.

A third round had torn a chunk out of his left bicep. The wound bled profusely across the table. His lower arm and left hand dangled uselessly. Nerves had been severed. A fourth bullet had grazed the side of his head, coming within an inch of taking the top of his skull off. His hair was matted to his forehead, coated in blood.

Finally, a fifth had struck him in the collar bone — just above the top lining of the bulletproof vest. That wound also poured blood.

The sixth shot had missed.

King admired his handiwork. Despite the tight confines of the tunnel, his instinctive sense of where Mikhailov was likely to be positioned had paid off. The man would cause him no more trouble.

Mikhailov's dark skin had turned pale around his cheeks and forehead. Sweat broke out across his brow. His eyes were wide and dilated, riding out the waves of pain that would no doubt be tearing through his system. His jaw had already started to swell from the head-butt earlier.

'Should have killed me when we first met,' King said. 'You had the chance.'

Mikhailov gazed at him with contempt. 'I thought it would be...'

'Easier?'

A nod.

'You don't know how many times I've heard that,' King said. 'You had the upper hand, though. I won't lie — that terrified me.'

Mikhailov smiled half-heartedly, then his features dissolved into a grimace. When he composed himself, he said, 'That's what I missed. That feeling of control.'

King regarded him now, lying pathetically amidst a rapidly-expanding pool of blood. 'Didn't really work out for you, did it?'

The man shrugged. 'You won't fare any better.'

'I think I just did.'

Mikhailov laughed — a scornful cackle that resonated through the production room. 'You think?'

King paused. 'I'd say you only have a couple of men left down here. They won't be much of a problem.'

'It's not my men that amuse me,' Mikhailov said. 'They are useless. You're tearing through them, as I thought you would.'

'You didn't think I'd tear through you, though.'

'You're right. But it's funny that you think you'll make it out of this country alive.'

'And why's that?'

Mikhailov gave a knowing smirk. 'They'll nuke this entire peninsula before they let you get out. They value their anonymity.'

'Who?'

'The viewers.'

'Really?' King said. 'You think bloodthirsty internet addicts are going to come hunt me down?'

Mikhailov shook his head, his eyes closed. He took a deep breath to compose himself before opening his mouth.

'I can feel it,' he said. 'Those cold fingers creeping up my spine. I think this is it. Which is why I don't mind sharing this.'

'Sharing what?'

'We broadcast to a very exclusive group of viewers,' he said. 'The oligarchs. The sheiks. Those men and women who seized riches beyond their wildest dreams when the Soviet Union dissolved. Many of them are old-fashioned. Set in their ways. They were dismayed by the new world. They missed the KGB days, the era of the secret police and the generous application of torture and brutality. Their instincts called.'

'That's who you're working for?'

'I work for no-one,' Mikhailov spat, like the very thought of being ordered around offended him. 'I sensed a business opportunity. I had many powerful contacts from my time of employment. I sent out probes, and they responded warmly to the idea. It takes the ruthless, psychotic types to become titans of industry. Nothing like turning innocent foreigners into savages to get the blood rushing.'

'Sick bastards,' King muttered.

'Sick bastards who pay millions for the experience,' Mikhailov said. 'An experience which also promises them total discretion. I have the identities of every viewer buried deep in the archives of these computers, encrypted beyond measure. You will never find them.'

'But they don't know that.'

'No... they do not. These are powerful people. Between them they are worth tens of billions. They effectively own

Russia. And you decided to inform them that a stranger had forced his way into the system while the stream was live.'

'So they'll retaliate?'

Mikhailov grinned wryly. He gestured to his wounds. 'That is why this doesn't bother me. I was a dead man the second you said that. We all were.'

'Then I win.'

'You win, but you'll die,' Mikhailov said. 'So will all your friends you came to protect. No-one will make it out of here alive.'

King felt his stomach constricting as the dread crept in. He didn't doubt Mikhailov. It was pointless for him to bluff. The man was in his death throes.

He stepped back into the tunnel and collected the two weapons on the ground. The MP-443 Grach, and Mikhailov's assault rifle. King snatched up the gun and stared at its make.

It was his own weapon.

The M4A1 carbine.

Mikhailov must have retrieved it from the cavern floor after kicking it off the walkway.

He shook his head in disbelief and stepped back into the production room. For reassurance's sake, he lifted the Grach and trained in on Mikhailov, just in case the man had some kind of final life-or-death attack to carry out.

Nothing.

Mikhailov hadn't budged.

Satisfied by the extent of the man's injuries, King approached the table, carrying the M4A1 under his right arm and clutching the handgun in his right hand. His left wasn't functioning. He tried to ignore the pain burning up that side of his body and concentrate on the task at hand.

Mikhailov lay groggily on the thin wooden surface, his face pale. The blood leaking from his wounds had spread, surrounding him with a giant crimson stain. King strode up to the man and pressed the barrel of the Grach against the side of his head.

'Where are you keeping the prisoners?' King said.

Mikhailov met his gaze with drooping eyes. He said nothing.

'Tell me,' King said. 'You're going to die anyway.'

Mikhailov moved his lips as if to speak, then his eyes closed completely and his head slumped back against the table.

King sighed and took the handgun away from the man's skull.

He dropped his guard for a split second.

That was all it took.

Mikhailov's eyes lurched open and he shot off the table like he had been electrocuted. The blood was drained from his face and his wounds were trickling crimson, but he moved as if nothing were wrong at all. King realised the grogginess and the dazed stupor and the slip into unconsciousness had all been a ploy.

The man was still hurt badly, and would likely die if he didn't receive medical attention.

But there was still fight left in him.

King realised this as he took a sweeping side kick to the right arm. He hadn't been expecting the attack whatsoever, and there was enough force behind the blow to knock him sideways into one of the tables. He sprawled across two computer monitors, shattering one of the screens.

He fumbled for the handgun and started to raise it…

…but by then, Mikhailov had taken off at a sprint.

King managed a single shot before Mikhailov disappeared from sight. The round went wide, slicing over the man's shoulder and ricocheting off the far wall of the tunnel. He had rushed the shot and failed.

Mikhailov tore around the corner and disappeared from sight.

King paused, stifling panic, suddenly alone.

'*Fuck*,' he whispered to himself.

Mikhailov knew where the other five prisoners were. He was the type of man to slaughter them all just to send a message — as he had done with Seth and Eli.

King couldn't allow him to get away. He had no other choice.

He slung the M4A1 over his shoulder and tightened his grip on the handgun. Spotting a small flashlight on one of the desks by the door, he snatched it up and flicked it on, sending a pale white beam of artificial light through the open doorway.

Then he took off in pursuit of Vadim Mikhailov for what he hoped would be the last time.

CHAPTER 38

The tiny flashlight turned the maze of tunnels into something out of a horror movie. The shadows were accentuated by the sliver of light coming from King's hand. He had to juggle the flashlight and the MP-443 in the same hand, keeping a pair of fingers poised to fire at any moment. His left wrist hurt to move — which made running awkward and agonising.

He trained the beam — weak as all hell — in a rapid pattern from left to right, searching every crevasse for the sign of human movement. He found nothing. The tunnel ahead twisted and turned, ascending into the upper levels of the mine.

He caught a burst of movement ahead and darted the flashlight over it.

Mikhailov.

The man disappeared around a bend — all King glimpsed was a brief image of his back, hunched over and sprinting. He had no idea how hard Mikhailov had been selling the extent of his injuries. The man could be in his death throes, only having acted after receiving a final burst of energy.

Like a last stand of sorts.

Or the ex-assassin could truly be indestructible and the bullet wounds could have been a non-factor to him.

King quickened his pace as best he could, keeping his left arm pinned to his side to minimise its swing. A few dozen feet later he stumbled, stepping into a slight dip in the tunnel floor. His ankle threatened to buckle, but he took the weight off it as fast as possible and pressed on.

He caught another glimpse of Mikhailov, hurrying through the tunnel in the distance. The man had no light to guide him. King realised he must know the tunnels like the back of his hand.

A minute later, he had an idea as to where Mikhailov was heading.

'Oh, shit,' he muttered, rasping for breath due to the steep climb of the tunnel floor.

He wheeled left, then right fifty feet later, following the brief views he received of the man. His suspicions were confirmed as he saw Mikhailov duck into the same tunnel King had arrived in.

'Elevator,' King said to himself.

He knew the consequences of Mikhailov reaching the mine shaft. As far as King knew, it was the only way out of the mine. If Mikhailov made it to the elevator and ascended to ground level, there would be a number of ways to prevent the cage from returning to King's level. Mikhailov knew the mine inside and out. He would know all kinds of override procedures.

King and the five WHO workers left alive would be trapped in the mine until the viewers of the live stream sent hardened killers down to finish them off.

A tremor ran down King's spine. He pushed himself as fast as he would go, compartmentalising the screaming pain in his wrist and the pulse-pounding headache in his skull.

Ahead, he heard someone wrench the mine cage shut, closing the mesh doors from within.

He's made it inside, King thought.

He shone the flashlight down the tunnel, illuminating the mine cage. The doors — made of metal grating — were firmly closed.

From inside the elevator, a voice rasped, 'Well played before, King.'

With a whirr of mechanical activation the elevator rumbled. The steel cable on top of the cage wrenched it up.

King fired a single shot with the MP-443, knowing it would prove futile. It ricocheted uselessly off the cage doors before the underside of the elevator disappeared from sight.

King stared in disbelief at the empty mine shaft ahead, dark and imposing.

He gulped back apprehension.

There was no other way to the surface.

He was trapped in the depths of the Russian Far East — badly hurt, in the middle of a spectacular failure of an unofficial mission. He wasn't supposed to be here. No-one in the United States government would come to his aid and risk a conflict of nations in the process.

It was on him to guide five innocent civilians to safety.

How he would achieve that, he hadn't the slightest clue.

All he could do was try.

He turned away from the now-empty mine shaft and set off in the direction of the cavern.

It was time to find the prisoners.

CHAPTER 39

The sheer quiet of the cavern struck him the second he stepped into the vast space. He strode out onto the same walkway Mikhailov had brutalised him on less than an hour ago. His boots — pressing against the flimsy metal — echoed all the way down to the cavern floor.

When he stood in one spot and peered out over the empty void, all sounds of his footfalls faded away. He couldn't hear a thing. Surrounded in all directions by a mile of rock, King felt a strange unease in the pit of his stomach. He wasn't ordinarily claustrophobic, but the setting affected him. He quashed the sensation and set off for one of the ramps, moving fast.

Each walkway was connected to the other by a multitude of access ladders and ramps. King made his way down the cavern, twisting his way around the walls. All the walkways hugged the perimeter of the cavern — none crossed the dead space in the centre. Rust coated most of the visible metal. Clearly it had not been a priority of Mikhailov's to keep the mine aesthetically pleasing.

It had served a ruthless and barbaric purpose, and now it would serve to contain an American intruder until he could be dealt with.

Or they could just leave us down here, King thought.

Sever the connection to the internet and wait for them to starve or die of thirst. Whichever came first. He shook off the fear and continued.

As long as he remained breathing, he would fight tooth and nail to stay that way.

He didn't have an ounce of quit in his body.

He reached the cavern floor and passed between the bodies of Seth and Eli, bowing his head as he did so. He wished he could have done something to save them. For a moment, he considered the fact that it had been his interruption which caused Mikhailov to put a bullet in each of their skulls.

He shrugged it off. If he hadn't done something, they would have beaten each other to death and lost all their humanity in the process. It wasn't his fault that Mikhailov was such a twisted fuck. He hadn't anticipated that the man would be so ruthless.

Even so, a quick death would have been preferable to being pummelled into oblivion by one of your co-workers. Succumbing to your injuries, helpless to stop them exacting their duty. King imagined all the similar bouts that had taken place on this floor.

He felt ill. He knew sociopaths and psychopaths were the first to succeed in business, which explained the high demand to view such a sickening and sadistic bloodsport amongst the elite of society. But it still chilled him to the bone. Striding across the cavern floor, he realised again why he had decided to re-join Black Force.

How could he sit in retirement when situations like this were unfolding across the globe?

He ducked into the steel door that he had seen Mikhailov and the British man walk through a half-hour previously. It led through to a high-ceilinged corridor — still carved out of the rock, but cared for a little more than the rough tunnels of the upper levels. The floor and walls were smooth to the touch. Dozens of doors branched off from this main corridor, all of them firmly shut.

King kept low, wondering if any of Mikhailov's thugs remained in the mine. He assumed he had killed them all.

Then again, he wouldn't put it past Mikhailov to abandon his men. One didn't succeed in such a ruthless industry without being concerned about no-one but themselves. They were on his payroll — nothing more, nothing less. He had no obligation to ensure their protection.

King heard the voices. They came from one of the rooms up ahead, low and hushed. Two men, murmuring back and forth in Russian. Their tones were stressed, their inflections harsh and discordant.

The last of Mikhailov's outfit.

Likely discussing their next move.

King hazarded a guess that they had been entailed with overlooking the remaining prisoners while the rest of the group hunted for the intruder. They were probably nervous, pent up from all the waiting.

King crept up to the closed door and hovered an inch from its frame, listening intently.

Definitely two men.

He gauged their rough position based on the volume of their voices. Then — delicately, cautiously — he placed the MP-443 Grach down between his feet. He slid the M4A1's strap off his shoulder and slipped a finger into the trigger guard, gripping the large carbine in his good hand.

With his left elbow, he leant forward and knocked on the door twice. Calmly. Gently.

As if everything was under control.

As if he were one of their co-workers, returning from successfully hunting the Americans.

He crouched low.

The door opened.

He killed the first man with a three-round burst to the face. The Russian mercenary's features simply exploded and he cascaded back into the room in a tangle of dead limbs. A cluster of panicked shouts echoed off the walls from somewhere deeper inside the room.

The prisoners.

He registered the sounds of their terror and thundered into the room, searching for the second man.

The final mercenary looked to be in his late forties, one of the older members of the group. His features were rough — complete with a heavily wrinkled forehead and leathery skin. It seemed male pattern baldness had struck over a decade ago. The guy's eyes were black and soulless, similar to all of the mercenaries King had met down here.

It took a certain type to accept a position in this kind of operation.

They all had to lack a conscience entirely.

The man was in the process of reaching for a Kalashnikov assault rifle resting in an otherwise-empty weapon rack. He got a single hand on the gun before King blasted his upper back to shreds with a volley of shots from the carbine. The guy hadn't been wearing any kind of body protection. He slumped forward into the metal rack, motionless.

For good measure, King put a final bullet through the rear of his skull.

He lowered the M4A1 and looked past the dead men.

Through a wall of steel bars, he met the gaze of five terrified World Health Organisation employees.

CHAPTER 40

The five men were on their feet, trapped on the other side of thin steel columns stretching from one wall to the other. Each of the bars were separated by only a few inches. The men stared at him with startled expressions, shocked by the sudden outburst of violence.

'Hey,' King said after a beat of silence.

No-one responded.

He didn't expect anything else.

'Sorry about that,' he said, gesturing to the two dead mercenaries. 'No other way to do it, really. Try not to look at them.'

'Who the fuck are you?' one of the workers blurted, his tone quivering.

King regarded the source of the voice. The man had a thick European accent — he couldn't pinpoint exactly which country he was from. He had long brown hair spilling down his back that would have ordinarily been lush, but was currently matted with sweat and dirt. His face was sharply defined, with high cheekbones and a pronounced jawline. He looked malnourished. King doubted the group had been fed since they were taken.

No need to satiate the contestants. They would die, anyway. In fact, being starved might have made them more rabid, more prone to obey Mikhailov when he commanded them to fight. King imagined Mikhailov's promises to release the victor were always completely false. All captives would be murdered eventually.

That's how they had remained undiscovered.

'I'm the guy who just went through hell to get you out of here,' King said. 'You could be a little more polite.'

'Sorry,' the man stammered.

'What's your name?'

'Léo.'

'Nice to meet you, Léo. I'm Jason.'

'You're a soldier?'

'Yeah. Kind of.'

'Kind of?'

'We'll have time to chat later,' King said. 'Are any of you injured?'

Four of the five — including Léo — shook their heads. The guy on the far left met King's gaze with a grimace. When he spoke, his voice was distinctly Australian. 'I think one of my ribs is broken, man.'

'What's your name?'

'Marcus.'

'Can you walk, Marcus?' King said.

'Yeah.'

'Then you're not injured.'

'Are you injured?' another one of the men asked, regarding King's left arm dangling by his side.

He glanced down at his wrist, which had now swollen to twice its usual size. 'I'll be fine.'

'Are they all dead?' Léo said, desperation in his voice.

King assumed he meant their captors. 'Most of them are. I'm good at my job.'

'What about…?' Marcus started, but he trailed off.

Like he didn't really want to know the answer to the question.

King met his eyes and softly shook his head, grimacing as he did so. He had been responsible for informing people that those close to them had died more times than he cared to think about. It never got easier. Marcus bowed his forehead and slammed it into one of the steel bars. He left it there, staring at the ground, breathing deep.

King saw a tear splash against the rock floor of the room.

The other four seemed shell-shocked. They stared vacantly at King, like they were seeing through him, not really aware that he was there.

Sarah. Jessica. Carmen. Seth. Eli.

Five workers dead. King imagined the ten-person party had formed a tight bond during their time spent as free civilians in the Russian Far East. An environment like this drew people together.

He knew news of their deaths would not be taken lightly.

He gave them a minute. Despite the sentiment, the timer in his head ticked down rapidly, reminding him each second that any time not spent in motion was time wasted.

That was the way things were on an operation.

King rarely ever had time to process what had occurred until after the fact.

'I know this must be crazy,' he said. 'It's a lot to process. But we have to move. We're not out of the woods yet. I need you all to follow everything I say until we make it home safe. Okay?'

A few blank stares. A couple of nods.

It would suffice.

King yanked a bundle of keys out of the rear pocket of the dead mercenary by his feet and unlocked the door fixed into the makeshift cell. He ushered the five men through. They followed his commands, but all of them seemed spaced out. Thankfully King had years of experience dealing with hostages of similar demeanour.

As long as they did as he instructed, he would manage.

He didn't want to alert them to the fact that they might all be trapped in the mine. Not just yet. Fear could break a man — staring into the empty mine shaft had almost broken him, and he considered himself one of the most mentally-hardened people on the planet.

If these civilians realised that there was no way out of the depths of the earth, nervous breakdowns weren't out of the question.

Before they reached the cavern, King turned on his heel and raised a hand. The men froze.

'Grab the shirt of the man in front of you,' he said. 'Close your eyes. I'll lead you through this part.'

'Why—?' Léo started.

King glared at him. 'Don't ask questions. Shut up and do what I say. Don't open your eyes for any reason.'

They obeyed, as he knew they would. They were more likely to respond to stern commands in the face of fear — hence his rudeness. When he was certain that each man had their eyes firmly shut, he led them in a rudimentary line across the cavern floor, past the dead bodies of their close co-workers.

The sight of Seth and Eli's lifeless forms with identical bullet holes in their skull might have been too much for the group to process.

When they made it to the ground level walkway, he let them open their eyes.

'Follow me,' he said. 'Keep your eyes trained on my back.'

As they ascended to the next level, King discarded the M4A1's magazine and chambered a fresh one home. He wasn't sure how close to empty the previous magazine had been, having lost count in the midst of battle. But it would pay to have a guaranteed thirty rounds at his disposal for whatever lay ahead.

He led them into the tunnels not far off the cavern floor, his mind reeling with thoughts.

What could he do?

Faltering in front of the workers wasn't an option. They would latch onto his weakness and fold mentally, which would in turn encourage him to give up hope. Once again, he resolved to act calm until he had drawn his last breath. It would keep him level-headed, and keep the workers from panicking.

King found the production room without much effort and ushered the five men inside. He glanced at a motionless body resting against one wall of the tunnel just outside the door.

The mercenary with the concussion.

Unquestionably dead.

The guy had succumbed to his injuries. A brain bleed, most likely. King was unperturbed by the development. He didn't hold an ounce of pity for these animals. It was one more spare bullet in his arsenal.

He followed the men into the production room and instructed them to stare at the rock wall.

'If I see you looking away from that wall, it's going to be trouble,' he said.

He wanted them focused on his rude commands instead of letting their mind wander onto stray thoughts.

Why isn't he taking us out of the mine?

Why can't we leave?

King also didn't want them looking out through the glass. There was an unobstructed view of Seth and Eli's bodies slumped on the cavern floor. He would have preferred not to bring them here, but there was matters that needed attending to as quickly as possible.

He needed to act before Mikhailov and his friends severed the connection, which King was sure would be done promptly.

He crossed to the nearest computer and shook the mouse, removing a plain black screensaver. He navigated to Google and muttered a silent plea that this avenue would prove successful.

'What are you doing?' Marcus said softly.

King turned to make sure the guy hadn't taken his eyes off the wall. Satisfied, he turned back to the computer and searched for luxury family resorts in St. John's, Antigua.

'I need to contact a friend,' he said.

CHAPTER 41

The landline phone connected to the internet cables rang for just under a minute, which felt like an eternity to King. He pinned the receiver to his ear by trapping it against his shoulder, at the same time drumming the fingers of his right hand against the surface of the desk.

'Come on,' he whispered. 'Come on.'

The ringing ceased, and a soothing male voice answered a second later. 'This is the Ocean Club. Francis speaking.'

'Hey, Francis,' King said, adopting a pleasant but insistent tone. 'My name's Jason King. I was wondering if you could do me an enormous favour.'

The man chuckled. 'That depends, sir. I am on the job, after all.'

King sensed the sly nature of the man's tone and adjusted his approach accordingly.

'Look, here's the situation,' King said. 'I believe that my brother is staying at your resort. He's an African-American man in his thirties with short black hair. He's in excellent shape and he's good looking. His accent is American. He'd stand out in a crowd. Do you know who I'm talking about? Have you seen him around?'

'I've seen him,' Francis said. 'You're certainly right, he's noticeable.'

King stifled a sigh of relief. 'Would I be able to speak to him?

A pause from the other end of the line. 'Your brother, you say?'

'Yes,' King said.

'Do you have a name for this brother?'

'That's the problem,' King said. 'He left the family home a few weeks ago. He got into a huge argument with our parents, and we haven't heard from him since. I'm desperate to talk to him about what unfolded. We were so close.' King paused, pretending to mask emotion. 'He would be staying under a different name. He doesn't want our parents to find him. Please — could you let him know that Jason King wants to speak to him? That's all I'm asking. You'd be doing me an unimaginable favour.'

Francis paused, considering the spiel. 'I cannot promise you that he will contact you back.'

'I'm not asking you to,' King said. 'Please just let him know that I called.'

'Jason King, did you say?'

'Yes.'

Another pause. King clenched his teeth as the stress leeched from his bones. This was a last-ditch effort. If it didn't work, he couldn't figure out a way to make it out of the mine. There was one way in and one way out. And if Mikhailov had been truthful, there would be a small army en route to their location.

'Okay, sir,' Francis said. 'Anything else?'

'No,' King said. 'Thank you, Francis.'

'Not a problem.'

The line disconnected. King took the phone away from his ear and stared at the receiver, deep in thought. Francis' tone had turned bemused towards the end of the conversation, like he was humouring an insane relative just for the sake of it. It didn't matter what the man thought of him. All he needed was for the name "Jason King" to reach its target.

Francis was unaware that the lives of five innocent civilians and a secret government operative rested solely in his hands.

A low cough behind King made him turn. He swivelled around in his seat to see the five health workers staring at him as if he were an asylum patient. Clear concern was plastered across all their faces.

Léo was the first to open his mouth. 'Have you lost your fucking mind?'

King allowed himself a wry smile as he realised how the conversation would have appeared to the workers. He hadn't briefed them on the context. To them, he had taken the opportunity to amend private family issues in the middle of an intensely dangerous situation.

'That wasn't what it sounded like,' King said.

'I hope not,' Marcus said. 'It sounded like you've lost the plot.'

King got the sense that Léo and Marcus did all the talking. The other three — all in their late twenties or early thirties, with slim builds and scruffy hair — had yet to speak in the brief time King had spent with them.

'I work for a certain division of the government,' King said. 'It's just myself and a select few others. One of my closest co-workers is among the most dangerous men on the planet. He's going to call me back and help us out of this situation.'

'What situation?' Léo said. 'Let's fucking go. I hate this place. We need to get home.'

'It's not as simple as that,' King said.

'Why not?'

'Getting out will be trickier than anticipated. Nothing I can't handle, though.'

He wanted to ease them into the news. Coming straight out the gate with the revelation that they were trapped in the abandoned mine until their enemies came for them would help no-one.

Sometimes, the truth had to be skirted around to keep everyone sane.

'We're stuck in here?' one of the three silent workers said in a voice barely above a whisper. His face had paled entirely, the blood draining from it as he made the realisation.

'Not exactly stuck,' King said. 'Just a few problems. I'm sorting it out.'

'What are you doing, man?' Marcus said. 'You don't need to be so vague. Just tell us.'

King shrugged. 'The only elevator out of here isn't working. There's some problems with it. As soon as I can get a friend to fix it up top, we'll be good to go.'

Selective information. They didn't need to know that the elevator had been intentionally disabled by a bullet-riddled madman, who was likely in the process of calling for reinforcements amongst his contacts in the Russian government.

'Are there friendlies on their way?' Léo asked.

King held up the satellite phone. 'That's what I'm working on.'

'Why are you calling a co-worker on holiday?' Marcus said. 'Why aren't you calling the fucking military or something?'

'Because he's the best,' King said.

The phone began to vibrate. King exhaled, letting out the built-up stress, and answered.

'Slater,' he muttered, the elation clear in his tone.

Will Slater paused a moment before responding. 'How the hell did you find me?'

CHAPTER 42

'You found me in Stockholm easily enough,' King said.

'I'm good with computers,' Slater said. 'You're an old man in comparison. Consider me surprised.'

'There were laughing children and splashing water in the background of our last call,' King said. 'I figured you were at a resort. Then it was just a matter of pinpointing which costs the most per night.'

Slater scoffed. 'I'm that simple, huh?'

'Expensive taste. I know that much about you.'

'So what do you want?' Slater said. 'I assume you're not calling unless you really need something.'

'I'm in the Russian Far East.'

'What the hell are you doing there?'

'Making mistakes.'

'Evidently.'

'It's bad, Will,' King said. 'I'm in deep shit.'

'Get Black Force to extract you. They have resources. You know that as well as I do.'

'I'm not here on Black Force's behalf.'

Stunned silence. 'You're kidding.'

'I wish I was.'

'What personal vendetta do you have in the Russian Far East?'

'It's not my vendetta,' King said. 'I was set up. There's plenty of time to fill you in later.'

'How bad's your situation?'

'Terrible. I'm trying to pull kidnapped health workers out of a gold mine near Shiveluch Volcano. We're trapped down here and there's all kinds of powerful people who don't want us out. I don't know what's coming for us.'

King sensed a palpable shift at the other end of the line. Slater had switched over to operational mode.

'Latitude and longitude,' Slater said. 'Now.'

King kept the receiver pressed against his ear and navigated through the nearest computer's directories with his good hand. Before long, he came across details of the mine itself — including a precise set of co-ordinates. He relayed them to Slater, taking his time to ensure each decimal point was accurate.

'Got it,' Slater said. 'I'll be there as fast as I can.'

'How fast will that be?'

'Depends,' Slater said. 'I can be twice as fast if you need me to go down that route.'

King thought of the time ticking away as Mikhailov schemed an assault somewhere far above. 'I think I do need you to go that route.'

Slater sighed. 'Haven't stolen a plane before…'

'There's a first time for everything.'

'Leave it with me,' Slater said.

He ended the call.

Most of the finer details had been left out of the conversation — but King knew they both had enough experience to only bother with the necessities. He hadn't informed Slater of what kind of hostility he would be facing on the ground — which meant he didn't know himself. He hadn't informed Slater of the reason why the health workers had been kidnapped — because it didn't matter. Now Slater only had to concentrate on the barebones nature of the situation. He could direct his energy and resources into solving the main problem.

What mattered was that they were trapped down here.

All the frivolities would be discussed later.

'That was your friend?' Léo said as King dropped the satellite phone onto the desk.

He nodded. 'He's on his way.'

'So what do we do now?'

King hesitated. He had been on the move ever since he'd set foot on Russian soil, always transfixed by the next objective, the next goal. Now he sat in the deathly silent sub-levels of the gold mine, wondering just what exactly he was supposed to be doing.

Nothing, he concluded.

'We wait,' he said.

As soon as he spoke the words, something in his subconscious shifted. A mental switch that had been set to full capacity ever since he'd dropped out of the B-1 Lancer's bomb bay suddenly relaxed. A wave of tiredness overcame him. He realised he had been roaring at full mental capacity for over twelve hours. In that time he had been beaten to within an inch of his life. Bones had been broken. Skin had been bruised. He imagined his brain had been rattled by some of the blows Mikhailov had landed.

And he had killed nearly twenty men on Russian soil.

He slumped back in the chair and battled down a sudden wave of exhaustion. With it came the cold reality that he was severely incapacitated. His wounds hurt more than ever as the adrenalin wore off.

Fighting the fatigue, he looked at the health workers, his vision shimmering unnaturally.

'Listen,' he said. 'You probably heard what I was saying on the phone. We have problems. We're not out of this yet. There might be more of your kidnappers' friends coming down to meet us.'

'You look like you're about to pass out,' Léo said.

'I feel like I might, too,' King said. 'I need to get to the tunnel that connects to the mine shaft. That's where they'll be arriving, if they come. You all need to barricade yourself into this room and open it for no-one. If someone forces the door open without announcing themselves, shoot them.'

They nodded in unison.

'But I need one of you to come with me,' King said. 'To keep me awake. I'm functioning on my reserves here.'

'I'll do it,' Léo said immediately.

King nodded and heaved himself to his feet. He snatched up the M4A1 and hobbled for the open doorway. 'Let's go.'

CHAPTER 43

They left Marcus and the other three men in the production room. King armed them with two of the MP-443 Grach pistols that he had collected from the dead mercenaries. They had been instructed to keep the barrels aimed at the door for as long as it took. He and Léo set off into the maze of tunnels. King had a tight ball of apprehension squirming around in the pit of his stomach — and he had faced situations like this countless times.

He couldn't imagine how Léo felt.

'Your friend,' Léo said. 'He's just as dangerous as you?'

'What makes you think I'm so talented?' King said.

'You killed the guys guarding us in a second or two. That shit only happens in the movies.'

'Just accuracy,' King said.

'Is your friend accurate?'

'I've only seen him in action once,' King said, recalling Slater's violent rampage through a horde of sex slavers on a luxury yacht in Corsica. 'But that was enough.'

'He'll get us out of here?'

'I hope so.'

They lapsed into silence. King listened to their footfalls echoing off the tunnel walls. At any second he anticipated the rush of rapid footsteps behind them, signalling an approaching attacker. He recalled the sheer helplessness as Mikhailov had tackled him from behind. A bolt of fear ran through him.

He would never let a situation like that unfold again.

'How are you holding up?' he said quietly, training the beam on the empty space ahead. They were close to the mine shaft.

'Okay, I guess,' Léo said. 'Trying not to think about anything.'

'That's the way.'

'You do this kind of thing for a living?' Léo said, flabbergasted.

'Yeah.'

'Are you used to it?'

King kept his gaze fixed firmly down the tunnel. 'I keep thinking I am. But there's no real way to get used to a career as volatile as mine.'

'At least you're alive.'

'Touché.'

They exited into a larger tunnel, wide enough to fit three or four men shoulder-to-shoulder. King recognised it.

'This is it,' he said. 'Elevator arrives somewhere down there.'

He trained his flashlight to the left, illuminating a sheer drop into nothingness fifty feet away from them.

The entrance to the empty mine shaft.

As he suspected, the elevator had yet to return to their level after Mikhailov's ascent.

'What do we do?' Léo said.

'Same as before. We wait, and keep an eye out for any activity.'

They clambered down onto the cold floor of the tunnel. King lay prone on the smooth rock, setting up the M4A1 on the ground in front of him. He let the front grip rest against the floor, acting as a stabiliser of sorts. He pointed the barrel in the direction of the mine shaft and settled in for what would likely be a long and uneventful shift.

A minute into the wait, King heard the distinct *thump-thump, thump-thump, thump-thump* of a heartbeat. He spent a moment attempting to calm himself before he realised the sound wasn't coming from his own chest.

'You nervous?' he said.

Léo stifled a panicked breath. 'Never done anything like this before.'

'I'd hope not. Breathe deep. In and out. Focus on slowing your pulse. You'll need energy for later.'

'Why?' Léo said. 'I don't know anything about what's going on.'

'Do you know what happened to Seth and Eli?'

'No.'

So the prisoners had no knowledge of the no-holds-barred fighting bouts before they were thrust into them. The surprise probably had its advantages to Mikhailov and his crew. The contestants had little time to think about their actions before they were forced to brawl for their lives. Compliance would be more likely.

'There was a sick game taking place in this mine,' King said. 'Fights between your group. To the death. That's why they were snatching people.'

'Seth and Eli fought?' Léo said, astonished.

'They were about to,' King said. 'I intervened.'

'They would never do that. They were friends.'

You have no idea what people will do to stay alive, King thought.

He remembered the manic glint in Eli's eyes. He had no doubt the man would have attacked his friend had he done nothing to stop them. Seth had remained level-headed. At least, until Eli laid a hand on him.

Then all bets would have been off.

King stomached his rage at the circumstances of the situation.

'There were people watching via cameras,' King said. 'Men and women in positions of power. Wealthy beyond measure.'

'Watching this?' Léo said.

King nodded. 'The world's a brutal place.'

'They know we're down here?'

He nodded again. 'They know I'm down here, specifically. They won't let it rest until we're all dead. Their anonymity is sacred.'

'So who's coming for us?'

'I know just as much as you do. More hired guns. Russian Special Forces. It could be anything.'

'Let's hope your friend beats them here.'

King grimaced. 'Yes, let's.'

The conversation died out. King focused on the flashlight beam, watching it shimmer and flicker as it pierced through the darkness, lighting up the visible portion of the mine shaft. His own vision began to waver. The light blurred into a shade of pale blue that slowly washed over him, warm and pleasant. The pain in his left wrist dulled slightly, fading.

Everything faded…

He slipped into some kind of trance. At least, that's what it felt like. It wasn't usual drowsiness. Maybe the head injury had dealt more damage than he originally thought…

The pale blue overwhelmed him and he sunk into the ground.

CHAPTER 44

Bang.

The rumble of metal sounded, close by. Limbs scrambled against rock. Panicked movement, all at once.

King was torn out of unconsciousness.

'*King!*' Léo yelled as he shot to his feet.

The syllable pierced the silence, ripping through King's eardrums. His head spun and his ears rang. His heart lurched, struggling to comprehend all the developments at once. At some point the flashlight had gone out. He was surrounded by black.

'Wha—?' he started.

He hadn't even realised he had been out. The darkness of the mine and the darkness of his unconscious state had blended into an amalgamation. Startled, he fumbled for his weapon.

'Elevator,' Léo hissed, breathing hard. 'It's here.'

The metal cage doors grated at the other end of the tunnel, sliding open. King froze on the spot as he heard murmured voices — at least five men, speaking Russian.

He went pale.

'*Don't move,*' he mouthed in a tone below a whisper.

The approaching party hadn't heard them yet.

King noticed the distinct sound of footsteps on the tunnel floor. At least one of the new arrivals had stepped off the elevator, into the mine. They were advancing towards their location.

King didn't know how many there were, or what kind of firepower they had. The unknown terrified him. He lifted his swollen left hand and touched it to Léo's chest, silently commanding the man to remain motionless.

Léo complied.

King let the wait grow to a horrifying length. Anyone else would have caved. His instincts screamed to take off in the other direction.

Now.

He unloaded half the M4A1's magazine down the tunnel. Muzzle flare ignited from the barrel, flashing like a strobe light off the rock walls. Dark silhouettes approaching from the elevator became apparent.

There were five.

As he suspected.

Two died in the initial burst of gunfire, twisting unnaturally off their feet. The other three dropped simultaneously, incredibly fast. King knew they hadn't been hit. They were responding out of instinct to the gunfire, minimising their target area just as he had been trained to do all those years ago.

They were elite.

And they would be training their barrels on the source of the barrage.

'Fuck.'

King swung his right hand around in a tight arc — still holding the M4A1 — and crash-tackled Léo to the floor. A moment later bullets ripped through the space above his head.

He wasted no time. The tunnel was a death trap. They would trade automatic gunfire until there was no-one left standing. In one swift motion he hauled Léo to his feet and set off at a full-pelt sprint in the other direction.

Thwack.

A sharp punch — vicious in its intensity.

He let out an involuntary yelp as the pain lanced through his upper back. He had been hit, but if the bullet hadn't impacted his vest it would have likely killed him. Instead it felt like blunt force trauma. Like a pro swinger had sent a steel baseball bat into his spine. The shockwave that transferred through the bulletproof material made him stumble and falter.

But he remained standing.

A second later he whisked Léo around a bend in the tunnel and they sprinted out of the line of sight.

King ran for his life, thrusting Léo ahead. The man got the message. He took off at an incredible pace down the tunnel, peeling away from King as the fight-or-flight mechanism kicked in.

King heard orders being shouted at full volume behind him. They echoed down the tunnel, ringing around his head. He couldn't understand a thing.

He had roughly fifteen bullets left in the carbine's magazine, and another full clip in his breast pocket.

It would have to suffice.

He and Léo burst out into the cavern ten seconds later, careering into the walkway's railing due to the speed they were travelling. Briefly, it groaned under their weight. King tore his bulk off the metal, terrified of falling to a grisly death.

That gave him an idea.

He forced Léo to the left, guiding him along the walkway. Then he pressed his back against the side of the tunnel's entrance and waited.

A half-second later, the first of the remaining attackers came sprinting around the corner. The guy wore a faded military uniform and a thick woollen balaclava that completely masked his features. He was as big as Mikhailov. Heavier than King. He was likely to pose problems in a fistfight.

Luckily, it wouldn't come to that.

The extra weight meant the man had built up momentum. He skidded on the flimsy metal walkway as he sprinted out in pursuit of King.

If King stayed put, they would have collided in a tangle of limbs.

Instead he side-stepped the charging attacker, wrapped a tight hand around the back of his neck and used the guy's momentum to his own advantage.

It took a single well-timed heave of exertion to hurl the man over the thin railing.

The guy smashed stomach first into the metal bar and tumbled over it, losing all balance as King launched him through the motion.

He disappeared noiselessly from sight, too terrified to even omit a sound. As soon as King recognised that the man was out of the equation he turned back to the mouth of the tunnel.

The two remaining mercenaries burst into view in unison. They fell on him in a savage heap, crushing him against the rock wall. King snatched for his carbine and managed to slip a finger into the trigger guard amidst the chaos.

A blow crashed off the side of his head. He grimaced and ducked away from the punch, bringing the assault rifle up as he did so. He squeezed off a short burst. In the quiet of the underground cavern, it blasted through the noiseless space. One of the men winced and backed off, hit somewhere.

King had no idea where.

He couldn't pay attention to anything for more than a half-second.

The other man thundered an elbow towards King's face. He ducked away from it. In the process, he inadvertently cracked his head against the wall behind him. One side of his face went numb and pain exploded across his vision.

Desperation seized him.

If he didn't seize the upper hand, he would die painfully.

He turned animalistic.

Due to the tight confines of the brawl he reversed his grip on the carbine and swung it by its barrel. The stock smashed against the man's jawbone, shattering it completely. King took him off his feet with a front kick, then turned his attention to the man he'd shot a second ago.

The guy hadn't been incapacitated, evidenced by the head kick that came darting towards King's unprotected face. He lurched backwards, narrowly avoiding the strike. The stumble put just enough distance between them to enable a burst of fire with the M4A1.

King spun the weapon again, scizing it by the trigger guard. He found the thin sliver of metal before the man could launch any further offence and unloaded the rest of the clip into his unprotected face.

The balaclava hid most of the gore, but King didn't get a chance to admire his handiwork any further. A powerful arm looped around his throat from behind.

It was the last man alive — whose jaw King had shattered moments earlier. The man's forearm strength was unbelievable. The choke hold cut off circulation to King's brain in a single squeeze.

He felt consciousness slipping away. He would be out within seconds.

Fumbling with an empty weapon, he panicked, eyes boggling. The guy squeezed tighter. The edges of King's vision started to blur, fading into sharp pinpoints of white light.

He knew what that spelled.

In a last-ditch effort, he dropped his hips and took a knee, implementing a judo technique. The man followed him down, intent on holding the rear naked choke until he was out cold. King used the momentum to haul the guy over his shoulder, rotating him an entire revolution in the air.

If the man simply kept his composure and remained latched onto King's neck, that would be the end.

But he didn't.

He panicked and eased his grip as he lost his balance.

King wrenched his head out of the choke, gasping for breath as he did so.

All kinds of undesirable symptoms washed over him. The cold sweat, the spinning vision, the loss of balance. He ignored them all and surged on the man in front of him, who was in the process of scrambling to his feet.

He knew the guy's jiu-jitsu base was strong. The rear naked choke had been applied with expert precision, targeting the carotid artery in his neck to deprive his brain of oxygenated blood and shut his lights out in the fastest amount of time possible. The squeeze had been vice-like, honed from years of practice. The guy had to be a brown belt or higher.

He clearly had experience in martial arts.

King kept that in mind as he charged.

He pinpointed a target just above the man's ear — the soft spot for causing serious neurological damage. Strikes like that — taking a running kick when the opponent was down — had serious long-term consequences if applied correctly, which was the reason they were outlawed in most combat sports.

But this wasn't combat sports.

This was life or death.

He rocketed the toe of his combat boot into the side of the guy's head, connecting perfectly against his temple. The man staggered away, still in the process of getting to his feet but reeling from the blow. King followed him along the walkway, biding his time, aware that there were no other combatants left to dispatch.

He could take his time with this fight.

He quickly realised that would not be in his best interests. The consequences of the previous brawl were rapidly dawning on him. He felt sick and dazed and debilitated all at once.

He threw caution to the wind and darted into range, desperate to finish the fight before he collapsed.

The guy sensed the urgency and threw a punch in retaliation.

To an observer, it would have seemed like a light jab — flicked out with minimal effort like a soft whip. It was true that the blow had little power to it, but it wasn't needed. That had been the intention. It made King realise the knowledge this man possessed in the field of martial arts.

It was the punches that sliced like lightning strikes that posed the most danger.

He couldn't take his head off the centre line in time. He saw a blur of movement, then something shattered under his skin.

The jab caught him square on the bridge of his nose, hard enough to crack the bone. King experienced every sliver of the pain that came with such a gruesome injury…

…but he pressed forward.

The natural reaction to a badly broken nose was to recoil. The man would have heard the sharp crack as he broke King's nose and expected hesitation.

King gave him none.

He wasn't prepared for that.

King delivered a staggering uppercut into the guy's ribs, then drew his fist back and repeated the move with the same hand — his left wrist was still unusable.

Bang. Bang.

The punches dealt horrendous damage, gifted with the kind of power that only came from the primal energy released by the urge for survival. The man buckled, unable to help himself keeling over to deal with the pain.

King dropped a thunderous elbow into the back of his neck, then wrapped both arms around his waist and lifted the man off the walkway.

He was heavy. Muscles straining, King let out a grunt as he picked up speed, taking several bounding steps with the man draped over his shoulder.

Just as the guy had started to recover from the barrage of strikes, King threw him over the edge of the railing.

CHAPTER 45

As the last of the threat dissipated, King's knees gave out. He fell on his rear to the metal, his senses disoriented and his vision swimming.

'Shit,' he said, wincing involuntarily.

He couldn't deny the condition he was in any longer. Before the hit squad had arrived, his injuries had been significant yet manageable. Now, with a broken nose and another fresh round of punches to the head to deal with, he had reached his limits. The repeated blows were starting to take their toll.

Bleeding profusely from both nostrils, he rested his head against the rock wall behind him and closed his eyes.

'*King!*' Léo cried.

He heard footsteps hurrying towards him, clanging along the walkway, getting closer and closer. He forced his eyes open as the man reached him.

'Hey, Léo,' he muttered through hazy vision.

'You did it,' Léo said, panting hard. He sat down opposite King and rested against the railing. 'You fucking did it.'

King could barely see. He felt the throbbing agony in his broken nose, in his broken wrist, in his skull. His ribs seared with each breath. He wondered if any of them were broken too.

'This isn't going to work, Léo,' King said, speaking low, at the edge of his limits. 'That was one team of mercenaries. There's plenty more where they came from.'

'How can you be so sure?' Léo said. 'You don't know what's up there. That was probably all their forces.'

King smiled wryly, exposing blood-stained teeth. He admired the man's optimism. 'Maybe so, Léo. But I doubt it.'

'We have to give it a shot. There's no other option. Let's get the others and get on the elevator.'

King perked up at the final statement. He felt a second wave of energy roll over him, threading feeling back into his limbs. He had forgotten about that.

He passed Léo the flashlight from his belt. 'Go check if the elevator's still there. That's our last chance. I need to deal with this pain alone.'

Léo nodded understandingly and set off back down the walkway. King watched him hurry into the tunnel they had come from and disappear into the shadows.

He let out a long and laboured breath.

The battle with his mind had begun.

He had been here before — on the verge of falling into a sleep he knew he would not return from. If he let unconsciousness take hold now, it would be hours before he woke up — and he might not be the same man when he did. If he gave up now, the five health workers wouldn't stand a chance. He wondered if they had ever fired a weapon in their life.

A death squad similar to the five men he had just dispatched would have a field day with a group of such inexperienced combatants.

So he needed to stay awake. It was paramount to their survival. It would be selfish to let death take him.

He thought of Klara nervously anticipating his return in Stockholm. He thought of Ray King making a life for himself in the small town of Aregno, Corsica. They both wanted to see him again.

He would make sure that they did.

He clambered unsteadily to his feet, and instantly a fresh wave of agony seared through him. He leant all his weight against the wall, sucking in harsh breaths of air.

There he waited.

Ten minutes later, Léo returned, flashlight in hand. The man's face sported obvious concern and disappointment.

King knew immediately what he'd found.

'The elevator's gone,' Léo said. 'They must have pulled it back up to the surface electronically.'

King nodded slowly. 'They have control of it.'

'How do we get out of this? What's to stop them continuing to send those squads down? How many do they have?'

King had no response to any of the questions. He stared at the health worker blankly, his alertness levels spacing in and out. On top of all the pain, a certain resignation began to set in. 'I don't know, Léo. I don't know.'

He had been banking on the elevator to be there. He would have likely died in a blaze of glory on ground level as the elevator reached the surface amongst a horde of Russian military and mercenaries, but if he could get the health workers out alive then he would be satisfied in the process.

They were his only objective.

He hadn't come this far to let them all die.

'Help me back to the production room,' he muttered. 'We're no use out in the open.'

Léo looped an arm around his back and helped him stagger toward the tunnel. They dipped back into the maze, a maze that King was all too familiar with by this point. He still lost his bearings, though, unable to focus on anything for longer than a few seconds. Each time he did, the agony resurfaced. He concentrated on the sensations, isolating each stabbing pain and compartmentalising it.

He wasn't succeeding.

By the time Léo found the door to the production room, King had become dizzy from the physical damage. Léo called out before he opened the door, announcing his identity to the four health workers.

Despite his warnings, they were met with two loaded handguns trained directly at their faces as they entered.

King managed a half-smile. 'Good job. Don't trust a voice until you're sure it's friendly.'

'Jesus Christ,' one of the men said.

The other three audibly gasped.

King imagined he didn't look too attractive. By that point his nose had swelled to three times its usual size, and the blood had caked dry across his face. Léo helped him over to the office chair and sat him down.

He fell into a heap on the plush material and focused on keeping his breathing measured and even.

'What the hell happened?' Marcus said. 'It sounded like there was a war echoing through those tunnels.'

'There was,' King muttered.

'And then—' the man said, gesturing out the pane of glass. 'That happened.'

King rolled his head groggily over, following the guy's line of sight.

'Oh…' he said. 'That's right.'

The bodies of two of the hitmen rested gruesomely on the cavern floor.

It had been a long way down.

King turned to the five men. 'Could…'

He trailed off.

Léo grimaced, aware of the extent of his injuries.

King took a deep breath before continuing. 'Could you guys step outside, please?'

'What?' Marcus said.

'I… I need to make a phone call.'

'Um, yeah,' Léo said, pondering the statement. 'Sure thing.'

They filed out into the tunnel reservedly, concerned by King's strange behaviour. When he was sure they were out of earshot, he scooped up the satellite phone and dialled a number with shaking fingers.

Ray King answered on the second ring.

'Hello?' the man said cautiously, likely wary of the unknown number.

'Dad,' King said. 'I know I promised to visit in a couple of days time. But I don't know if I'm going to make it back to Corsica. I…'

Then he choked on his words and forced back tears, waiting for his father to respond.

He had never wanted it to come to this.

CHAPTER 46

'Where are you?' Ray said.

King half-smiled. Always optimistic, his father was. 'Nowhere you can help me.'

'I can try my best. You're my son.'

'Trust me,' King said.

'Jason…you're not going to die, are you?'

Ray spoke the words as if he were suggesting that an impossible feat were about to take place. His voice faltered with each word. King sensed the pain in the question.

'I'm human, Dad,' King said. 'I'm not invincible.'

'You said you just had to take care of things while your organisation got their shit together. You promised you'd be back.'

'I know.'

'How bad is it?'

'I don't know yet.'

'Then you'll be fine.'

'Dad…'

'You're not dying.'

'I don't know if…'

'Hang this phone up and get back to work,' Ray said. 'I won't even entertain the possibility. Look what you've done in your lifetime. There's no way you're dying now.'

'I needed to call,' King said. 'Just in case.'

'Get your ass out of there, Jason. Wherever you are. You don't need me to tell you that.'

'I'll try my best.'

'Good lad.' Ray's voice cracked on the last word, distinctly noticeable. The machismo demeanour threatened to disappear.

'If I don't,' King said, his voice stuffy due to both nostrils congesting with blood. 'I wanted to say thank you. For everything. I lived a full life. I don't want it to break you. I want you to keep living your own life, okay? Happily.'

A pause. 'O-okay.'

'I'll have died doing what I'm best at.'

'No you won't. You'll make it out.'

'I don't know,' King said. 'It's looking grim.'

'Don't say that.'

'But it was my choice to come here. Mine and mine alone. So it's no-one's fault. Don't blame anyone if it happens.'

'Okay.'

'Goodbye, Dad. I'll fight tooth and nail to get out of here. This call is just in case I don't make it.'

'Wait—'

King ended the conversation with the click of a button. He didn't want to drag it out unnecessarily. He let out an exhale filled with all the pent-up emotion in his chest. Staying on the phone any longer would have amplified the hurt.

And the fog of unconsciousness was settling over him with each passing second.

Emotionally and physically exhausted, pushed to the literal edge of what was tolerable, his eyes drooped and he fell into the sleep he had been so desperate to avoid.

CHAPTER 47

He didn't dream. His mind went dark. Every now and then a bolt of sensation from any one of his injuries penetrated the murky depths of his subconscious, reminding him that he was still alive.

He resurfaced from the darkness to a sea of bright lights above. He squinted against the glare, coming around slowly. He realised someone was tilting his head back, trying to force something between his teeth.

He raised a hand in protest.

'Painkillers,' a distant voice said. 'Found them in the cabinet. Swallow.'

He gulped the tablets down, beyond the point of protesting. He couldn't see who was delivering the medicine — some of his senses were still muddied, in a semi-conscious state. For all he knew, Mikhailov could have found him and forced poison down his throat.

He could have just complied to his own death.

The thought was ridiculous.

A bullet was faster and more efficient.

He almost welcomed the quick end. Anything to put him out of his misery.

Then — sometime later — the pain dulled slightly. Nowhere near enough to restore his abilities, but enough to clamber out of the slumber one last time.

He opened his eyes and gazed around the room.

The five health workers sat on the opposite side of the tables, watching him intently. He noticed their concerned looks.

'How long … have I been out?' he muttered. Sweat coated his face and the inside of his khakis.

Léo checked a grimy watch on one wrist. 'Almost seven hours.'

King's pulse rose. 'Fuck.'

He started to scramble off the chair but his nose burned hot and painful, forcing him back into the seat. He grimaced and felt his neck muscles twitch. The familiar headache sprouted back into life and his wrist became agonising.

He was nowhere near out of the woods yet.

'You haven't heard anything?' he said through clenched teeth.

Marcus shook his head. 'Nah, man. We kept wandering up to the mine shaft and checking it out. The elevator hasn't come back down yet.'

A thought flashed through King's mind.

Slater.

Was it possible? Had he eliminated everyone above?

'When's the last time you checked?' King said.

'I went twenty minutes ago,' Léo said. 'It doesn't sound good.'

'Sound?'

'There's noises drifting down from above. You can hear them pretty clearly. It sounds like there's twenty men up there. Speaking in Russian.'

Shit, King thought.

He ruled Slater out.

The Russians were gearing up to make a move. They didn't know how injured he was. Maybe they thought he had dispatched the first squad with ease.

They're preparing for an all-out assault…

'You're right,' King muttered. 'That doesn't sound good.'

'You can't fend them off any longer,' Léo said, looking him up and down. 'That's clear enough.'

'No,' King admitted. 'I can't.'

'I can't think of anything else to do except try. We can't hide. They'll flush us out.'

King nodded. Even that hurt. He grimaced and leant back in the chair.

They all heard it simultaneously. The soft metal thud of the elevator cage slamming home in the sub-levels.

King's pulse quickened.

Its arrival spelled their death.

Rising on shaky legs, he hefted the M4A1 off the table near his chair. He fished the final magazine out of his breast pocket and reloaded the carbine.

Thirty bullets.

That was all that was left.

The weapon was intensely heavy in his hands. It felt like a foreign object. He wondered if the injuries he'd suffered had affected his cognition…

There was only one way to find out.

'Stay here,' King said softly. Defeated before he had even set off into the mine.

'We're coming with you,' Léo said. 'More firepower.'

King shook his head. 'You stand more of a chance in here. Don't let anyone through that door. You hear me? Fight until the end.'

None of them responded. It seemed the sobering truth of the situation had finally struck them. Maybe they had been waiting for King to surface out of unconsciousness with a foolproof plan to survive.

He had nothing for them.

He could barely walk.

He limped to the door and swung it open. He stepped out into the gloomy tunnel and switched on the flashlight on the underside of his rifle. He swung the beam in the direction of the mine shaft and prepared to set off in what could only be described as a suicide mission.

Before he took his first step, he heard the approaching party.

There were at least ten of them this time. The sound of their gear rattling and shaking as they descended towards the production room spelled his inevitable death.

Then he picked up a fresh sound.

Close by.

In fact — right behind him.

The beating he'd suffered had thrown off his reaction speed. Before he could even begin to turn around, the cold barrel of a handgun touched the base of his neck.

'There is more than one way into this mine, my friend,' a voice said, laced with sadistic glee.

King bowed his head, recognising the inflection.

Mikhailov.

'Drop the rifle,' the man commanded.

King dropped the rifle.

'Hands on your head.'

King placed his hands on his head.

'Inside.'

Barely even making it a step out of the production room, he turned and strode through the open doorway. When he stepped back into the room the five workers stared at him with a mixture of confusion and panic.

Then they noticed the hulking brute holding a gun to King's head, and they froze in place.

Mikhailov gripped King by the back of the neck and hurled him into the same chair he'd been sleeping in moments earlier. He landed hard, sending pain flaring through his skull.

He let his shoulders roll forward, dejected. He had no weapon. No energy. His entire body throbbed with the culmination of the last twenty-four hours. He hadn't been expecting success when he stepped out of the production room. In fact, he had been mentally preparing himself for his own death.

The fact that he hadn't had the chance to die in combat crushed his morale.

And it would not be a faceless mercenary wearing a balaclava to do it.

It would be Mikhailov.

The one man who he wished nothing but death upon.

Through half-closed eyes he got a proper look at Mikhailov for the first time. The man was in similarly terrible shape. The blood had drained from his face, to the point where his skin had turned a mottled grey. It leaked from various bullet wounds which he hadn't had the chance to clean yet. As a result, his tattered uniform was coated in his own blood from head to toe.

He looked demonic, like something out of a horror movie.

Mikhailov stared around the room with rabid eyes, crazed by his injuries. His gaze flitted from man to man, sizing up the health workers, checking for weapons, satisfied that he had managed to gain the upper hand.

'You really think you could win?' he said to King.

King shook his head. 'No.'

'But you still marched forward anyway.'

'Yeah.'

'You faced your death like a man.'

King said nothing.

'I admire that,' Mikhailov said. 'At least you can die with some dignity.'

The big man turned to the party of health workers, leering at them. 'As for you five. Fuck, you have caused me some issues. You will die slowly. Pathetically. I'll enjoy it.'

'What makes you think you'll be the one to do it?' King said.

Mikhailov turned to him. 'What?'

'You told me yourself. The viewers aren't going to be happy that you compromised their privacy. You'll die alongside us.'

'They might kill me. But I have time. Time to prepare.'

'No you don't.'

Mikhailov hesitated.

'Didn't you hear the elevator arrive?' King said.

'You're bluffing.'

King laughed.

It seemed that Mikhailov's hearing had been affected by his wounds. The man was likely swimming in a state of delirium — just as King was. Clawing along with the satisfaction that he would get the last laugh. He thought he would be the one to put a bullet into King's skull.

'You haven't been in contact with anyone since you left the mine,' King said, vocalising his realisation. 'You've been hiding up top. Licking your wounds. Scared to get in touch with your superiors because they'll kill you for it.'

Mikhailov stared at him blankly, his face just as pale as before.

'You have no idea what's going on,' King said. 'They're already sending teams of mercenaries into the mine. I've dealt with one already.'

The commotion outside the production room reached a fever pitch. Rapid footsteps echoed down the tunnel as the second hit squad descended on them.

'Here's one now,' King muttered. 'Good luck talking your way out of this.'

They swarmed in through the open doorway like wraiths, silent and determined. King had been close in his initial estimate. Eight men filed into the room one-by-one, each dressed identically to their previous comrades. They were big, imposing, hard men — wearing fatigued Russian military uniform, their faces all covered by woollen balaclavas. The masks exposed nothing but their cruel eyes, eyes that passed clinically over the room, sizing up the situation.

There was no need to open fire just yet.

Their manpower was too strong.

All eight men wielded giant Kalashnikov assault rifles, all state-of-the-art, all brand new. As Mikhailov had confirmed before, the viewers had money to spare. The men fanned out inside the suddenly cramped room, training the barrels of their weapons on its occupants.

Mikhailov watched them enter with wide eyes. He let out a burst of panicked Russian, attempting to reason with the mercenaries. They disregarded him. One of them raised his Kalashnikov silently and pressed it against the back of Mikhailov's skull. The man muttered something low and threatening.

A command.

Mikhailov complied, dropping his weapon. He fell to his knees, landing heavily against the rock floor.

King scoffed and closed his eyes. 'You die with us, my friend.'

The mercenary closest to him barked an order in Russian and aimed a Kalashnikov at the side of his head. King understood.

Shut up.

He slumped into the chair, forcing himself not to hyperventilate. He couldn't fight back. There were too many of them. Even if he killed one, or two, or three, the rest would gun him down in a heartbeat.

In his current state, he didn't think he could even manage getting out of his chair.

He let the pain in, hoping that would take him before the Russians could. Maintaining an illusion of calm was his only objective. He wanted the health workers to die as painlessly as possible. If they didn't see him panicking, they might maintain some semblance of hope.

One of the masked men moved behind King's chair and seized him by the throat, clasping a gloved hand against his neck — which had already turned purple from the choke hold applied hours earlier. He yanked King into an upright position in the chair.

King spluttered, all his bones aching. He closed his eyes and waited for the killing shot through the top of his head.

That was the most effective way to do it.

The mercenary leant down and muttered in his ear, 'You might need this.'

King felt cold steel in his right palm.

He froze.

He had just been passed a weapon…

But that wasn't what made him hesitate. He had been shocked by the voice.

It wasn't Russian. He recognised the accent.

American.

'*What the fuck,*' he muttered through split lips.

Will Slater — his features still covered by the thick balaclava — lurched up and unleashed a storm of gunfire upon the room.

CHAPTER 48

Pandemonium struck.

In the confined space, the unsuppressed Kalashnikov rounds were deafening. King lost his hearing within the first three shots — but he didn't need it to survive.

He surged forward with the fully-loaded MP-443 Grach that Slater had placed in his hand a second earlier. Newfound energy seized him, invigorating him.

He gunned Mikhailov down first.

The brute only had time to widen his eyes at the revelation before King brought the barrel of his pistol up and blasted his forehead into pulp. Mikhailov collapsed to the floor, unequivocally dead.

The four mercenaries around him — two on each side — jolted and jerked as lead ripped through their delicate skin. Slater unloaded his weapon with the clinical precision of an elite soldier.

Two shots per man, targeting the neck and face, causing irreparable damage to everything his bullets touched.

Health workers and mercenaries alike dove for cover.

King sprawled onto the ground, still capitalising on the confusion. He fired twice more, gunning down the man closest to him. The guy keeled over, dropping his weapon in the process. In a single swift manoeuvre King caught his Kalashnikov in the air and turned it on the remaining mercenaries.

He and Slater fired at the same time — two sets of pinpoint-accurate automatic gunfire that decimated the last two men. They didn't even have time to return fire. Bullets plastered the wall behind them, with the rest slicing through internal organs and tissue.

They fell in unison.

The deafening gunfire ceased, replaced with barrel smoke and an intense ringing in King's ears. He staggered, shocked by what had unfolded. The carnage had begun so quickly that he hadn't had time to process anything. Now, he stood in silence and registered the chaos that had taken place.

Eight men — including Mikhailov — were dead, their vital organs torn to shreds by his and Slater's rounds. The health workers had flattened themselves to the ground, pressing their hands over their heads in a vain attempt to protect themselves from crossfire.

It had worked.

For a fleeting, terrifying moment, King thought they were dead. Then they lifted their heads — one by one — surveying the scene in stunned awe.

King opened his mouth to reassure them, but he had gone temporarily deaf from the blistering reports. He flapped his lips like a dying fish, still stunned.

He turned to Slater.

The man peeled off his balaclava, revealing the same pearly white teeth and high cheekbones that he remembered from Corsica. King hadn't seen him since he had commandeered a private chopper and fled from Black Force over a month ago.

Slater said something, but all King heard was a high-pitched whining in his ears. A wave of nausea overwhelmed him and he dropped back into the same chair, breathing hard.

The adrenalin of the shootout had come from somewhere primal. There hadn't been a shred of energy in his body when Slater handed him the pistol. He had called on his final reserves, drawing from a place deep inside his subconscious to aid him one last time.

Now, he had nothing left in the tank.

The tinnitus dulled, providing slight relief. The whining had become near unbearable, piercing into his skull with all the grace of a charging bull. Now it settled, and certain sounds returned to the edge of his hearing.

Slater crouched in front of him. King tried to focus on the man but his sight had seemingly lost its ability to function properly. Blurry shapes swam on the edges of his vision.

'You're in bad shape,' he heard Slater say.

'Yeah,' he mumbled. 'Not good.'

'Let's get you lot out of here.'

King paused. 'How… did you get here?'

'I hijacked a private jet at V.C. Bird International Airport. A Gulfstream. The pilots were refuelling for their client — some kind of energy tycoon. We barely made it off the ground — ATC suspected foul play as soon as we requested to take off early.'

'You flew straight here?'

'They had enough fuel. And — thankfully — an emergency parachute on board. I left the aircraft over the exact co-ordinates you gave me. Landed a mile away, in the middle of nowhere. Rough landing, too…'

'They saw you coming?'

'No-one was watching.'

'Your uniform,' King muttered, gesturing to the dull khakis Slater was dressed in. The kit was identical to the dead mercenaries' outfits.

'Took me twenty minutes to find the place. By that point, this lot had arrived. They weren't paying attention to approaching combatants. All of them were focused on gearing up for the descent. Preparing for combat. They didn't expect a thing.'

'How'd you do it?'

'One of them had stepped away from the rest of the group. He lit up a cigarette — psyching himself up for the big attack, probably. I dealt with him and changed clothes.'

'Goddamn…'

'It was chaos up there — you should have seen it. They were all shitting their pants. Had you already killed some of them?'

'Five men,' King said softly. 'The first team they sent in. They didn't come back.'

'That unnerved them,' Slater said. 'From what I could gather, they'd been sent with minimal orders from Moscow. All they knew was that the mine had to be cleared. Everyone had to be killed.'

'So you mingled?'

'It didn't take long. I hovered around until they decided to head in. I couldn't kill them up there. Too much open space. I needed close-quarters carnage. Tight spaces and confusion.'

King gave a half-smile. 'Great minds think alike.'

'You need a hospital,' Slater said. He scooped an arm around King and helped him tentatively to his feet. 'Where's Isla?'

No response.

'King,' Slater said. 'Where's the pick-up point?'

'I don't know.'

'What?'

'I'm kind of winging it here.'

Slater hesitated. 'That's right. This is your personal thing, isn't it?'

'No,' King said. 'It's Isla's.'

Silence.

After a long beat, Slater said, 'She sent you in here?'

King nodded.

'You didn't know it was unofficial, did you?'

King shook his head.

'That fucking *bitch*.'

'Tell me about it,' King muttered. 'Let's focus on getting back on home soil first. Then we can deal with all that.'

'*You* can.'

King turned his head to look at Slater. 'Will…'

'I'm not going back,' Slater said. 'They'll kill me. Or lock me away in a military prison for the rest of my life.'

'They didn't kill me,' King said. 'And I did the same as you. They welcomed mc with opcn arms.'

'You didn't just disappear. I went AWOL. They won't forgive that. You know it as well as I do.'

'I don't think I can get back on my own,' King admitted, wincing as more agony coursed through him.

'I'll help you back,' Slater said. 'Then I'm gone.'

'They'll arrest you.'

'I don't think so.'

King cast his eyes over the production room floor, littered with the dead bodies of Slater's enemies. He shrugged. 'Point taken.'

Slater leant over the desk and snatched up the phone. He handed it to King. 'Make the call.'

King's vision wavered. He reached for the number pad with trembling fingers, then stopped. 'Dial for me. You know her private line.'

Slater hesitated. Then he punched in a long string of numbers and handed the phone to King.

The call connected immediately, and was answered with reserved silence. King paused, unnerved by her unresponsiveness. Then he realised the number was unknown to her.

'Isla,' he said. 'It's King.'

'Oh my god!' Isla yelled. 'I've been doing everything to get in touch. What the *fuck* have you done?!'

He paused, shocked by the outburst. 'What…?'

'What did you do? Who did you piss off?'

'What are you talking about, Isla?' he said.

'Please don't tell me you're anywhere near Shiveluch Volcano.'

He paused. 'I am.'

'*Get out*,' she demanded, her voice more panicked than he had ever heard it. 'Get the fuck out, right now.'

'What's going on?'

'I don't know who you infuriated, but the Russians are trying to wipe you out. They just launched an ICBM. It's directed at the Kamchatka Peninsula. They're bombing themselves with the most powerful non-nuclear ballistic missile in their arsenal.'

CHAPTER 49

Terror seized King in its icy grasp. He felt it flood through his limbs, lending him a sudden spike in his heart rate. He sat up straight in the chair.

'*Isla*,' he hissed. 'Get in touch with your superiors. Shoot it down. We'll all die if you can't.'

'I'm not hiding this from my superiors,' she said. 'As soon as I lost contact with you, I turned myself in.'

'Where are you?'

'Don't worry about me. It's too late for me. I'm responsible for my own mistakes. Get yourself out of there.'

'Shoot it down,' he repeated.

'We can't. There's nothing we can do to stop them bombing their own territory. Do you want the exact co-ordinates of the suspected impact zone?'

'Yes.'

She relayed them to him. He checked them against the latitude and longitude still displayed on the computer monitor and swore viciously.

'That's us,' he said. 'They're destroying the mine and all the land around it. Eliminating all evidence.'

'What?'

'Don't worry. You're sure it's not a nuke?'

'We don't think so. Get yourself as many miles away as you can. If you avoid the blast radius you should be okay.'

How long?'

'Six minutes, by our calculations.'

King tossed the phone away.

Slater stood poised in the centre of the room, charged with nervous energy. 'What the hell was that about?'

'We need to be miles away from here in six minutes,' King said. 'The Russians just launched a missile at us.'

Slater froze. He gestured to the dead men around him. 'Why would they do that? They still think their men are in here.'

'Collateral,' King said, rising off the chair. 'They don't care. They're turning all record of this operation into a scorching crater.'

'Why?'

'Protecting their identities.'

King saw it dawn on Slater's face that the situation wasn't infeasible. He watched the man suppress panic and spur the five terrified health workers into action.

'The elevator!' he commanded. *'Go.* Right now.'

They took off in a cloud of fear, limbs scrambling against the rock. One by one they tore around the open doorway and sprinted into the darkness of the tunnels.

King lurched forward and stumbled off-balance. He screamed silently at his legs to work, but his body wasn't listening to his mind. He thought he might pass out from the exertion.

Slater seized him under the arms and hauled him towards the door, carrying most of King's weight across his straining muscles. King staggered as best he could. They rounded the corner and plunged into the depths of the mine.

'Leave me,' King muttered.

'Shut up.'

'I'm serious.'

'So am I.'

'I shouldn't have asked you to come.'

'We can make it.'

King heard Slater bare his teeth and pick up the pace, desperation charging his system. He willed himself forward with everything he had left, focusing on putting one foot in front of the other.

'*Five minutes,*' he whispered, terrified.

'Don't think about it,' Slater said.

'Do you know where you're going?'

'Not a clue.'

King grunted in frustration and slapped the side of his head with his good hand, trying to shock his system into focusing. Barely able to keep conscious, he brought up the makeshift map of the tunnel system in his head. It was up to him to guide them out of the maze. Otherwise they would get lost in the shadows, and a ballistic missile would detonate above their heads.

The mine would implode.

They would be crushed under millions of tons of falling rock.

He shook the thought away and concentrated. Sweat dripped off the bridge of his shattered nose.

'Right, here.'

Slater wheeled him around the bend. They powered up an incline. King felt himself slipping. One of his legs gave out, and he scrambled for purchase on the smooth ground.

For a terrifying instant, he toppled backwards.

Slater snatched him by the collar and wrenched him back on course. 'Don't you fucking dare give up on me now.'

'Understood,' King whispered. It was all he could manage.

Head pounding, eyes watering, nose and wrist screaming for relief, senses fading, he ran.

Once he built up momentum, he tore Slater's hands away from supporting him.

'Let's go,' he snarled. 'I've got this.'

Together they sprinted through the underground maze, running with animalistic fervour. King let instincts take over. He wasn't sure how he stayed upright. He pumped his arms and legs like pistons, tearing down the cramped tunnel towards the mine shaft.

'What if the elevator's not there?' Slater said.

King shook the thought off and pushed forward. If anything sapped his will, his legs would give out and he would be helpless.

He couldn't see. Couldn't hear. Couldn't think.

'*Left!*' he roared.

In unison they exploded out into the wider tunnel. If he had got it right, the mine shaft was directly ahead. As they skidded into the final stretch, King heard panicked shouts of encouragement up ahead.

Running blind, he forced his legs to reach top speed.

The elevator was there.

The five health workers waited inside.

They screamed for Slater and King to hurry.

They powered through the open cage doors and crashed into the far wall of the elevator. King collided with someone at full pelt, who let out a grunt of surprise.

It was Léo.

Still thriving off the terror of time ticking away, King snatched blindly for the remote fixed into the side of the elevator wall. None of them had a flashlight to see with. They were fumbling in sheer black.

He found the steel device and crushed all the buttons at once, pleading for the elevator to ascend.

The steel cable — fixed into the roof of the cage — groaned.

With a jolt of momentum, they started to rise.

It was slow. Painfully slow.

There was no way to speed up the process, so King slapped himself in the cheek as the elevator crawled towards the surface.

Stay conscious, he begged with himself. *Just stay conscious.*

He heard panicked rasping close by. One of the health workers was hyperventilating.

'Breathe deep,' Slater commanded. Somehow, he managed to keep his voice from wavering. His calm tone allowed the man to settle.

'Th-thanks, man,' the guy spluttered. It was Marcus.

The seven of them pressed shoulder-to-shoulder in the cramped cage, all silently willing the elevator to rise faster.

'How long do we have?' King said. His head drooped involuntarily, nostrils flaring with what felt like liquid fire. He let out a gasp and forced the pain back down.

Not now, he thought. *Not yet. Stay awake.*

'I don't know,' Slater said. 'Don't focus on that.'

'What vehicles do they have up there?' King said. 'We need to be ready.'

'There's a few all-terrain vehicles,' Slater said. 'Like modified rally cars. I'd say that's how they got into the peninsula so quickly.'

'Anything else?'

'I saw a cluster of snowmobiles.'

King let his commanding instincts take over, instructing the health workers even on the edge of consciousness. 'You five pile into one of the big ATVs. I'm assuming you'll be able to start it up, but if they've removed the keys, move to the snowmobiles. Two men per snowmobile. Fire them up with the pull start mechanisms and get the fuck away from the warehouse.'

They murmured their understanding. Léo piped up. 'What about you?'

'I'm slower,' King said. 'Don't want to hold you back. Focus on yourselves.'

Light spilled into the mine shaft above their heads. King craned his neck and saw the faint glow of the warehouse lights.

They were close.

'You all ready?' he said.

He saw their outlines now. The five men nodded in turn. He saw their terrified faces, their shaking hands and quivering legs. He saw the sweat dripping from their pores.

This was a different kind of fear.

'Don't look back,' King said. 'Just drive. Got it?'

More nods.

The elevator slammed home, jolting to a stop at ground level. The mine cage took a second to open as an internal mechanism activated the doors. They swung outward, spurred by an electronic command.

The seven occupants of the elevator ran for the vehicles like men possessed.

CHAPTER 50

Two steps out of the elevator, King blacked out.

There was a sharp pop inside his head, horrifying in its intensity. His vision disappeared — like a sheet had been draped over his head. He still had feeling in his limbs, but he felt them give.

He had reached the point of no return.

He couldn't take another step.

He fell face-first towards the concrete floor of the warehouse.

A strong hand slammed against his chest, halting him in his tracks. He felt his feet lift off the ground, and something hard and bony drove into his stomach. He blinked hard, and his vision returned for an instant.

A single flash of colour.

Slater had him draped over one shoulder, powering across the warehouse floor with King in a fireman's carry. King's head dropped and he lost all consciousness.

Bang.

For what felt like the hundredth time, he jolted back to reality. It hit him in a whirling pool of distorted images. Nothing felt real.

Except the gravity of the situation.

This time, he stayed conscious.

Overwhelming brightness flooded his vision.

Daylight.

It had been far too long since King had experienced it.

Despite his shaky grasp on reality and the unbearable pain searing through his nerve endings and the ballistic missile roaring toward their location, he felt relief as the claustrophobia fell away.

He stared out at open plains for miles in all directions. It was a gloomy day — he guessed mid-afternoon. The sky held a canopy of grey, overcast storm clouds. King glanced up at them and gulped back terror.

None of them would see the missile coming until it was right on top of them.

Slater had dumped him on the back of a snowmobile. The impact had shocked his system into activation. Through half-closed eyes he saw the health workers piling into a military-style buggy with thick all-terrain tyres. Léo leapt into the driver's seat and stamped on the accelerator. The car rocketed away in the other direction, speeding into a patch of forest and disappearing from sight.

King glanced down at the snowmobile he rested on and noticed how different it was to the ones he had previously commandeered. This looked to be five times the price and five times the horsepower. Mikhailov had resources to spare, it seemed.

'How long... do we have?' he said, struggling to form the words.

Slater didn't respond. The man pull-started the snowmobile with a single, vicious tug of the ripcord. The engine roared to life.

There was sheer desperation in Slater's eyes. He was focused on nothing but getting them away from the impact zone, ignoring everything else.

'How long?' King barked, louder.

'A minute,' Slater said. 'Maybe two.'

Slater swung a leg over the seat, slotting into the space between King and the handlebars. He wrenched the throttle before he was even seated. The rear tracks screamed into motion, kicking up two plumes of white powder behind the vehicle.

The snowmobile shot off the mark.

It was certainly high-powered. King snatched the back of Slater's jacket with sweaty hands, preventing himself from tumbling off the back of the seat from the burst of sudden momentum. He held tight as Slater hunched low and gave the engine everything it had.

Biting wind whipped at their clothing. King's vision blurred against the intense chill. He shielded his eyes with a single hand and twisted in his seat, looking back at the warehouse. The building — and its surroundings cliffs — shrank into the distance with each passing second.

Would it be enough?

He could hardly see. Snowmobiles with this kind of power required helmets and visors to protect from the elements. Falling snow and sleet lashed against his face. They tore through the gloom, pushing faster, abandoning all caution.

Slater turned his head and screamed over his shoulder. 'What's the blast radius?!'

'I don't know!' King roared back. 'Could be up to a mile. Depends what kind of firepower they're using.'

Slater glanced at the speedometer behind the handlebars. 'We're not there yet.'

They shot forward into a stretch of land devoid of all vegetation. The ground was dead flat for as far as the eye could see. King cocked his head as he looked out over the desolate plain. It contrasted with the mountainous terrain he had become accustomed to in this region.

Something wasn't right.

'What is this?' he yelled. 'Where are we?'

'What do you mean?'

'It's too flat.'

Slater paused. 'Let me check the map.'

He kept the pressure on the throttle, but reached into one of the pockets built into his khakis at thigh-level. He extracted a small weatherproof device with a digital screen displaying a satellite image. He squinted and shielded his eyes from the slicing wind, peering hard at the picture.

'Oh, fuck.'

King went pale. 'What?'

Slater tucked the device back into his pocket and snatched the handlebars in shaking hands. Eyes wide, he changed course, aiming the snowmobile diagonally to the right. The rear tracks almost slid out on the ground below. For the first time King noticed the change in texture. The land beneath their snowmobile felt hard.

Like ice.

'We're on Kharchinskoye Lake,' Slater yelled. 'All this ice is going to break when the missile hits.'

'Jesus Christ...'

They heard it. An ominous rumbling in the sky, growing steadily closer. King twisted again and peered back.

'*Go!*' he roared at Slater.

The missile shot through the clouds, just over a mile behind them. It could have weighed thousands of pounds for all he knew. From this distance, it appeared as a flaming streak that sliced through the gloomy canopy of the storm. He glimpsed it arcing toward the cliffs for a brief second.

Then it flashed against the peninsula — impacting almost directly on top of the mine — and detonated.

King turned away, shielding his eyes from the blast. Without any kind of visual on the explosion, it became a waiting game.

The shockwave hit first.

The ground all around them screamed and rumbled as the vast sheet of ice coating the frozen lake tore apart. An invisible barrier of displaced air punched King in the back, smashing all the wind out of his lungs.

He gasped as the sensation blasted through him.

They were far too close to the impact zone.

The snowmobile underneath them almost lifted off the ground from the force of the shockwave. Its rear tracks went airborne for a split second. Slater careered into the handlebars, precariously close to hurtling over the hood.

When the vehicle slammed back onto the ice, it found nothing to support its weight.

The front skis dipped into the freezing lake, catching against the dark body of water.

With such a drastic loss in forward motion, the snowmobile simply stopped.

King went airborne. He twisted, limbs flailing. Wind and snow and shattered ice pounded his face, numbing him to the experience. His swollen nose had almost forced his eyes shut entirely, blinding him to the landing area.

He hit the surface of Kharchinskoye Lake upside-down at close to fifty miles an hour.

Silence.

CHAPTER 51

The impact didn't knock him out, but it might as well have.

Immediately, he lost all sensation from the neck down. The water was arctic, so cold that it took a horrendous, gut-wrenching effort just to tread water. The icy swell splashed over his face, aggravating his wounds.

He had foolishly lifted his broken wrist in front of his face before landing, an instinctual reaction to being thrown from a vehicle at speed. The plunge into the lake would have ground the broken bones against each other, worsening the injury.

At least he couldn't feel it.

The effects of exhaustion took over. The sheet of ice had almost entirely disintegrated, shattering under the force of the blast radius. Fragmented chunks had drifted away from where King and Slater had landed. He spun uselessly, searching for anything to hold onto.

It only took a few seconds for the lake to start dragging him down.

The weight of his gear swamped him. The heavy combat boots, the thick khakis, the cold-weather jackets and bulletproof vest. It all tightened around him, constricting him as the material filled with water and dragged on him like a deadweight.

His nose and mouth dipped below the surface. The last shreds of energy left in his bones began to fade.

A firm hand seized the back of his collar, wrenching him above surface level. He gasped and spluttered, treading water to complement the added help. He spun to see Slater dragging him through the icy water, face scrunched up in determination.

The man's eyes had turned hard and emotionless. All his attention was focused on a single objective — survival. He had shed his heavy jacket, wearing nothing but a tight compression shirt. He kept King from sinking with one hand, and used the other to swim. He kicked out, his strokes measured and powerful.

King swam weakly, lending what assistance he could, but it proved futile. Slater was responsible for almost all of the effort. Without his help, King knew he wouldn't last ten seconds above water.

It was a terrifying predicament.

Broken, beaten, vision swimming and ears ringing, his pathetic strokes gave way to exhaustion. A moment later they stopped altogether. He lost all sense of time, succumbing to either the mind-numbing pain in his broken bones or the hypothermic reaction to the arctic waters.

Either a minute or an hour later, his hands drooped…

…and touched solid ground.

With a final, all-encompassing heave of effort, Slater thrust him ashore.

King sprawled into a dirty puddle of snow and slush. He reached through the mushy layer and felt hard earth beneath. His teeth chattered relentlessly. Steam clouded in front of his face with each breath, and freezing water leaked from all facets of his clothes.

He dropped his forehead into the sludge and willed for his breathing to return to normal. Each inhale came in a rattling gasp, and the subsequent exhales sent him into spluttering coughing fits. He lifted his head to see a gargantuan plume of smoke rising in the distance. The blast had obliterated an entire section of the peninsula.

The mine — and all evidence of its secret purpose — had been demolished in a single attack.

Slater crawled onto the shore beside him and slumped in a heap, breathing just as hard. They lay in the sludge as the minutes ticked by, surrounded by desolation and emptiness. King wished for a relief from the agony. He wished for a warm bed and a long period of time where he didn't have to worry for his life.

He looked back to where they had swum from. Kharchinskoye Lake dwarfed them. The ice had shattered to reveal a sweeping stretch of dark arctic water. If the missile strike had destroyed the ground underneath them a few moments earlier, they never would have made it to shore. The distance would have been too great.

Slater's last-second effort to correct course for the nearest edge of the lake had saved them.

'That was a hell of a swim,' King said through shaking teeth.

Slater groaned as he rolled onto his back. The journey had sapped him of all strength. 'I didn't make it this far to die in a fucking lake.'

'I would have. I don't know how you did it.'

'I haven't taken the same amount of punishment as you. You looked like you were on death's door when I found you.'

'I still am.'

'Well, don't knock yet. We're almost out of this.'

King took a moment to gaze out in all directions. Nothing for dozens of miles.

No civilisation.

No aid.

'How?' King said. 'How do you propose we get out of this?'

Slater extracted the slim satellite device from his pocket. 'I can make the call.'

King hesitated. 'You said you wouldn't do that. You know Black Force won't be happy if you return.'

'I don't see an alternative.'

'Wait for the WHO guys to find us,' King said. 'Then disappear. Stick to the plan.'

'I don't know, King. I feel like you're going to need me.'

'What do you mean?'

'You said you were here unofficially.'

'I am.'

'Isla sent you.'

King paused a beat, considering whether he should share the news. 'One of the workers was Isla's sister.'

'Sister…' Slater muttered.

King knew what he was thinking. Slater hadn't seen a woman in the mine.

'She's dead.'

'Oh.'

'And you're right,' King said. 'We're fucked. Her and I both. I decided to continue through with it, even after I found out it was a ruse. We're both accountable for it.'

'What was your thinking behind that?'

'I knew the workers were in trouble. I wanted to bring them back silently. Without making a scene. I thought I could manage.'

Slater turned to look at the gaping wound in the peninsula. As the residue from the blast cleared, King noticed that the land had been scorched, the snow incinerated. The wind turned and the sweeping trails of smoke began to arc in their direction.

'You certainly made a scene,' Slater said.

'I know. So you need to get out of here. They don't know you're here. Keep your profile low, and maybe they'll forget all about you while they deal with Isla and I.'

Slater shook his head. 'I'm in this with you. You only returned to Black Force because of my departure. I'd be a coward to run away a second time.'

'Slater…'

It was too late. By then the man had dialled a number and pressed the device to his ear.

'Isla,' King heard as he slumped back into the snow. 'It's Will Slater.'

CHAPTER 52

The fishing village rested on the edge of the Kamchatka Peninsula, tucked into an alcove of the craggy landscape. It was composed of a small community of identical weatherboard houses designed to withstand the raging coastal storms that buffeted the coastline. Sturdy warehouses lined the piers that jutted out into the churning waters of the Pacific Ocean. Large commercial trawlers and smaller vessels were docked in a plethora of marinas, most left unattended. The disastrous weather had limited operations for the day.

King's jaw rattled as the buggy bounced across uneven terrain. It screeched to a halt at the top of a mountain trail that spiralled down towards the coastline. From his position in the back seat, he had an unobstructed view over the village. He pulled the official WHO jacket a little tighter around his quaking shoulders and sucked in a deep breath through his open mouth.

'This is it?' he called over the howling wind.

'I think so,' Slater said, sitting behind the wheel. 'Could have picked a better day for the rendezvous.'

He touched the accelerator and set off precariously down the narrow gravel trail.

The five health workers had found them several hours ago, only minutes before King was set to turn hypothermic. He had experienced the sensation before, and knew all the warning signs. First, the loss of feeling in his limbs. Then a strange warmth in his core, a natural reaction as his body began to cave into the mind-numbing cold.

His vision had started to fade when the crunching of dirt under all-terrain tyres sounded nearby.

Léo had taken the initiative, peeling most of King's soaked clothing off and replacing it with dry garments from the workers' own bodies. Slater received similar treatment, as his temperature had also plummeted after the call with Isla had ended.

King hadn't heard much of the conversation that Slater had with his old employer, but it had certainly seemed terse.

They had been instructed to make the journey to the nearest coastline and await further instructions.

Now, the storm raged all around them as the buggy descended into the fishing village. Slater steered through potholed dirt streets, attracting the curious gazes of a handful of weather-beaten locals. King inhaled freezing air, unable to breathe through his nose due to the swelling. His eyes and the inside of his mouth stung from exposure to the elements.

He had experienced enough cold for a lifetime.

The five health workers were squashed into the available seats. All of them sat in stunned silence. They had barely spoken since rescuing King and Slater from the edge of Kharchinskoye Lake. It could be due to any number of reasons — shell-shock from the narrow escape, a depletion of their energy reserves or simple overwhelming sensory overload.

King wasn't bothered.

He didn't exactly feel like talking either.

They reached a rundown marina — home to several groups of fishermen unloading their haul from moored trawlers. Perhaps the conditions had been right for fishing this morning. Rain lashed the piers, but the hardened men and women seemed accustomed to the conditions. They set about their work with weather-lined faces, uninterested in the storm.

Slater shepherded the health workers out of the vehicle, gesturing for them to make their way single-file down one of the piers. He looped an arm around King's waist and helped him along the slippery wood. King appreciated the assistance.

He had reached the end of his limits.

They were approached by an ageing local, shocked by the appearance of outsiders. King imagined the remote location of this village meant that visitors were an astonishing rarity.

Slater took the lead, striding forward to shake the man's hand. King couldn't hear what was said above the wind, but the conversation lasted just over two minutes. Slater spoke animatedly — King quickly realised the man was fluent in Russian. He gestured first to the modified buggy, bringing the expensive vehicle to the man's attention. Then he pointed to one of the smaller boats in the marina — a rusting carcass of a vessel, barely holding itself together.

The man shrugged, then nodded.

He exchanged a set of keys with Slater.

Slater returned to the party, jangling the keys for them all to see.

'We have a boat,' he said.

'Why do we need a boat?' King said.

'Isla's on a Nimitz-class aircraft carrier, several hundred miles off the coast. They're sending a Navy chopper to extract us a few miles offshore — we attract less attention that way. I called her when you were passed out on the drive here.'

Léo turned his gaze to the frothing waves slamming home against the coastline. 'We're going out into that?'

'You can handle a few waves,' Slater said. 'Especially given what you've been through over the last day.'

'True,' the man said.

King had no words of protest.

He had no words at all.

In fact, by this point he didn't think he could manage an audible syllable.

They filed down to the ancient fishing trawler and climbed aboard one-by-one. Slater went first, leaping over a sizeable gap. He found a wooden plank resting against one of the plastic benches and shimmied it across to the pier. The health workers crossed the board precariously. King went last, taking his time with his footing. When he made it onto the main deck he slumped into one of the hard plastic seats and drooped his head, ignoring the rain lashing against him.

A hand clamped down on his shoulder.

Groggily, he raised his head.

'All good, brother?' Slater said.

King nodded.

'We'll be home soon.'

King grimaced. 'That's what I'm worried about.'

'Don't be. You've got me by your side.'

King smirked wryly and shook his head. 'You're only going down with me, Slater. Now's your last chance. I'm telling you. They won't forgive this.'

'They shouldn't have to forgive this. You did the right thing.'

'Not in their eyes.'

'Whose, exactly?'

King shrugged. 'We'll find out.'

Slater gave him a reassuring look, then climbed a rusty steel ladder and disappeared inside the wheelhouse. The five health workers dropped into the seats all around King as the trawler chugged to life.

'How the hell does he know how to drive one of these things?' Léo muttered.

'He knows a lot of things,' King said. 'Resourceful guy.'

'What were you two talking about before? I overheard something, but I wasn't sure if I was interpreting it the right way.'

King closed his eyes as the trawler peeled away from the marina and churned through the seawater, heading out into open ocean. 'That's a long, complicated story, Léo. Let's just worry about getting you home safe.'

'Are you going to be okay?'

'I'll be fine.'

They crested a sizeable wave and the deck rattled, aggravating King's injuries. He gulped back nausea and hunched lower, bracing against the storm.

CHAPTER 53

By the time the Russian shoreline had faded into a hazy blur, King had thrown up twice in the space of a minute. He wasn't sure if it was his injuries that had made him so nauseous.

He didn't ordinarily get seasick.

If he did, he never would have made it through SEAL training all those years ago.

The six of them sat rigid on the main deck, clenching nearby handholds with white knuckles. Slater was somewhere in the wheelhouse, guiding the trawler through the madness. Their surroundings were an unidentifiable blur of dark clouds and dark waves. Sheets of rain lashed the side of the boat, slashing sideways through the air due to the scything wind.

The painkillers given to him in the mine hours earlier had all but faded away. Their effect had been futile, but they had enabled him to function. Now, every waking moment was spent concentrating on the mental torment. He figured one of his ribs was broken. Although it had been dulled earlier, each breath came with a rattling jolt of pain in his mid-section. He couldn't breathe out of his nose. His left hand had swollen beyond belief. Patches of skin around his wrist were starting to turn purple, as was much of his face.

He needed serious medical assistance — and an extended vacation.

Something told him that would not be on the agenda anytime soon.

A few minutes later, the distinctive sound of thrumming helicopter propellers sounded on the horizon.

They heard the aerial beast well before it came into view. The low-hanging storm clouds masked visibility, but the roar of the chopper drowned out everything else.

'Can you hear that?' Léo gasped, shocked by the intensity of the noise. All five of the health workers cast their eyes skyward.

'That's them,' King said.

He heard Slater kill the engine. The trawler halted its forward trajectory and settled to a halt in the roiling seas. King gripped a nearby handrail to steady himself and looked for the military chopper.

It sounded like a CH-53E Super Stallion.

That was the only kind of helicopter capable of creating such an imposing sound.

The behemoth descended into view, directly above them. King peered up at the vast steel underbelly of the Sikorsky chopper. He spotted noticeable differences in the design — specifically a wider cargo hold, easily capable of fitting a Humvee within its fuselage.

Slater stepped out of the wheelhouse, dropping onto the deck beside King.

King pointed up at the chopper. 'You ever seen one of those?'

He scrutinised it. 'Last I heard they were still in production.'

'They're bigger.'

'I'm guessing this is a prototype.'

'What are they?'

'CH-53K's,' Slater said, then regarded King with a grin. 'King Stallions.'

'You're joking.'

'I can assure you the name's a coincidence. Unless you really are the stuff of legend amongst the Armed Forces.'

'I don't think the Armed Forces know either of us exist.'

Slater grimaced. 'We might not exist for much longer.'

Before King could consider the weight of the statement, the CH-53K came to a hover about a hundred feet above the trawler. The gargantuan rear ramp descended, and thick cables unspooled off the edge. King counted four separate hoists — each outfitted with a search-and-rescue style safety harness.

The cables thumped onto the deck, one after the other.

King and Slater set to work.

Between them, they had over two decades of training in hostage extraction. They moved clinically to each of the WHO workers, instructing them on what was about to occur before strapping them into the full-body harnesses. With four cables to deal with, they secured all the men but Léo, who would go up with King and Slater on the following round.

When safety checks had been completed, King stared up at the hovering beast and flashed a thumbs-up with his good hand.

The four terrified men were whisked into the air.

As King waited for the first wave to disembark into the military chopper above, a thought struck him. He felt the trawler shudder underneath his feet as a frothing wave lashed at its hull.

'They could leave us here,' he muttered to Slater. 'This boat's going to fall apart. It'd eliminate the problem of having to deal with us officially.'

'They won't deal with us officially anyway,' Slater said. 'Nothing about us has ever been official.'

'You still have the chance to leave.'

'Not anymore, brother.'

The empty harnesses dropped off the rear ramp again, signalling that the first four men were secure on board. They unspooled quicker than the first time, hitting the deck within seconds.

Slater secured Léo while King struggled into one of the harnesses. As he slipped the worn material over his left shoulder, he caught his broken wrist in an awkward position. He gulped back another wave of pain and secured the automatic locking system against his chest.

Slater did the same.

A moment later, King felt the sharp tug under his armpits and the trawler fell away from his feet.

The unmanned boat rocked and bucked in the storm, pounded by the churning seas. King squinted as he rose in the air, rain blasting him in thick sheets. Finally, the cables dragged them over the lip of the rear ramp and they touched down on the metal.

King got to his feet, looking through to the interior of the chopper.

The CH-53K's fuselage was enormous, at least thirty feet long and nine feet wide. There was only a couple of inches to spare height-wise. King ducked into the dim space and helped Léo undercover.

Four Navy soldiers in standard military gear greeted them. They ushered Léo to a section at the rear of the cabin, where the other four workers were seated side-by-side. Two Navy personnel — neither of them in uniform — were crouched opposite the group, likely briefing them on what procedures lay ahead in order to get them back home to their families.

King had seen it all before.

He and Slater waited cautiously as the rear ramp ascended behind them. With a resounding crash, it locked into place, sealing them off from the weather outside.

The four Navy soldiers didn't budge an inch.

Simultaneously, they drew sidearms from their holsters.

'We've been instructed to ask you not to move,' one of them said in a voice laced with tension.

'By who?' King said.

A voice near the back of the cabin said, 'By me.'

A grizzled man in unblemished military uniform strode across the empty fuselage. He wore nothing to identify himself by rank or position of authority, but King knew his type. He came from somewhere invisible to the public eye, a branch of the military that operated in the shadows.

Maybe Black Force.

Maybe something else.

He stepped between two of the soldiers and regarded King and Slater with his hands crossed behind his back. There was clear anger in his eyes.

'You two don't know me,' he said. 'But I know you. I've been running your careers for the last few years.'

'And you are?' King said.

'I'm one of the guys who slaves away behind-the-scenes. You see Isla. You see the fancy toys and the meeting rooms and the facade that shields you from the inner workings. You see the shopfront. You don't see the production facility that keeps it running.'

'I thought that was intentional.'

'It was.'

'We've been talking to Isla on the phone,' Slater said. 'We'd prefer to speak to her now.'

'That's not going to happen.'

'Why not?'

'Isla's in a prison cell. Just as you two will be an hour from now. She was instructed to guide you back over the phone.'

'And why are we all being thrown into a prison cell?' King said.

'Well, it appears the shopfront we put up to separate us from our operatives left room for corruption. It left room for one of our most trusted handlers to send you into Russia on a personal knee-jerk reaction.'

'I stayed of my own accord,' King said. 'I take full responsibility for my actions.'

'I know you do.'

'I came of my own accord, too,' Slater said. 'I'm—'

The man turned with something close to disgust in his gaze. 'I know who you are, Will. I know everything. You two don't seem to get that.'

'We get it,' King said. 'We're just wondering what happens now.'

'Black Force is done,' the man said coldly. 'You two wreaked havoc in a foreign territory with zero permission. You killed countless people without any authorisation. And I don't know who the hell you pissed off down there, but Russia isn't talking to us. All sorts of diplomatic ties are currently severed.'

'If we did nothing, those five men over there would be dead.'

'I guess you consider a world war less dangerous than a few missing health workers. This is why you two are the muscle. This is why we keep you out of everything that goes on behind-the-scenes.'

'I'll say it again,' King said. 'What happens now?'

'We're detaining you,' the man said. 'As of now, you're considered rogue operatives. If need be, we'll turn you over to the Russians to be prosecuted there. I imagine they want blood. At the moment, I'm happy to give it to them.'

'You think we'll go along with that willingly?' Slater said.

The man didn't respond. He cast his icy gaze over the two of them. 'I don't care what you go along with. Neither of you have a choice. Cut the macho bullshit.'

While two of the Navy soldiers trained their loaded weapons on King and Slater, the other two stepped forward and produced steel handcuffs. King's mind passed briefly over the thought of retaliation, but he disregarded it. He had willingly accepted the consequences of continuing the mission in an unofficial capacity. He wouldn't shy away from them now.

He offered out his hands, hoping to deter Slater from bursting into action. The ramifications of laying a hand on official military personnel would be disastrous. He was fully aware of the man's penchant to fly off the handle.

He silently pleaded with Slater to obey.

The steel bit tight into his broken wrist, making him grunt. He broke out in a cold sweat. Slater glanced at him briefly, then looked at the approaching soldier.

'*Don't,*' King whispered, barely audible.

'He's right,' the nameless man said to Slater. 'Listen to your friend. You make a single move and we'll put a bullet in your skull.'

Slater stayed frozen, still as a statue, like a lion stalking its prey. The tension amplified as the Navy soldier reached hesitantly for his wrists.

The soldier locked the handcuffs into place.

Slater bowed his head and let out a long exhale. King imagined he had been milliseconds away from action.

King let out the breath that had caught in his throat.

They would live to see another day.

Shackled by the wrists, the soldiers led them to a darkened corner of the cabin. King and Slater were thrust into the hard plastic seats. Their handcuffs were fastened to steel rings near their groins.

They weren't going anywhere.

The nameless man checked — then double-checked — their restraints. Satisfied, he gave a curt nod to the soldiers and made for the door at the other end of the fuselage.

'Back to the carrier,' he said. 'We'll throw them in with Isla until we sort out this mess.'

The chopper's nose dipped as it took off. King's stomach dropped. Freezing water dripping off his clothes pooled on the seat below. He shivered involuntarily.

The realisation that he was a prisoner washed over him.

He exchanged a glance with Slater as the ramifications of what they had done began to set in. There were no records of their employment — or even their existence. They had spent a decade working for the most secret government organisation on the planet, toiling away in the shadows as contracted warriors.

They could be locked away in a military black jail for the rest of their lives — and no-one would be any wiser.

The CH-53K powered away from the Russian coastline.

King closed his eyes, rested back against the hard plastic headrest, and sighed.

He knew that from this point on, nothing would be the same.

JASON KING WILL RETURN...

Read Matt's other books on Amazon.

amazon.com/author/mattrogers23

Printed in Great Britain
by Amazon